Looking for Lulu

Carl Granger

Copyright © CARL GRANGER 2020

GS

GRANGER-SCHMIDT PUBLISHING

The author asserts the moral right under the Copyright, Designs and Patents Act 1988 to be identified as the author of this work.

All Rights reserved. No part of this publication may be reproduced, stored in a retrieval system, or transmitted, in any form or by any means without the prior written consent of the author, nor be otherwise circulated in any form of binding or cover other than that in which it is published and without a similar condition being imposed on the subsequent purchaser.

This is a work of fiction. Names, characters, places and incidents are the product of the author's imagination or are used fictitiously. Any resemblance to actual persons, living or dead, events or locales is entirely coincidental.

ISBN: 978-2-901773-51-1

To Pete,

thanks for the cat -

you bastard.

1.

08:31 - MONDAY MORNING

Oscar Smith yawned wide enough to crack his jaw. Stretched and farted, one hand carefully holding the top of his head in case it lived up to its latent threat of exploding. Belched comprehensively then realised, with a groan, that there was more to come.

He thrashed his legs to untangle them from the stained sheets, then almost tripped over the empty Bergfeuer bottle next to the bed.

Fuck. If he'd drunk what was in there the night before, he was in a worse state than he thought. He managed to stagger the short distance to the bathroom where, as he sank to his knees in front of the lav, jumbled memories started to come back, together with most of the contents of his stomach.

There'd been a woman, at some point, he vaguely remembered. Young. Not too young, he hoped. Blonde. Not bad looking. He'd no idea how he'd managed to pull her.

But he could remember banging her. Vaguely. She'd been a lively one, for sure. Someone from work, perhaps.

That could be embarrassing. She might remember him, even if he couldn't pick her out on an ID parade.

Once his stomach had stopped turning itself inside out, he rocked back on his heels to stand up. Took a step back and landed in something wet.

The rank smell nearly made him throw up again.

Grabbing some bog roll, he stood precariously on one leg to wipe his foot, glaring at the large ginger tom cat which sat smirking at him from just outside the door.

'Clive, you little bastard, if you don't stop pissing on the bathroom floor, I'm going to have your bollocks off,' he told it, to its apparent indifference. 'And not at the vets, you little git. I'll do it myself with two bricks.'

He considered having a shower. Decided it might be more than he could manage. Opted instead for waving the shower head around a bit to get rid of the worst of it, then shoved his toothbrush round inside his mouth a few times.

He glanced at himself in the mirror. Rubbed a thoughtful hand over his raspy chin. That must have been like sandpaper, rubbing up against some of the places he had a vague memory of visiting the night before. It was about a five-day stubble now, but it would have to stay another day at least before he could fancy tackling it.

He found his suit and tie in a crumpled heap near the foot of the bed. He couldn't be arsed to do anything other than give it a few token shakes. He turned up a sort-of clean shirt draped over a chair in the kitchen. Sprayed a good dose of deodorant under his arms before he pulled it on. That should help a bit.

Then he was good to go. He picked up the car keys, telling Clive to behave himself, as he opened a packet of the ridiculously expensive gourmet food which was currently all the little sod would eat, and went out, slamming the door to the flat behind him.

He'd clearly been anxious to get inside with whoever the hell it was he had brought home because his works vehicle was parked at an angle, with one front wheel up on the kerb.

He was almost certainly still well over the limit, if he got stopped. But if any Plod fancied being brave enough to breathalyse him, he'd soon find out the deep shit that would get him into.

He drove the quick route to work, parked in his usual space, then fished out his ID card to let himself in. He stuck his head round a doorway, caught the eye of the woman on reception and gave her a saucy wink.

'Morning, Edith, you're looking particularly gorgeous this morning. A real sight for sore eyes,' he told her, not meaning a word of it but knowing it meant a lot to her.

She had the ear of people in high places, so it never hurt to keep well in with her. He needed all the allies he could get.

Before he went on his way upstairs, he paused for a moment to square himself up and try, at least, to look as if he was in charge.

As he did so, he thought to himself, as he often did, 'Detective Inspector Carl Smith has entered the building.'

Time to bash on. Arses to kick, cases to crack.

* * *

09:23 – MONDAY MORNING

No point in being the Gaffer if you couldn't rock up at whatever the hell time you felt like it. Smith's men knew that whoever might be looking for him any time he wasn't at his desk the answer was always the same: 'The DI is out following up a lead.'

Smith was a big man. Tall, broad shouldered, heavy on his feet, most of the time. Every step he took as he trudged slowly upstairs to the main CID office sent a lancing pain up from the ground to his head, with the potential to blow off the top of his skull.

He knew he should pack in the good German schnapps

before it got the better of him. His excuse was that, with a German mother, three German grand-parents, and much of his childhood, and his military service, spent in Germany, he sometimes felt more German than British.

He spoke the language fluently. The name on his birth certificate was Oskar Schmidt but he'd legally changed the spelling as soon as he was old enough to. He'd got fed up of constantly being called a Kraut in the Services Education schools he'd attended as a child.

He had a German ex-wife somewhere, too. A kid, allegedly, although he had no way of knowing if it was his or not. He'd never paid any of the maintenance she'd claimed. She'd never been able to find him to enforce payment. She certainly couldn't now, with his new role in civvy street.

He shoved open the door to the main office and headed, on autopilot, to the coffee machine in the far corner. He didn't speak immediately. It would take a strong hit of caffeine before he felt human enough to do so. Nor did he so much as nod in response to the, 'All right, guv?' greeting from his DS, Tony Taylor. At least he could trust Taylor to have everyone's nose to the grind.

There was a very pointed note above the double-shot espresso button he was the only one to use. It had been there for some time. Now it was emphasised in red felt-tip. Lots of underlining and exclamation marks everywhere.

'Guv. Coffee subs. Long overdue. Please pay!!!'

Smith reached in his back pocket for his wallet. Found it was missing.

Fuck!

No wonder the girl had been all over him like a rash. He'd thought she was simply as randy as a bitch on heat when she'd been squeezing his arse and checking out the bulge in his trousers. And he had been bulging, by that point. He'd nearly come in his shreddies at the thought of what lay ahead.

He was trying to think if there was anything vital or

incriminating in his wallet. A couple of emergency Johnnies, for sure, which he couldn't remember using. He hoped she hadn't repaid him with a dose of something nasty, as well as nicking his cash.

He took a big swallow of his espresso, looking round the room to see who was doing what. At least DC Dai Evans, sitting nearest to the coffee machine, had his head down over his work, for once. Lazy bastard.

Then Smith realised that the DC's head was bowed, not studying the paperwork on his desk, but because he was asleep.

The DI could move quietly when he needed to. Military training did that for a person. He made no sound as he took the few short steps necessary to bring him up close behind the sleeping detective. Then he fetched him such a slap round the back of his bald head that the sound rang out round the office and made everyone look in that direction.

'Ow, fuck, what the...'

His hand went up to massage his skull as he looked round to see who the assailant was. He nearly jumped out of his seat when he saw the DI standing over him, glowering.

'Wake the fuck up, Evans. The taxpayer doesn't pay you to sleep on duty. What's the excuse this time?'

'Sorry, guv,' the DC said contritely. The name was Welsh but the accent was pure Estuary. 'The kid was awake and screaming all night so I didn't get a wink of sleep.'

'Drown the bastard,' Smith growled, and sounded like he meant it. 'Or chuck the woman out and tell her to take the snivelling brat with her. Now get on with whatever it is you're meant to be doing.

'Tony,' he turned his head, slowly and cautiously in case it really did fall off, towards his DS. 'Give me half an hour then come and find me and tell me everything we've got on currently.'

'Will do, guv. Oh, and the Det. Sup. has been trying to get hold of you. He's phoned twice already. He said he'd call back.'

'Shit,' Smith commented, as he headed for the sanctuary of his office to finish his coffee.

Tony Taylor was a good DS. He accepted it as part of his job to cover for his DI – lie for him, if necessary – and to keep him up to speed at all times.

As Smith had expected, there were papers waiting for him on his desk with a summary of everything he needed to know. Smith would pick over them and no doubt find questions still unanswered. He had the kind of incisive mind which always did that. But at least he'd be on top of things when the Det. Sup. caught up with him.

As if on cue, his desk phone rang. Detective Superintendent Murray Aird, Divisional Head of Serious Crime. The person to whom Smith was answerable for everything he did.

'Oscar,' he said, by way of greeting. 'These robberies with violence. Time you had them wrapped up. What's taking you so long?'

'Manpower, guv,' Smith told him, one hand instinctively making jerking gestures as he listened to the softest hint of a Scottish note in the voice, overlaid by the many years his immediate boss had spent living south of the border. 'I could do with a couple more officers to get it sorted.'

'And there you have it,' Aird retorted. 'Your choice of word. Manpower. I could send you two cracking good DCs by tomorrow, but they're both women, and I know you.'

It was an open secret that Smith's team was always 'No women, no suntans' as he was known to put it. He kept getting away with it, too, because he was clever. He always had a cast iron reason for turning down any officers from either category that he was offered. Besides, his clear-up rate was good. He might need chasing sometimes, but he got the results. Outstanding ones. Quite likely often by methods the Det. Sup. preferred not to think about. But he was an asset to the divisional clear-up rate figures. It was why his officers stuck loyally with him and would never speak out against him.

'I've got nothing at all against women officers, guv. Nor against women in general,' Smith told him glibly.

It was perfectly true. He'd had plenty of himself up against whoever the mystery blonde from last night was. The robbing bitch. Most of himself up against her, and up plenty of other places, too, now that his memory was starting to come back, albeit still in a fragmented way. But he didn't like them in the work place. Too distracting, for a rampant red-blooded man like him.

'I need a result this week, Oscar,' the Det. Sup. told him.

'On it, guv. Have a nice day.'

Smith only said that because he knew how much it irritated Aird.

He scan-read everything DS Taylor had given him. One of Smith's biggest strengths was the speed with which he could extrapolate info from reports and pounce on exactly what action needed to be taken. It wasn't quite a photographic memory. He had to look at every word for it to register. But it was rare that any more than one read-through was ever needed for him to have the details off pat. It's why he sailed through theory exams with no effort.

He stamped out into the main office, bellowed a bit, told the team their fortune, set them on the right course which should give them the result they needed within the time-frame.

Then he helped himself to more coffee, ignoring the note this time, before trudging back to his office on the pretext of doing paperwork, whilst secretly hoping the second espresso would reboot his memory enough to relive the previous evening's antics. And hopefully, to pick up some sort of a clue about who the mystery woman was. He planned to pay her another visit. And not just to get his wallet back.

2.

14:23 – SUNDAY – THE PREVIOUS DAY

He heard her scrabbling about in the garden next door before he saw her or heard her speak. The old biddy had put something up against the fence again so she could stand on it to peer over into his garden. She wouldn't be able to reach without whatever it was.

'I see you're having another barbecue, then?'

He ignored her whilst he carried on basting his meat with the sauce. He could still see her out of the corner of his vision. Beady little eyes peering. Her nose twitching. She looked like a ferret, he thought. Or a rat. Yes, more like a rat, with that long pointed nose, always sticking into someone else's business.

'That's right,' he told her finally, keeping his tone patient and civil, whilst imagining how long her severed head would take to cook, now that the charcoal was glowing red hot.

'You have a lot of barbecues.'

It sounded more like an accusation than an observation.

'I like barbecues,' he told her, still without losing his temper, which he could so easily do. She brought out the very worst in him.

'Spare ribs again?' she sniffed. 'Is that all you ever cook

these day? You're always having spare ribs lately.'

'I like spare ribs. They're my favourite.'

'Is that all you ever eat?'

He must check with the local council. Perhaps there was some by-law of which he was unaware which limited the number of times you could eat spare ribs in your own back garden. Was the restriction per week or per month, he wondered. And were there barbecue wardens who patrolled the neighbourhood, sniffing out the evidence of any infringements? Or would his interfering old bag of a neighbour rush indoors shortly to phone them up and drop him in it.

Hopefully, if it was council-run, there may be no one on duty on a Sunday afternoon.

'Sometimes I eat liver, with fava beans and a nice Chianti,' he told her, accompanied by the appropriate slurping sounds.

The Hannibal Lecter reference was clearly lost on her as she continued, in the same disagreeable tone, 'The smell is very sickly. Sweet. Cloying. It carries into my house when the wind is blowing this way.'

He was trying to stay patient but it was getting harder with each pile of drivel she spouted.

'That will be the sweet and sour sauce, you see. The clue is in the name. Sweet. And sour.'

It was a shame that nosy old pensioners like her didn't have to come into the offices where he worked to justify being paid, like the benefit seekers he dealt with had to do. He'd love to be in that position of power over her. He'd sanction her for anything and everything. Starting with having a twitchy nose.

He'd have her begging him to give her what she no doubt felt was due to her. She'd tell him about how she'd paid into the scheme all her life and she only wanted what was rightfully hers.

'Would you like to try some?' he asked her instead. 'I've made enough for two. I always do.'

Her nose wrinkled even further as she looked at him as if he had made an obscene suggestion.

As if. He wasn't into necrophilia and she looked as if she had one foot in the grave. He'd no need. Not when he had it on tap, whenever he felt like helping himself.

'Is it foreign? It smells it. I don't eat foreign.'

'Oh yes, it's very foreign,' he told her. 'Very, very foreign. All of it. Definitely nothing you will have eaten before. Not round here, at any rate.'

'I won't, then,' she said, not bothering to hide her disgust. But then the remnants of good manners got the better of her and she went on, 'But thank you for the offer. Enjoy your meal.'

She disappeared from sight as he piled the ribs onto a plate and headed towards the kitchen. He divided the food up. A generous half he put onto another plate which he transferred to the oven and put on a low light. The second plate he carried with him, with a good handful of paper kitchen towels and a clean tea towel. Ribs were such messy things to eat, but that was part of the attraction.

As usual, when she'd heard his footsteps on the stairs, she'd pulled herself as far back into a corner of the room as she possibly could. As far as the rope which tied her two wrists together and then in turn to the radiator under the window, where the blind stayed firmly down all the time, would allow.

Her eyes, above the gag in her mouth, were huge. Her eyelids were pulled back so far he was sure the eyeballs would pop out one of these days.

Like a very stylised Bambi from the cartoons.

He put the plate of ribs on the floor in front of her then crouched down so that his face was level with hers when he spoke.

'I've brought you something delicious to eat. You're really going to love this. And you do need to eat something. You're getting too thin. So first of all, I'm going to take the gag off. And you're going to promise me that you aren't going to scream. Not even the sound of a little mouse. Aren't you?'

When she hesitated, his tone instantly hardened. His eyes glinted, and he put his face even closer to hers.

'You're not going to make even one little squeak, are you? Because you know that if you do, I shall have to punish you again. Harder, this time. And I don't like having sex with you. I really don't. You just lie there like a dead fish. Like a dry, dry dead fish. It hurts me to do it. But you've shown me how much it frightens you, so I do it to punish you.

'Now, if you don't want that to happen to you again, you're going to stay so quiet when I take off this gag. Aren't you?'

Her nodding was so frenetic, those wide Bambi eyes filling with pitiful tears, that it was hard for him to untie the gag.

He picked up the plate and held one of the sticky, sauce-covered ribs out to her.

'You'll like this. A lot. This was Number Three. You'd have liked her, too. I think you would have got on with her. She looked a bit like you.'

He only just managed to drop the plate and clamp his hand over her mouth as she began to scream.

And scream.

And scream.

Then she fainted. Her lids closed over the doe eyes to spare them from further horrors.

* * *

22:43 – THE DAY BEFORE – SUNDAY

Lulu, she'd called herself. It was starting to come back to him as he went over the day's paperwork. Smith was a skilled multitasker. It was another of his strengths. His eyes and part of his brain were concentrating on the file on the armed robberies, while the rest of him was reliving the night before.

He'd been on his own at the bar, as usual. Billy No Mates. Scanning the spirit bottles to see if there was anything he would consider remotely drinkable. Desperate as he was for something, he'd not yet sunk low enough to touch peach schnapps.

He settled on vodka. At least he knew the brand was a bit better than piss water. He asked for it on the rocks, then was turning to go and find a quiet corner when he walked smack into her as she was heading for the bar.

The close encounter was not unpleasant. She had the proverbial tits like watermelons. She was a lot shorter than he was and as his suit jacket was hanging open as usual, he copped for her nipples in his midriff. He could feel through his shirt that they were hard, too.

He'd instinctively held his glass up high – the serious drinkers' need to protect their next fix at all costs – so there was no spillage. It didn't stop her looking mortified.

'Oh, God, I'm so sorry. Did you spill any? Trust me to be so clumsy. Let me buy you another.'

He was eyeing her up with predatory appraisal. Imagining experiencing the same feeling of those boobs against his body with no clothing between them.

Some hopes, he reckoned. But he could still dream. It had been some time since he last got lucky.

'It's fine. Really. No spillage, no harm done.'

His gruff voice was slightly husky and he knew some women found that attractive. He gave her what he hoped was more charming smile than sex-crazed leer. Then he decided he might as well give it a go.

'Look, are you with someone? Or could I perhaps buy you a drink to show there's nothing to apologise about, and no hard feelings.'

The way she was gazing up at him, all wide-eyed and moist lips risked making something hard, though. The old one-eyed trouser snake was starting to stir.

'That's really kind of you. I was meant to be meeting my boyfriend but I'm late and he's not here, so perhaps...'

Smith shrugged, feigning an indifference he wasn't feeling. To put it mildly, he was gagging for it.

'Up to you. No pressure.'

Except there was. Increasingly. Down below. Christ, those tits looked like a right handful.

She had her phone in her hand now and was scrolling through, not looking at him as she spoke.

'I say boyfriend but this was meant to be a first date. We were meant to meet up here for a drink then go on to a club. There's no word from him, though.'

'His loss. Look, let me buy you that drink, at least. Oscar,' he told her, holding out a big hand. The old German habits died hard, even after so long. 'What will you have?'

He was hoping she'd have a serious rogering later on, if things went the way he hoped.

'Lulu,' she told him, slipping her soft hand into his paw. 'What are you having? What was it I nearly made you spill?'

He was careful to play the gentleman over the first vodka on the rocks when she asked for the same as him. Keeping a demure distance between them at all times. Not encroaching on her personal space.

By the second drink, when she seemed to be listening with rapt attention to everything he said, he risked letting his thigh touch hers fleetingly as he sat down. Casually let his hand brush against one of those boobs as he reached across to put her glass in front of her.

She appeared to be hanging on to his every word. When she asked what he did, he played it cool. Military Police sounded more sexy than being an ordinary copper, especially when he hinted that he was on something of a special undercover mission.

'Oh, my God, are you some sort of a spy?' she'd asked

him.

He'd shrugged modestly. Falling back on the old gag.

'You know what they say. If I tell you, I'll have to kill you. And that would be a pity.'

From there to inviting her back to his place to sample some of Germany's finest liqueur had been a piece of cake. And he couldn't believe his luck when she was all over him the minute they got through the door. Although with the benefit of hindsight, he could almost pinpoint the exact moment she'd pocketed his wallet.

He could console himself with the thought that she'd still gone to bed with him after that, so presumably the cash hadn't been all she'd wanted from him. There wouldn't have been all that much in there, although he didn't know exactly how much. It was almost worth it.

He'd been going at it in fine style while she writhed about underneath him. If it had been all show on her part then she was a bloody good actress.

At one moment, just as he thought he couldn't hold on any longer, he felt a light touch against his scrotum which drove him wild. A slight tickling feeling against both of his balls at the same time, as if she was touching him teasingly with that fine, soft, blonde hair.

But how could she be? Her face was on the pillow under his and his tongue was halfway down her throat. Her hair wasn't that long. Was she some sort of kinky contortionist, touching him with her feet?

Then he felt a sudden sharp pain in both buttocks at the same time. Lancing. Like so many booster jabs simultaneously, administered by a medic with a serious drink problem and a shaky hand which was struggling to find its target.

He withdrew his tongue hurriedly and arched his whole powerful body upwards, which had the effect of driving him deeper still inside her as he bellowed towards the ceiling, 'Fuck!'

She was grinding her hips against him now, panting

with anticipation. If this was fakery, he wasn't the only Oscar she deserved.

'Yes, yes, that's it! Fuck me! Hard! Fuck!' she screamed in his ear.

He made one last effort to hold on but it was a lost cause. As he came with a shuddering climax he groaned, 'Clive, you little bastard, I'm going to pull all your sodding claws out with a pair of pliers.'

3.

09:57 - MONDAY MORNING

The tap on Smith's door was hesitant. Timid, almost. He grunted a response and his DS, Tony Taylor, came into the room. Smith had seen squaddies up on a court martial look more relaxed than Taylor did.

Smith ruled by fear. None of all the touchy-feely supportive crap he was supposed to do these days. They kept sending him on courses about it. He'd occasionally get a lecture from a senior officer, reminding him that it was the twenty-first century. Things were evolving and he needed to as well.

He couldn't give a shit. Anyone who didn't like the way he worked could do one, as far as he was concerned. He got the results. Plenty of people knew he broke most of the rules in the book to do so. But he got away with it. As long as he kept getting the convictions, and wasn't stupid enough to get caught doing anything he shouldn't, there was not much anyone could do about it.

Anyone joining his team who couldn't live with the way he worked quickly moved on. So far, all of them had been wise enough not to say anything about why they wanted to transfer, other than 'personal reasons'.

Most of them, like Taylor, chose to stay. Few other teams in the division, or even in the wider force area, enjoyed the conviction rates of Smith's team. Taylor chose to bite his tongue and basked in the reflected glory. For now.

'Guv, sorry to bother you.'

Taylor had been in Smith's office many times. He was never invited to sit down. He imagined rank had been much more of a thing in the Military Police than it was these days in most police services in civvy street.

Smith raised eyes which were still bloodshot from whatever he'd been up to the night before. Taylor suspected, from the look of his boss, that he'd blow positive on a breath test, yet no doubt he'd driven in to work in his service vehicle. Again.

'It's the coffee fund thing. It's getting like the national debt.'

'Seriously? You've got nothing better to occupy yourself with than me owing money for coffee? I'll pay it. I've said I would and I will. I just can't at the moment. Someone robbed my wallet last night so I've got no cash.'

'Shit, guv, that's a bugger. What about your cards?'

'Just how thick d'you think I am, Tony? Cards are in a separate place. I'll get some cash next time I go out. Now, haven't you got any proper coppering to get on with?'

'I have, guv, that's what I came to see you about. We've got a suspect in our sights for the armed robberies. We've been keeping an eye on him and we know he's at home, right now, so I'm going to go and bring him in for questioning.'

Smith had been visibly the worse for wear. Tony's words were like throwing a switch in his brain. He sprang to his feet so abruptly that his chair shot backwards on its castors and crashed into the filing cabinet behind. He then grabbed his crumpled jacket from the coat-stand and started pulling it on.

Tony hesitated. The last thing he needed to deal with was a clearly still half cut DI who was known to knock suspects about for the fun of it, even when he wasn't hung over.

'I can manage fine, if there's stuff you need to be doing, guv. Sean and Craig are already there on obo and I was going to take Nick with me...'

'So now you've got me instead. What are we waiting for?'

Luckily the DI didn't object to Tony driving. He must have realised himself that it was the best solution.

Tony risked another question.

'Is everything all right, guv? Only I can smell something. Is it TCP?'

It was. Smith had needed to put something on his arse where Clive had stuck his claws in. He had some vague notion about something called cat scratch fever, and he wasn't about to find out the hard way that it wasn't just an old wives' tale.

It hadn't been easy, sloshing liquid on his own backside and trying to get it accurately on the claw marks. It had stung like a bastard, too. He didn't realise how strong the smell was until he was in the close confines of the service vehicle with the DS.

He chose to ignore the question altogether. To change the subject, he asked for full details of the person they were going to lift. Someone with form, though not for anything as violent as the latest spate of robberies. If they had the right man, it would be a big tick on the books.

Provided the DI didn't blow it for them by getting too slap-happy, Tony was thinking to himself. He knew from experience that after a short time in the DI's company, most suspects were ready to admit to any unsolved crime outstanding in any of the four corners of the country during the last ten years or more.

One day, he was going to go way too far. Tony fervently hoped it wasn't on a day when he was following Smith round and trying to keep some sort of control over him.

Tony parked not too close to the target property,

behind another vehicle in which two team members, Craig Stephens and Sean Walsh, were keeping an eye out for the suspect leaving. Both looked immediately on edge to see the DI there, looming over the car in which they sat.

'Still inside?' he asked them.

'Yes, guv. He got back a couple of hours ago and hasn't moved since.'

'Right, we're all going in. Whatever he says and whatever happens, I want four identical versions of what actually happened, against whatever he claims.'

The look the three detectives exchanged wasn't lost on Smith. He didn't give a shit what they thought. They were going to put a piece of scum away by whatever means necessary. That's all he cared about.

The robberies were vicious and getting worse. If they didn't stop this bastard, and soon, they were going to be looking at a murder case instead.

Smith thumped long and loud on the front door, holding his ID up ready. He'd sent Sean round the back. He looked the most formidable of them, after the DI.

A man opened the door warily and peered at them. He was in his underwear. One glance at Smith towering over him, filling the doorway, was enough. He turned and bolted for the back door, to find that exit blocked by the lesser, though still impressive, bulk of Sean Walsh.

A steel-blue puppy raced out of a room off the narrow hallway, barking in fury. Only a little thing. Young-looking. But it sounded fierce and it had sharp teeth in the open pink mouth.

Smith stuffed his large booted foot in between its jaws and as soon as it was distracted, grabbed it by the scruff and held it at arm's length while it snarled and yelped alternately.

'Don't hurt the pup! It cost me a fortune!' the man they'd come to bring in shouted at them. Devlin, his name was. Ivan Devlin.

'Well, I'll tell you what I'm going to do for you, Ivan,'

Smith told him, his tone pleasant enough. 'We're going to go into your kitchen while we ask you a few questions. And if your memory should fail you, or if you don't give me the answers I want to hear, I'm going to see how long this little mutt,' he waggled the puppy by the scruff as he spoke, making its yelps go up to screaming pitch, 'can hold its breath under water. Do we understand one another?'

Devlin gave an enraged bellow and lunged at the big man holding the puppy. Craig, who had followed the DS in behind Smith, and Sean moved as one to restrain him.

Smith led the way into the kitchen, which was surprisingly clean and tidy. The sink was empty and sparkling, with a lemony fragrance wafting in the air. He put the plug in and filled it with tepid water as far as the overflow.

Devlin kicked and swore and pleaded. When Smith plunged the squirming animal's head below the surface, Devlin started to cry.

Seconds ticked by. Tony Taylor started to get anxious.

'Guv, let it up to breathe, for God's sake.'

'Bastard, bastard, bastard,' Devlin wept, then, 'all right, all right, I'll tell you what you want to know. Just don't hurt the pup any more.'

At his words, Smith lifted the little creature out of the water. It immediately started to cough and sneeze and retch. He reached for a towel from the rail by the sink then thrust that and the half-drowned puppy at Craig.

'Get it dried off, then call the nick and get someone who knows about such things to come round here. It looks like an illegal pit bull to me. Then wait here for the Woodentops to arrive and oversee a full search of the place. Inside and out. I want nothing missed, and I do mean nothing.

'Sean, you come with us. Sit in the back with Devlin to make sure he doesn't get any ideas. Put some clothes on, Devlin. We can't take you in like that.'

Smith and Tony went outside to the car while Sean

took Devlin to get dressed. Craig was wrestling, as carefully as he could, with the wriggling puppy which was now beside itself with fear and rage.

'Guv, that was pushing it too far. What if he says something? We'll never get a conviction if it comes out that whatever he tells us was obtained under duress.'

'Tony, is your maths not very good?'

'Good enough, guv.'

'How many coppers were in that house?'

'Four, guv.'

'And how many coppers are going to say exactly what I tell them to, if they're asked?'

Tony Taylor hesitated for the briefest moment before he said reluctantly, 'All of them, guv.'

'Is the right answer.'

* * *

18:31 - MONDAY EVENING

He closed the door quietly behind him and turned the key in the lock before he approached her. He never took any risks. He always left them securely tied but there was a remote chance one of them might be clever enough to slip free.

'I've brought you some liver and onions this evening,' he told her conversationally. 'You really need something to keep your strength up.'

As soon as he appeared she cringed back as far as she could into the corner once more. At the beginning he'd thought the Bambi eyes were attractive. They made her look alluring. Her vulnerability aroused him, to a degree.

The novelty was starting to wear off more quickly with this one than with any of the others, though. The bucket thing, for one reason. It was never enjoyable, emptying them. But this one kept saying she had some sort of a medical condition. He'd never seen anything like it. It was a big turn-off. He never fancied touching her much after dealing with that.

She wouldn't eat, either. Hardly anything. She kept saying she was a vegan. She didn't eat meat. She even kept turning her nose up at Number Three and she was his favourite. That's why he still had some left, even now.

But he needed to make more room in the freezer, so he was stuck with this one until he could do that. Acid was so messy. He'd only tried that once before and vowed never to again. Besides, it was such a waste and he couldn't abide waste of any sort.

He put the plate down on the end of the bed, out of her reach, while he let himself out of the room to go and empty out the bucket and slosh some disinfectant in there to stop the stink.

Perhaps when she could smell how delicious the meal was, she might get something of an appetite. He'd found it delicious, at least. Succulent, tender, with a sweetness to it.

He'd done all the things he'd read about to tempt her to try some. A small portion. Nicely presented on the plate. Some of the liver, in its own delicious juices. A tiny portion of fluffy, creamy mashed potato. Carrots and beans cooked so they kept just enough crunch. Not fava beans, of course. He'd never been a fan of broad beans. Nasty, leathery things.

He'd always hated them, from being a little boy. His mother would force him to sit at the table until he ate them all. If he hadn't done so by the time his father got home from work, he'd get a proper leathering. Mind you, he'd get one most days, anyway. There was always some reason for it, whatever he did. No matter how many revolting broad beans he ate.

Up until that day. He'd just turned sixteen, when his father had lifted a hand to him once too often. He didn't see the sharp, shining steel of a kitchen knife in his son's hand. Not until it was too late and it was buried up to the hilt in his chest.

His mother was away when it happened. She'd done one of her regular flounces and gone to stay with her older sister on the other side of town for a few days. She knew her absence made it ten times worse for the boy, but she didn't care. Her survival instinct was intent on looking after Number One – herself.

He took advantage of her not being at home to teach himself the best way to butcher and dispose of a body. When she came back, he greeted her with a tasty, rich stew which she'd greatly enjoyed, and had even asked for seconds.

He explained his father's absence by saying he'd come home from work in a violent temper on the day she'd gone away, which had got worse when he discovered his wife was not there. He'd gone back out, to the pub, the son told her, and he hadn't seen him since.

Good riddance, they both agreed.

He also told her that he'd become interested in cooking after watching something on television. She was more than happy to come home every day to the tasty stews and casseroles he prepared for her. He told her he was thinking of making a career out of it.

All was peaceful and harmonious, for the first time he could remember in his life. Until the fateful day when there had been a power cut and she'd got home before him. She'd thought to check on the contents of the freezer, out in the garage, and had come face to face with the frozen severed head of her late husband.

She was made of stern stuff, having put up with the violent man for years, so she didn't scream the place down, alert the neighbours, and get the police arriving at the door. She simply waited calmly for her son to come home and to demand an explanation from him.

He was surprised and disappointed that she didn't see his point of view and understand what he'd done. It seemed she could live with the fact that he'd murdered his father – her husband. That was understandable, given the circumstances. But for some reason she thought it unreasonable to have been a party to disposing of his body, although she'd thoroughly enjoyed every meal and was always asking for more.

It was when she started ranting that he was insane and in need of the help of a psychiatrist that he realised he couldn't trust her not to do something stupid.

He hadn't bothered to give his father a number. He'd assumed he would be the only one. But once his mother joined her late husband, or what was left of him, in the freezer, he took to referring to her, fondly enough, as Number One.

That was how he'd discovered that the meat of the female of the species was sweeter and more tender than the male, and he'd developed a real taste for it. He'd also convinced himself that the sweetest meat of all was that fed on its own kind.

'I'm going to take your gag off so you can eat the lovely food I've prepared for you. So you know the rules. Don't make a sound. Or I will have to punish you. Do you understand?'

She did that rapid nodding again, eyes blinking frantically. He hesitated a moment. Could he really trust her? She'd let him down before. Best to be prepared.

He went to the wardrobe in another corner of the room, opened the door and took out two pieces of wood.

As soon as she saw what he was doing she started to shake uncontrollably all over, then tears sprang to her eyes.

'This is just a precaution,' he told her, his tone reassuring. 'It's entirely up to you whether or not I need to use either of them. You understand that, don't you?'

She tried to get enough control of her body to nod in response. The trembling made it hard.

He carefully laid the items on the bed where she could see them. Both of them looked like broom handles, although modified for a different purpose to their original one.

One, thicker and more sturdy than the other, was perhaps three feet long. It had holes drilled through each end, with rope threaded through and formed into loops. Not thick rope, but very strong. Like something a climber might use. Something which wouldn't easily break.

The other was shorter. The surface polished smooth. The end carefully rounded. It was this one her eyes locked onto, their expression one of repelled fascination. A rabbit mesmerised by a stoat.

He gave her a second warning, then moved to take off her gag. Next he offered her a drink of water and helped her to take it in steady sips. He knew the gag made her mouth dry and he was not inhuman. Or so he told himself.

'There, now. That's better, isn't it? So much better for us both when you don't scream.'

Her eyes had a look of cunning now.

'I promise never to say anything to anyone. Ever. If you let me go. I won't tell them you kidnapped me and kept me here against my will. Nor that you raped me or anything. I promise. If you just let me go.'

He'd picked up the plate to start spooning the delicious food into her mouth. He lowered the spoon, frowning at her.

'But I haven't raped you,' he said, a note of offence in his voice. 'Never. I told you what the rules were, and what the consequences were for screaming. You accepted the rules, but you chose to break them. So you had to be punished.

'I didn't get any enjoyment out of it. You know that. Sometimes I didn't even do it myself, I had to leave it to Tickler.'

'But that's still rape!'

Her voice was going up again. That shrill, hysterical tone he hated.

'Be quiet! You know the rules. Be quiet, stop saying such wicked things, or you'll have to be punished.'

She tried to calm down. Had one last vain try at

reasoning with him.

'I need to go home,' she pleaded. Crying now. Tears and mucous running down her face in a most unattractive way. 'Please. Please let me go. I promise not to say anything. Not to anyone.'

He was angry now. His face darkening and twisting in fury.

He grabbed the handle with the rope at each end, dropped to his knees on the floor in front of her, and forced her legs apart as wide as they would go. She wore nothing under her skirt. He left her that way, always, so she could use the bucket whenever she needed too, without struggling with undergarments while her hands were bound.

Once her bare feet were firmly secured in the improvised stirrups, he reached for the polished piece of wood.

That was the point at which she fainted.

4.

09:37 – TUESDAY MORNING

Smith's desk phone was ringing as he walked through the door of his office. He knew it would be the Det. Sup. He'd been trying to get him on his mobile since just gone eight. Smith had been studiously avoiding his calls.

'Morning, guv,' he said as he picked up the phone.

'Where the hell have you been, Oscar? I've been trying to get hold of you since first thing. Your DS said you were out chasing up loose ends from yesterday. I thought you had that sewn up and a prime suspect in custody?'

'We have, guv. Tony and I are going to start interviewing him now. There were just one or two more pieces of the puzzle I needed to sort out.'

Aird grunted his disbelief. He knew Smith well enough by now to detect the sound of crap excuses, even over the phone.

'It was that arrest I wanted to talk to you about, anyway. I had your suspect's solicitor bending my ear last night. She says anything her client has said or is likely to say will have been obtained under duress. She claims you intimidated him and tortured his puppy to make him confess.'

'Me, guv? Torture a puppy?' Oscar Smith's feigned innocence was an acting performance which deserved an award of the same name as his. 'I love animals. I've got a moggy of my own at home.'

'Then I pity the poor sod,' Aird growled. 'Anyway, his brief's not letting go of this one, so I hope to God you have a reliable witness.'

'Three, guv,' Smith told him glibly, glad the Det. Sup. couldn't see his smug smirk of satisfaction. 'DS Taylor and DCs Stephens and Walsh.'

'Four?' Aird's voice went up a notch. 'Four CID officers to bring in one suspect? If he was considered that much of a threat, why didn't you get armed back-up?'

Smith was back to making gestures down the phone. One of the reasons he dodged his boss on his mobile, preferring to talk to him via the desk phone so he couldn't see him as they spoke.

'More of a flight risk than a threat. Stephens and Walsh were keeping obs in a vehicle outside the front, so when DS Taylor and I arrived, I sent the two of them round the back, just in case our suspect decided to leg it. They were there while I spoke to the suspect then arrested him. Walsh came in the back of the car with us while we brought him back to the nick. So there were at least two witnesses to everything which happened between me and him before I took him to the custody suite and let him call his lawyer.'

'You didn't question him straight away?'

'By the time he'd finished crying on his brief's shoulder, it was getting late, so I decided to let him sleep on whatever fairy tale he was thinking of spinning us, and question him this morning. Guv.'

'So what about the puppy, Oscar? Did you touch it? And I want the truth, not your usual line in bullshit. This could get serious.'

'I did touch it, guv. That part is true. Only a little bastard, quite young, but very feisty. It kept going for us, all teeth bared, so I picked it up and gave it a cuddle until it calmed down. Not just to stop it biting any of us but because the poor little sod was clearly frightened.'

'Put the bloody fiddle away, Oscar. You're not breaking my heart, you're making me want to puke. I don't want anything to go wrong on this one. It's a bloody good tick on the books for all of us if we can put this filth away. But I don't want it going pear-shaped because you've decided to rip up the rule book and do things however you might have done them in the military.

'What happened to the pup, anyway, if you've got your man in custody? And where were you earlier on? I've been trying to get hold of you since first thing.'

'Sad news about the pup, guv. I thought it looked like a pit bull so I got the experts round to check and it is. So it's been seized, which means it will probably be put to sleep, once they get a court order. That's where I've been this morning, sorting things out about the poor little doggy.'

'My arse, you were. And that's not a job for a bloody DI anyway. Just make sure you get a solid conviction on this one. I don't want your usual pissing about and bending all the rules to get in the way of us putting a dangerous offender away.'

Smith's bellow of 'Fuck off, you smug-arsed bastard' as he slammed the phone back down, must have been audible outside in the main office. Tony Taylor's knock on his door shortly afterwards was even more timid than usual.

'Are you ready to question the suspect, guv? Only time's getting on a bit...'

'Don't you start, Tony, for fuck's sake. I've just had the Det. Sup. on, bending my ear saying the suspect's brief has been speaking to him complaining that I tortured the puppy. But you and the others can confirm I did no such thing. Can't you, Tony?'

Tony hesitated for just a few seconds. He wished he had the balls. He really did. To stand up to the DI. Tell him exactly what he thought of him and his rule-breaking. And then to go and drop him right in the shit by telling the truth to the Det. Sup. And to any top brass who wanted to hear it.

The truth was he was scared stiff of the man and he admitted it to himself. He'd seen what he was capable of. Too many times not to be. He spent sleepless nights wrestling with his conscience. What if he reported him and wasn't taken seriously? His word against that of a DI and former Military Police Captain with an impressive clean-up rate in both forces.

And that part was true. Even if Tony sometimes felt like throwing the towel in and asking for a transfer, he knew he'd not find a gaffer anywhere within the force area with the same clean-up rates. Tony had been doing things Smith's way for so long now, he wasn't sure he could remember how they were meant to be done.

For now, it was safest to nod and agree. One day the DI would come crashing down. Tony hoped that if he kept his own head down, worked hard, studied for promotion, he could be long gone before that happened. Then he could have a try at doing things the proper way.

At least the guv looked in slightly better fettle than he had the day before. His suit was less crumpled, his shirt was clean, if not ironed, and he'd had a shave. That only served to highlight the livid scar which ran down from his temple to pucker one corner of his mouth, giving it a permanent half-grin which only served to make him look even more evil.

Smith was fond of hinting that it was a wound acquired on active military service. Only Smith himself knew it was the result of a drunken brawl in a Berlin night club which had resulted in him getting himself arrested by the German police.

Luckily, his fluent German, his military ID and the impressive yarn he'd spun them had seen him walk away from that one with nothing more than a polite request to modify his behaviour – plus a good few stitches in the wound when he was seen and treated by the medics.

When Tony opened his mouth to speak, Smith interrupted him. Reaching in his pocket, he pulled out a cheap new wallet, took out a banknote and handed it to his DS.

'Here's what I owe the coffee fund, give or take, if you were about to start banging on about that again. Now let's go and see what our puppy love friend has to say for himself after a comfy night in a cell.'

'I wasn't, guv, but thanks. I wanted to give you this and see if you thought we should follow it up. Joe Barnes brought it up with me this morning.'

Joe Barnes was Smith's oppo from the uniform lot. The Woodentops, as Smith insisted on calling them, amongst other uncomplimentary terms. Smith was supposed to liaise with him but the two were like cat and dog, so he delegated the task to his DS. Barnes was far too bloody politically correct for Smith's liking.

Smith glanced at the printed report Taylor handed to him then look up with a scornful sneer, emphasised now the twist to the side of his mouth was more visible.

'Mispers? Fuck sake, Tony, we're serious crime. Runaways hardly fall into that remit. Chuck it back to the Woodentops and tell them not to bother us unless it's something a bit more up our street. Now, shall we go and knock seven bells out of our guest?'

He saw the look on the DS's face and said, 'Joke, Tony. Joke.'

'Guv, I really think we should take a closer look at this report. These are not your usual runaways. They're young women, in work, no problems at home, no reason to go on the run. Early twenties, no history of anything similar. There are four missing from our patch alone in the last year. Joe thinks it's possible some from other divisions may be linked.

'Guv, what if we have a serial kidnapper at work and we write it off as just runaways?'

That piqued the DI's interest. Something like that would be a big feather in his cap if he could solve it. He glanced again at the report, then tossed it onto his desk for later.

'That's worth a look, at least, once we've finished with our new visitor. So let's go and make a start on him, shall we? See if we can get him to sing for his supper. Have you got the knuckledusters?'

Then he rolled his eyes to the ceiling at Taylor's expression and said again, 'Joke, Tony. Joke.'

5

09:57 – TUESDAY MORNING

Smith left all the routine shite to Tony Taylor. He knew the drill. They'd worked together often enough and Taylor knew just how the guv liked to play things. Smith simply leaned back in his chair, making it creak ominously, while Tony started the recording and got all present to identify themselves.

'Ms Channing, representing Mr Devlin,' the solicitor announced in her usual purse-lipped, prissy fashion. 'And before you go any further, Inspector, let me register my formal objection to your presence during the interview of my client. You should know that I have already made a complaint to your superior officer about serious allegations made by my client. Allegations that you tortured and nearly killed his puppy. A little dog of which he is very fond, and of which he has had no news since he has been held here overnight on what I consider to be spurious allegations, based on the so-called evidence which has been disclosed to me so far.'

Smith immediately straightened up in his seat, sensing some fun to come. He disliked Muzzz Channing, as he always insisted on pronouncing it – more so since it was obvious how much it annoyed her – and welcomed any opportunity to lock horns with her.

He was pretty certain she was a dyke, for one thing.

With her short-cropped hair, her masculine suits and her tailored men's shirts. All she needed was a tie to complete the picture. Even her shoes were butch. Highly polished Oxfords.

'I've already spoken to Detective Superintendent Aird about this, Muzzz Channing. I explained that I was simply restraining the puppy which was becoming aggressive and distressed. I think he was fully satisfied with my explanation.'

He often wondered what it would be like to shag her. He'd give it a go, if the opportunity ever arose. For the novelty factor, if nothing else. He'd bet money on her liking it doggy fashion.

'I wouldn't count on that, Inspector,' she smirked at him, the rank sounding like a swearword coming from her pussy-faced mouth.

He didn't understand the reason for her knowing look. He thought he had it all smoothed over after his conversation with the Det. Sup. But Channing the Dyke looked as if she knew more than he did, and he didn't like that.

He was about to question her further when the door opened quietly and Detective Superintendent Murray Aird came into the room.

Tony Taylor shot to his feet, looking ready to cack himself. Lying for the guv was something he was used to. Having to do it on the record in front of the Det. Sup. was something else entirely. Yet he knew he was going to have to do it. He couldn't trust Aird to give him the round-the-clock protection he would need if he dropped the DI right in the shit.

Smith did little more than nod in acknowledgement of his boss's presence. He'd had more than a bellyful of all that saluting and snapping to attention bullshit in his Army days. He certainly wasn't about to do it for Aird.

'Detective Superintendent Aird has entered the room,' the Superintendent announced, for the purposes of the recording, looking round for a chair.

Taylor grabbed the one he had been sitting on to pass to him, hoping fervently that this was his chance to slope off and make himself scarce.

He was thwarted when the Det. Sup. told him, 'Thank you, Sergeant. Please go and find another chair for yourself and come straight back. I want you in on this interview, and I have a feeling we may be some time, so no doubt you would prefer to be sitting down.'

Everything about Aird was rounded. His shaved bald head, shiny and polished like a billiard ball. His slightly prominent beady eyes. The paunch only just contained within the buttons of his suit jacket. And especially the way he had smoothed off almost all traces of what had once been a distinct Scottish burr to his voice to replace it with something anonymous.

Once the DS was back with a chair, on which he sat, right at the edge, looking nervously from his own boss to the Det. Sup., Aird kicked things off.

'This may be a little bit unorthodox but as Mr Devlin has made a complaint against you, Inspector Smith, via his solicitor, Ms Channing, I thought it might be profitable to air that issue first, all of us, on the record, before I decide whether it would be proper for DI Smith to carry out this interview. If nobody has any objection?'

His look round at everyone, as he said it, made it clear that he was asking for the purposes of the recording only and none would be welcomed.

Smith wondered suddenly, in a lightbulb moment, if the two of them were at it. Aird and the Channing dyke. He couldn't imagine any other reason why Aird would be here, wasting everyone's time, with some shite about him torturing a bloody yapper. It would explain why she'd been in a position to contact him directly to complain.

'Thank you. DS Taylor, I understand you were also present for the arrest. Could you please tell us, in your own words, exactly what this alleged incident with the puppy tapped out. He'd been pale before, when t came in. Now his face was drained of all colour and he kept needing to lick his lips. Smith suspected the only thing stopping him reaching for a drink of the water put ready on the table was that his hand would be shaking too much to pick it up.

Sneaky bastard, Aird was, Smith thought next. He must have been already in the building, or out in the car park at the very least, when he'd been talking to him earlier. He never gave any hint of his intention to appear, and certainly not to be at the interview.

Taylor cleared this throat and tried again. He had to get this right. The thought of what Smith might do to him if he didn't was too bleak to even contemplate.

'Sir, when we were trying to speak to Mr Devlin, the little puppy became very agitated and kept trying to bite everyone. DI Smith picked it up carefully and tried to calm it down, for its own good. But that made it struggle and try harder to bite him, and in its excitement it started to pi...'

He quickly revised what he was about to say, looking at the solicitor and saying, 'Excuse me, ma'am, it started to piddle everywhere, all over itself and the DI's arm. So he, the DI, took it to the sink to wash it clean in warm water, and to clean up his hand and his jacket at the same time.'

Smith was impressed. As yarns went, it was an absolute cracker. He almost found himself believing it. He had to make a conscious effort not to grin or to let his eyebrows shoot up.

'When they were both cleaner, he found a fluffy towel to wrap the puppy in then he handed it to Craig – to DC Stephens, sir – and told him to make sure he dried it carefully so it didn't catch cold.'

Smith had to look down and cough into his hand at that point, afraid he was about to lose it. The fluffy towel to swaddle a baby puppy in was the perfect touch.

'I see,' Aird said levelly.

He wasn't a stupid man, Smith knew. Not by any stretch of the imagination. A pain in the arse and a stickler for everything by the book. But he hadn't got where he was without recognising a load of baloney when he heard it. Confronted with a straight-faced testimony like that, from a Detective Sergeant with a blameless record, Devlin was outmanoeuvred and he knew it.

'Ms Channing, are you, on behalf on your client, satisfied with the Sergeant's explanation?'

Devlin was on the point of saying something. Or of spontaneous combustion. It was hard to know, from his expression, which was the most likely. Channing motioned with an upraised hand to stop him from saying anything at all.

'For the record, I am still far from happy,' she said. 'But I'm prepared to accept what the sergeant has said. For now. And it seems I can't do anything to prevent Inspector Smith from interviewing my client. But I want your assurance, Superintendent, that all of the procedure will be recorded, both audibly and visually, and that we will have copies of both.'

'But of course,' Aird spread his hands as he spoke. 'That's standard procedure. And for your extra reassurance, please know that I shall be remaining in the building, though not in the room, until the inspector has finished interviewing your client. You have my phone number. Please feel free to call me back at any time if you feel my presence would be of further help. And of course, you and I should get together once you have all finished here so you can discuss any further concerns with me.'

I can just bet what form that discussion is going to take, you randy old goat, Smith thought, noticing the look which passed between the two of them. Then he jerked his attention back to the present as he realised the Det. Sup. was addressing him once more.

'So perhaps before I leave the room, Inspector, you could kindly update Mr Devlin on news of his little dog.'

Smith put on his most sombre expression. In both of his policing careers, he'd had to break the worst possible news to grieving relatives. He tried to adopt the same tone now.

'Mr Devlin, I told you at the time that I suspected your little puppy was of the banned pit bull type. I'm sorry to have to tell you that expert opinion has confirmed my suspicions. The pup has now been impounded while a court order is sought for its destruction.'

Devlin let out an anguished wail, more heart-rending than some Smith had heard from bereaved next of kin of a human casualty. Tears were flowing freely from the man's eyes.

Smith was in need of a slash and of more coffee, so he took the golden opportunity.

'Muzzz Channing, perhaps you would like a short break for your client to recover his composure before we continue? I can arrange for someone to bring you both some tea, perhaps.'

'Coffee for me, Inspector. And it's Ms Channing. Not Muzzz, as I believe I have had occasion to tell you before.'

The three officers left the room together and Aird despatched Tony Taylor to sort out refreshments.

'This isn't over between us, Oscar,' Aird told him. 'Tony's a good DS but that was the biggest load of bullshit I've ever heard and you've clearly been leaning on him to stick to the party line. You and I will talk more, later.'

'Yes, guv,' Smith told him, flicking the finger at the round-shouldered retreating back of his superior officer.

* * *

10:18 – TUESDAY MORNING

'Right, Mr Devlin, Muzz Channing,' Smith shortened the Ms slightly, to show willing, though still left it long enough for her to roll her eyes and sigh audibly. 'If you've had time to compose yourself after the upsetting news about your little dog, perhaps we can continue.'

Smith sat down heavily. He liked to make a point of his size. The proverbial throwing his weight around. Showing all present that there was only one Alpha male in the room.

DS Tony Taylor took his seat next to the guv and once again went through the formalities for the recording. Smith would have bet money on the Det. Sup. being glued to the monitors to watch every minute of the interview. Which meant he would have to be careful about whatever he said and did.

In a sense he'd already shot his bolt. Now the man knew he wasn't going to get his pup back, or even to be able to sell it on if he did find himself going down for a stretch, Smith had less to hold over his head to get a full confession on record. He was still confident he had plenty in his arsenal, so he was looking pleased with himself as he started to set out his stall.

'As I explained to you, Devlin...' he began, before the solicitor interrupted him.

'Mr Devlin, please, Inspector. You will kindly address my client correctly at all times, until he is convicted of something.'

'Oh, but you've been convicted of plenty in the past, haven't you, Mister Devlin,' he drew it out as much as he did with the solicitor's prefix of choice. 'And I doubt you were called Mister whilst inside serving time.'

The Channing woman was clearly about to cut in once more so Smith inclined his head slightly in concession. He needed to crack on.

'But moving on, as I explained to you before we left your house, we had a warrant to search your property and I've just had the final results of the search.'

He put papers in front of Devlin and his solicitor as he went on, 'Apologies for the late disclosure, but I have only just received these myself.'

'You never told me you were searching,' Devlin said accusingly.

'Oh, I did, I assure you, Mr Devlin. You were perhaps a bit preoccupied thinking about your dog. I'm sure the sergeant here will confirm that for you. DS Taylor?'

Tony looked unwaveringly across the table and made eye contact with Devlin. He knew the suspect had been told of the search, and shown the warrant, because he had done it himself. But if the guv wanted to claim the credit himself for some reason, so be it.

'For the recording, I can confirm that I personally witnessed Mr Devlin being told of the search and being shown the appropriate warrant.'

'Thank you, Sergeant,' Smith told him, then turned his attention back to Devlin.

'If you both look at the list of items found and seized at your property, you'll see the first one listed is a sawn-off shotgun. Of exactly the type used in the armed robberies we are investigating.'

'Is there any camera footage of this search?' Channing demanded, pouncing like a dog on a bone. Like a pit bull on its prey, Smith couldn't help but think to himself. 'Body cam footage from any uniformed officers who may have taken part?'

'We wouldn't usually film a search of any property, Muzzz Channing.'

He stretched it to its fullest once more, trying to get a rise out of her.

'And where was this shotgun allegedly found?'

'Allegedly? Are you implying that the weapon was not, in fact, found at the property? I have a team of officers prepared to testify that it was. It was in the garden shed.'

She turned to her client with a look of triumph on her face.

'Mr Devlin, are you in the habit of locking your garden shed?'

He picked up the clue without needing any prompting.

'No, never. No one round there would rob from me. They know I ain't got nothing worth robbing, for a start.'

'The weapon has, of course, been sent off to be checked for fingerprints,' Smith told him. 'And of course we already have yours on record.'

Then he almost laughed aloud when, with a smirk as of pride at his own cleverness, Devlin replied, before his lawyer could do anything to stop him, 'There won't be any prints on it.'

'You're sure of that, are you? How could you know that there would be no prints on the weapon, unless you were the person who handled it last, and you know that you were wearing gloves at the time? If it was indeed planted there, you can't have any idea if there were prints on it or not, can you?'

'You're putting words into my client's mouth, Inspector,' the Channing woman snapped at him, then, to Devlin, 'please don't say anything further before we have had the opportunity to discuss these further developments.

'Inspector, is there anything else you intend to spring on my client without notice, like that?'

'Oh, I'm afraid there is,' Smith told her, not bothering to hide his delight. 'Your client was told that we had CCTV footage which appeared to show him, holding a shotgun, at the scene of the latest robbery. I have, this morning, shortly before joining you here, received the digitally enhanced copies of those shots.'

He reached into his document folder and laid out the prints across the table, like a croupier dealing out cards, facing towards the two people sitting opposite.

Devlin's face drained of colour as he looked at them. The person in the photo who was brandishing the sawn-off had a scarf round the lower half of his face, but it had slipped slightly and showed the nose. Devlin had a highly distinctive nose. Hooked, broken and reset at quite an angle.

'Correct me if I'm wrong, Mr Devlin, but I think your record shows that you in fact had your nose broken for you by the victim of one of your earlier robberies, for which you went to prison. You beat a shopkeeper very badly with a similar weapon to the gun in this photo, but not before he had hit you full in the face with the baseball bat he kept behind the counter for his own protection.

'So, your solicitor will no doubt correct me if I'm wrong, but this is the way I see it. The prosecution is, of course, going to produce these photos as evidence, and will rely heavily on the unique shape of your nose for identification. And that will inevitably lead to details of that particular previous conviction coming to light before you would want them to.

'Because that story doesn't really show you in a very good light, does it? And naturally, the victim of your attack on that occasion would be called as a witness for the prosecution to relate exactly what damage he did to your nose.'

He saw the Channing woman flush red from her neck up, clearly in fury, so he carried on while he was well into his stride.

'This is the point at which I think we should adjourn this interview to give you the opportunity to consult your solicitor about these latest disclosures. What I propose, therefore, is that we arrange for your release now on pre-charge bail, which DS Taylor here will sort out.

'There will be reporting conditions and a requirement of residence at your known address. Then, once you've had the opportunity to discuss things at length with your solicitor, she will no doubt advise you on your best course of action in response to the charges you will be facing.

'So shall we all agree to reconvene here at, say, ten o'clock tomorrow morning?'

He picked up his folder, feeling smugly pleased with himself. Ten – nil he made that one, in his favour. He'd particularly enjoyed watching the Channing woman getting so furious.

He swept out of the interview room into the corridor, heading for the stairs and the sanctuary of his own office. And coffee. He felt he'd more than deserved coffee after that satisfactory sparring match.

He got as far as the door to the room which housed the monitors, connected to the cameras in the various interview rooms. The door opened and Aird said brusquely, 'In here, Oscar. A word.'

Bollocks, Smith thought to himself. He thought he'd played that rather well. He couldn't quite see what the Det. Sup. would have to whinge about. They were getting close to banging up someone who was best off out of the way before he finally killed someone.

'Cutting it a bit fine with disclosure there, Oscar. And I hope to God that gun wasn't really planted. But then, I don't think even you would be stupid enough to pull a stunt like that.

'Wrap this one up, by the book. All the paperwork in order. No rough stuff with the suspect. This will be a nice tick on the books if we get it to court and get a sound conviction. Let's not count our chickens too soon, but good work so far. Tell the team I said so.'

Smith hid his surprise well. In fairness to Aird, because he would deliver bollockings right, left and centre where needed, he did follow up with praise when it was well earned.

While he was on a roll, Smith couldn't resist a cheeky question, out of curiosity.

'Guv, how come the Channing woman has a direct line to you? If you don't mind me asking.'

Not that he gave a fish's tit whether he minded or not.

'Oh, you didn't know, then? I thought the jungle drums in this nick were better than that. Jayne Channing is, er, of the other persuasion. She currently happens to be dating my eldest daughter, who lives at home. So she's a not infrequent visitor to my house.'

6.

16:59 – TUESDAY AFTERNOON

'I have to go out now, Edith, so I wondered if I could drop you off home on my way. It's about your knocking-off time, isn't it? Only it's not all that far off my route for where I'm heading, so it would save you getting cold and wet standing waiting for your bus.'

Edith, behind the reception desk, was already halfway into her coat and gathering up her bag, lunch box and umbrella. She was always a clock-watcher. She was reasonably diligent at her job but the pay wasn't enough to persuade her to give away even one minute of her own time for free.

'Oh, that's so very kind of you, Inspector. It's raining cats and dogs out there and I have to stop at the shops on my way.'

Even had he not been a perceptive detective, Smith would have had to be on another planet not to pick up on the heavy hint behind the words.

Sighing inwardly, he told her, 'Well, as long as you don't have a week's worth of shopping to do, I could take you via the shops and then drop you to your door, if that would help?'

It was worth it in the long run, he reminded himself. The fact that she had not tipped him off about Aird's presence unannounced in the building today only served to confirm his suspicions. The Det. Sup. had been so determined to try to catch Smith up to no good, he must have sneaked in the back way, steering clear of Edith's watchful eyes, and loitering in the building waiting to pounce. Either that or he'd waited in his car until the last possible minute and managed to dodge Edith when he had come in.

Smith could play the gentleman when he chose. He opened the passenger door for Edith and saw her safely settled, with her seatbelt on, before going round to get in to the driver's seat. Luckily she preferred one of the smaller supermarkets on the edge of town rather than the big hypermarkets on the commercial centre which gave him the heebie-jeebies.

He meekly pushed the trolley round while she selected the items she needed. Mostly a collection of fairly uninspired basic groceries and some ready meals. He knew she was unmarried and lived with her widowed mother.

'I need to get a box of chocolates for my mum,' she told him, leading the way to the confectionery aisle.

He rightly took it as a hint and played the chivalrous knight once more.

'Let me get those for her, as a little treat. Which does she like? What about these?'

He picked up a popular brand. A smallish box, nothing inspiring.

'Oh no, mum likes something much classier than those,' Edith told him, looking affronted. 'No, she much prefers good quality continental chocolates. She was very well travelled in her younger days, you know.'

She picked up something very select. A box almost twice the size of the one in his hand and more than twice the price.

Bloody hell! He did a double take as he looked again at the cost. Nearer to three times, in fact. She'd better not let him down the next time his boss tried to sneak up on him. At this rate it would be cheaper to hire a private detective and have him put a tracker on Aird's car.

'If that's what she likes, then that's what she shall have, with my compliments.'

He dropped her off at her door, waving away her effusive thanks for the lift and the chocolates. As far as he was concerned, it was an investment like any other.

He'd finally remembered the name of the pub where he'd picked up the mysterious and light-fingered, Lulu so he was heading back there to see if he could find out anything more about her. In particular, he wanted to know where he could find her. There was unfinished business between them, as far as he was concerned.

'Lulu? You'll be lucky if you see her again. Not in here, not for a long while, if you're looking for her for the reason I think you might be.'

The young man behind the bar had given him a pitying look when he'd trotted out his tale of having met her, spent a pleasant evening with her, but forgotten to get her contact details. It sounded as if he was not the first to be caught out by her.

'I'm guessing you woke up with no wallet, or something like that?' the barman asked him.

He was as camp as Christmas but his tone was sympathetic enough, rather than laughing at the thought of a big bloke like Smith, who certainly looked as if he could handle himself, getting robbed by a slip of a girl like Lulu.

Smith grinned ruefully.

'Something like that. Look, mate, if she should happen to show her face in here again, I'd be really obliged if you'd give me a bell. I'm not far away and I really would like to see her again. Here's my card.'

He took one of his work cards out of the new wallet, carefully folded a tenner around it and handed it over to the young man, who deftly pocketed the banknote, looked at the card, then glanced up, wide-eyed, at Smith.

'Oh, my days! You're the Lily Law? Gawd, Lulu's bitten off more than she can chew this time.'

'Make the call, won't you? And don't worry, I don't hit

women.'

He didn't expect he'd hear anything, but at least he'd tried. Although it was turning into a costly evening so far. He decided to spend a bit more money on a chip supper. He was hungry, but he knew that by the time he got home, he'd probably not feel like cooking.

Clive the cat was sitting waiting for him in the hallway, managing to look both smug and reproachful at the same time. Whatever he'd been up to, it had probably been more fun than Smith's day. Although there was at least the prospect of a nice solid conviction in the offing, if he kept cracking the whip over the team.

His fish and chips eaten, Smith slipped his shoes off, chucked his tie on the floor and sank into his favourite armchair, pulling up the footrest. Then he picked up the phone and called a saved number.

'*Hallo, Oma*, this is Oskar.'

He slipped automatically into flawless German to speak to his paternal grandmother. The only person in his life he had ever truly loved.

'I know perfectly well who it is, Oskar. I may be old but I am not yet senile.'

He laughed as he replied, 'Sorry, *Oma*. Of course you aren't. How are you?'

'How am I? I'd be a lot better if you could convince these stupid carers you pay for that I'm not an infant so they shouldn't treat me like one. Speak to them, Oskar. Sack them all, preferably.'

'Oma, you've just turned ninety. You need a little bit of help at your age. That's all.'

She gave a snort of contempt so he sighed and agreed. It was always simpler that way.

'All right, I'll talk to them again and remind them that you still have a very active brain, and to speak to you with a bit of respect.'

'Good, thank you, Oskar. Now, how are you? Do you still have your little cat? What was his name? Clive, is it?'

Smith moved the phone so she could hear the tomcat's loud, contented purring where he lay stretched out on his master's stomach.

'Yes, Clive. That's him saying hello.'

'And when are you coming to see me, Oskar? It seems so long since I saw you last.'

'I'll try and come soon, I promise. Things are just a bit busy at work at the moment. I have quite a big case to wrap up. Then I really will try to come over. And I can talk to the carers in person, to remind them.'

They talked a while longer. As ever, his grandmother wanted to know everything about his life. Was he seeing anyone? If not, why not? What about work? When would he get promoted?

She wasn't wrong about her state of mind. She remembered almost everything he ever told her and often came back to things they'd discussed in previous calls.

She finally let him go and said her goodbyes, Smith promising faithfully to visit her as soon as he could, she reminding him that there were no certainties at her time of life.

Smith had never known his biological father. His mother had been a young single parent with a small baby, German, from a decent enough family who had frostily tolerated their illegitimate grandson throughout his life but shown him neither love nor affection.

His mother had managed to ensnare a British soldier not averse to taking on someone else's bastard child for the sake of a very attractive wife who was an excellent cook and home-maker.

He'd aspired to the rank of corporal but had zero ambition. The product of a British Army father and a German mother – Smith's beloved Oma – Smith's new stepfather had treated him well, always provided for him, took him to endless rugby matches, in which the young Oscar had played, despite having no interest in the game himself.

He'd been kind to him without ever showing him any overt signs of love, and although he had adopted him as his own son, he had never given him his name. That had left Oskar Schmidt with the German name growing up, which saw him known constantly as Schmidt the Kraut, Oskar the Sausage-gobbler and other worse names throughout his school years.

The step-father corporal's German had also been fluent, with a German mother, so his work role was as an interpreter. He seemed to drift along perfectly happily through life with no ambition at all, but no sign of any discontent.

It came as a shock to everyone who knew him when one day he simply went off for a walk in the woods and when he failed to return, was found hanging, blue-lipped with tongue protruding, from a tree.

The young Oscar, barely into his teens, was shipped off to live with his paternal grandmother, by then a widow, until he was old enough to apply for and go off to Sandhurst to become an army officer.

He never saw or heard from his mother again.

* * *

18:46 – TUESDAY EVENING

'I made you some nice thick broth. I thought that would be easier for you to eat, and you really do need to eat something to keep your strength up. You're losing too much weight. It's vegan, too. You see, I listened to what you said. Potatoes, oatmeal, vegetables, that sort of thing. Here, try some.'

It wasn't vegetarian, never mind vegan. He'd made it with some of the brains. He thought that was quite an altruistic gesture on his part, as they were his favourite bit.

He'd adapted various recipes from those for calves'

brains and was both pleased with his ingenuity and proud of the results. For this fussy guest, he'd had to be a bit imaginative. There was no oatmeal in the broth, but he'd had to think of something which would explain the texture and colour, once he'd blitzed it in the liquidiser.

'I'm not hungry.'

She was starting to get that flat, listless tone to her voice. Her eyes, too, were different. The spark had gone out of them. All the will to survive was extinguished already. He'd thought she might have some fight left. He liked it much better when they fought to the bitter end. He climaxed much faster when they did that.

He was disappointed with this one, though. She had reached this stage earlier than any of the others had. If that was linked to being a vegan, he was glad he'd never once thought of going down that route himself.

As far as he was concerned, birds and animals, and their by-products, had been put on this earth by whatever supreme being anyone chose to believe in, for one purpose alone. To serve Man and to provide for him to the end of their lives and beyond.

'You must eat something,' he told her, not unkindly. 'You've lost so much weight. I can't possibly let you go free looking like this.'

The doe eyes suddenly widened. A faint but discernible light of hope was kindled within them once more. He noticed that the skin on her face looked taut and fragile of late. Blue veins showed through distinctly at the temples.

'You're going to let me go?'

Her voice was weaker now, too, he noticed. He had to pull her back from the brink somehow. She was no use to him in this state.

'Well, of course.'

He managed to insinuate a small note of reproach in his voice. To show his disappointment that she had not believed what he had told her.

'I always told you that I would set you free, didn't I? It

hurts me that you clearly didn't believe me. And yet I've done nothing to make you suspect that I'm not a man of my word, have I?'

She was a fraction late in replying. She was scanning his face as he spoke. Hanging on to every word with increasing desperation. Wanting so much for him to be telling her the truth. Not daring to believe that he was.

'Have I?'

His voice came out as a sharp bark now which made her wince visibly.

She tried not to flinch in fear at his tone. But despite her efforts to stay calm, she felt herself shrinking back, found her eyes blinking rapidly in terror, and in a desperate effort not to let tears start to flow.

'No,' she said hastily, her voice softer than she intended it to be.

She tried again, 'No, you haven't. You're really going to let me go?'

Her voice broke slightly as she asked, her eyes anxiously scanning his impassive face for any sign of hope she could cling on to.

'I've told you. As soon as you look a bit more presentable, I'm going to set you free. So until then, please try to eat up some of this delicious broth I've made for you. That will help to put flesh on your bones.'

He could even say it without any trace of irony. He'd practised saying it to himself, in front of the mirror in his bathroom. Until he could say it, every time, with a straight face.

The first few times he'd tried, he couldn't stop the laughter breaking from his lips. He could tell from the minute he went into the room afterwards that the sound of him laughing to himself, alone in the bathroom, had sent his guest into a frenzied panic which drove him wild with desire.

He wasn't proud of his behaviour on that first occasion. It was the intensity of the fear which his manic laughter had provoked which had driven him beyond all self-control.

At the height of the most intense climax he could ever remember having, somehow his hands were round the white throat. Gripping, throttling.

Her eyes, looking up at him, silently pleading with him to stop, seemed to lose their light at the very moment he started to come.

The feeling of her legs flailing against the carpet underneath him, the froth appearing at her lips, already starting to turn blue, were such powerful erotic stimuli, he thought he would never stop.

He was so ashamed of his complete lack of mastery over himself that once he'd finished his ritual – the one he'd learned first with his mother – the careful, reverential washing of every part of her body in his bath – he'd dealt with himself.

He'd learned to strip naked to perform the ritual. He loved the intimacy of feeling once-warm flesh against his own bare body as he worked. This time, once he'd washed her clean, he'd laid her carefully on the floor of the bathroom and knelt at her feet, begging her forgiveness.

He'd taken the leather belt from his trousers and beaten himself mercilessly on every part of his body that he could reach, until he was weeping from the pain. Far worse than any of the countless thrashings he'd known from his father. Then he'd turned the shower on to its coldest and hardest setting and stood there under it, still weeping. Shivering, miserable. Promising himself he would learn some self-control.

He mustn't ever again let himself be so over-indulgent. That was the way errors were made. Errors which could see an end to everything he now lived for.

It was the memory of that shame and of the pain he had inflicted upon himself which helped him to keep control now, in the face of her provocation.

He kept his voice soft and calm as he held out a

spoonful of the greyish-fawn slop.

'Try some of this,' he told her. 'Please do try some. I'm sure it would do you good. And then you have my word. I will set you free.'

7.

09:27 – WEDNESDAY MORNING

'So, Tony, your Mispers. I said I'd look at the file and I have. And I think you might have a point. The four missing on our patch have too many similarities for it to be pure coincidence. Aside from the fact that any copper who accepts that coincidence is even a thing should be shot, never mind removed from the job.'

The DI sounded as if he might have meant it. Tony Taylor was never sure.

Smith took a slurp of his double espresso before he continued talking. The rate he went through them when he was in the office meant he'd soon run up a hefty tab once more, unless Tony kept chasing after him.

Smith had the file on the table in front of him but it was closed and he didn't have any notes to hand. Taylor knew that one single read-through was all the gaffer needed to have all the info off by heart. One reason no one on the team could ever get away with turning in sloppy reports. If they slipped up on the smallest detail and Smith read their work, he would spot it. Then he would kick arses right round the office and back and demand a total rewrite of the offending document.

'All of them blonde, or fair-haired at least, and always natural. Similar ages, roughly the same height and build. If this is the work of one person, they're going for a particular type.'

'So he has his favourite profile, you mean? A particular sort of look that's meaningful to him, for some reason?'

'Who says it's a bloke, Tony?' Smith looked at him at he asked the question.

'Well, I assumed it would be a bloke, snatching women...'

'Is not the answer I expect from a DS. So many reasons why it's not necessarily a bloke, so for the time being, we treat them as a total unknown, until we have some concrete leads to go on. It wouldn't be the first time a male serial kidnapper, or even a killer, has used a woman to bring his prey to him.

'Young women these days tend to be wary of going anywhere with strange blokes, but they might be less suspicious of a woman befriending them and suggesting going off for a drink or a meal somewhere.'

Unless they were thieving bitches who were more interested in getting into the man's wallet than his trousers, Smith was thinking to himself. He was still bitter about falling for the oldest trick in the book with Lulu and not being able to find her to exact his revenge.

'Fair point, guv. So you think we might be looking for a couple, working together?'

I don't think anything yet, Tony, it's far too early. There's been no public appeal for information yet, is that right? Do we know why? Have the Woodentops not pressed for it?'

'Joe Barnes said he has been pushing to get someone higher up to do that, but they're wary of starting public panic if they're seen to link all four cases to the work of one man too soon. One or more persons, I should say now. I think they're still holding out for the faint chance that one, at least, of them might turn up safe and well and give them some answers.'

'About as likely as me joining a seminary to become a priest, after this much time since the first one went. Not with the strong possibility of a link between them,' Smith scoffed.

Tony made that prissy face he did when Smith said something which touched a nerve in him. His mouth pursed up like a puckered arsehole. Smith knew he was a god-botherer who didn't approve of his boss's rampant atheism nor his colourful speech, which in Tony's books amounted to blasphemy.

'I'll talk to Aird about it, see if we can't stir something up a bit,' Smith told his sergeant, seeking to change the subject. 'And talking of the Det. Sup., did you know his daughter was a lezzer? The gossip mill mustn't be working to full capacity as I hadn't heard that. Just as well I didn't say anything to put my big foot right in it, eh?'

Tony Taylor's mouth seemed to screw up even more. He looked, for a fleeting moment, as if he might finally grow a pair and tell his boss exactly what he thought of him. Smith didn't allow him the opportunity, but instead gave him both barrels of his hardest stare, until the DS looked away.

'Right, so assuming there is a link, where could our kidnapper be encountering these women? What, other than looks, do they have in common?

'Sally Rogers, 24, medical centre receptionist. Kathy Morgan, 23, estate agent. Vicky Garcia, 21, beautician. Gill Burrell, 26, primary school teacher.'

Smith trotted out all the details faultlessly from memory. Tony Taylor had to look down at his own notes to check everything, although he knew he had no need to. His boss wouldn't have made a single mistake in what he said. He never did.

'All single, no steady relationships, according to the info from the Plods, assuming they managed to ask the right questions and note the correct answers,' Smith continued.

'So, let's go on the premise, for now, that our kidnapper is one person, of either gender. So where might they have come across these four suspected victims?'

Even as he posed the question, he imagined Tony Taylor suggesting some sort of church social, or whatever they called them these days. He underestimated his DS though.

'Someone who's buying a house,' Taylor said without thinking. 'With one or more children in school. Someone who might need a medical certificate in connection with a mortgage application.'

Smith nodded and asked, 'And what about the beautician?'

'If it's a woman, they want to look their absolute knock-out best to go and talk to the bank manager. Or the building society, about taking out a mortgage. And if it's a man, he wants to treat his wife or his girlfriend, or bit on the side, while they still have a bit of money to spare, before it all goes on loan repayments.'

'Impressive, Tony,' he told him. 'You say the Woodentops have spoken to family, friends, work colleagues, that sort of thing?'

'They have, guv, plus employers.'

'Right, get me all of those reports. Everything. I don't want edited versions, either. I don't trust that lot not to miss something which might jump straight out at one of us. And get some of the team onto trawling for other similar cases in other areas. Ditto for those, I want all the interview notes, every letter of them.'

'You're thinking this might be one for Serious Crime after all, then, guv?'

'We've potentially got four bodies somewhere on our patch. Or at the very least, four young women being held against their will. We've had no sightings, no personal effects found, no bodies, or even any body parts.

'In short, it's starting to look for all the world as if this is something beyond the scope of our lowly friends in uniform.

'You were right, Tony. It seems very much as if we

could have a serial kidnapper, potentially a killer, too, on our manor. And a nasty one, at that.'

* * *

19:46 – WEDNESDAY EVENING

'What are you eating tonight, Oskar? And don't speak with your mouth full. You were brought up better than that. Fish and chips again? You should eat properly. Take care of yourself. Cook fresh food. You know how to do it.'

'I'm having a curry, Oma. Chicken. Akbari Chum Chum.'

They were speaking German, as ever, except for the Bengali words for the takeaway he was eating. Or at least which he would like to be eating, rather than getting his ear bent by his Oma.

She gave a loud snort of derision.

'What kind of a stupid name is that for proper food? Why do you eat that foreign stuff? What's wrong with Bratwurst? Or Käsespätzl? You used to love my Kartoffelpuffer when you were little. Why don't you eat proper German food?'

He let her listen to Clive purring for a moment to give him enough time to swallow his latest mouthful. It was very good.

'You can't get German food round here, Oma. Not like you used to make it, for sure. And I don't have time to cook. I'm too busy trying to catch criminals.'

Again she scoffed down the phone at him. Loudly. When he did find the time to go and visit her, he must check if she needed new hearing aids. She was tending to shout more often than to speak.

'You need to find yourself a woman, Oskar. Someone who can cook properly, and keep house for you while you're at work. A nice German girl who could look after you and feed you up with the right meals.

'You could come and marry one of these stupid carers you insist on me having. One or two of them can at least cook a Wurst without burning it. And if you marry one and take her back to England that would be one less for me to put up with.'

'Why would you want to inflict one of them on me if they're not good enough for you?'

'Because, Oskar,' she began, with an acerbic tone suitable for wilful small children or people of low intelligence, 'the things you would expect from a wife are but a distant memory to me, and even then, not with another woman. Or rather, only once, and that was because we were both very drunk indeed.'

Smith nearly choked on the large mouthful of Chum Chum he had just taken. His Oma had always spoken frankly in front of him. Always, even when he had been a young boy. But the image she had just put into his head came under the definite category of Too Much Information. Especially when he was trying to eat his supper.

'A woman wouldn't put up with me, though, Oma. Don't forget I've tried that before and it didn't work out.'

'Nonsense!' she told him firmly. 'Remember what I always told you when you were learning to ski. So you fall over. So what? You get back up again and you keep on doing it, until you can stand up on your skis and go wherever you want to. You've spent far too long lying in the snow feeling sorry for yourself, Oskar. It's time to get back up. Start with your Stem Christie turns and it will soon all come flooding back to you.'

She'd been an excellent downhill skier in her day. Championship standard. A fierce and fearless competitor who hated to lose. She'd taught the young Oskar to ski, often taking him on holiday to Bavaria, where the best slopes were.

Her husband, Oskar's Opa, hadn't been remotely

interested in skiing or any other sport. He'd been more than happy to sit in the nearest bar at the foot of the slopes, reading a book, sipping the Glühwein, always putting his hand in his pocket to pay for their passes and anything else they needed. Oma always said it was because of his sedentary nature that he had died relatively young.

'Oma, any woman would be a fool to saddle herself with a copper for a partner. We're not good marriage material. There's no telling what hour of the day or night we might get called out.'

'Stop making excuses, Oskar. So get yourself a mistress. Come and try out some of these useless carers. You can use the spare room to give them a trial run in bed. When I take my hearing aids out, I won't be able to hear if you're doing well enough to make the headboard bang against the wall.'

Smith had to laugh at that. It was so typical of the bluntly spoken Oma he had adored all his life.

'Oma...' he began before she cut across him.

'Oma what? You're a decent looking man, Oskar. You should be having sex, and plenty of it.'

'I have to go, Oma. I still have work to do. I'll try to come and see you as soon as I can. But I'm not promising to sleep with any of your carers. I thought you said most of them were ugly, with moustaches, anyway?'

'Don't be naive, Oskar. You don't have to look at a woman while you're making love to her. I thought you knew that.'

'Good night, Oma. I love you,' he told her firmly, to wind up the conversation.

'Good night, Oskar. I am so very proud of you.'

'And there you have it, Clive, my little friend,' Smith told his cat as he ended the call. 'Oma is proud of me. But has she ever loved me? She's never said so. Nor has anyone else. Well, the ex-wife, maybe. But screaming *ich liebe dich* while I was shagging her doesn't really count. It's just a thing you say when you're having sex, a lot of the time.

'I don't suppose you have to worry about such niceties, do you? I suppose it's just a case of wham, bam, and not even a thank you, ma'am, in your case. And yes, I am a bit jealous of you. Your life is a lot simpler than mine. At least no other cat ever stole your wallet while she was checking out your crown jewels.'

The cat was purring at him, its eyes slowly crossing as it started to nod off, sitting on the arm of his chair. It had already had an experimental sniff or two at the Chum Chum, Smith gently pushing its inquisitive nose out of the way.

'I love you, you little sod,' he told the cat, running a hand the length of its back, watching it arch its spine in response to the gesture. 'For all your faults. But keep that between the two of us. I'd never live it down if it got out round the nick.'

Clive opened his eyes wider, then lifted a back leg and began to give his own balls a good licking.

'Well, perhaps not all of your faults,' Smith told the cat, as he took his plate to the table to finish off his meal without the distraction.

8.

WEDNESDAY – EARLIER IN THE DAY

'Guv, about these missing women on our patch. I think it's something me and the team should pick up and run with,' Smith told the Det. Sup., Murray Aird, over the phone. He'd made time to call him after he'd finished his daily discussions with Tony Taylor, plus made sure the file on the armed robberies was progressing and was watertight in every detail.

There was a short pause then Aird's voice, dripping with irony, asked, 'Who are you and what have you done with Oscar Smith? The Oscar I know and try to love, despite his many faults, is usually trying to offload cases onto the humble mortals in uniform, rather than wanting to take stuff off their hands.'

Smith gave what he hoped sounded like a polite chuckle, then went on, 'Seriously, though, guv, I think we should do a televised appeal for the public's help with this one. We're not making enough progress on it.'

'Top floor are against it, Oscar. I have mentioned it before. They're afraid of causing panic if the cases aren't really linked. Show me a palpable connection and I'll try again.'

'On the basis of similarities alone there has to be a link there. It seems clear that someone is picking a certain type of victim. Height, colouring, age. Even to the fact that they are all in work, in decent jobs, doing quite well for themselves. This isn't someone selecting random slappers off the street or picking them up in seedy bars.'

'Uniform have passed this on to you?'

'Joe Barnes brought it up with Tony, guv.'

Aird gave a grunt of disapproval. The animosity between Barnes and Smith was an open secret both in the nick and throughout the division.

'The pair of you, you and Joe, should bloody well grow up and start liaising with one another direct, like you're supposed to. You need to get off your high horse about uniformed officers, Oscar. Most of us started out that way. Unlike you and your ex-Army executive officer friend, who covers your arse for you whenever you screw up too badly.'

There was no mistaking the anger in the Det. Sup.'s voice now. Smith tried to keep his tone the right side of civil as he responded, 'Guv, the RMP isn't exactly the Brownies, you know. I've done my fair share of front-line policing. And believe me, young subalterns still wet behind the ears get all the shit jobs going.

'I'm happy enough to liaise with Barnes, if it will get us anywhere. And I strongly suggest you push the top floor once more to consider a public appeal. I'll even front that myself if you think it will give it more clout. The longer we leave it without coming clean about possible links, the more the public are going to hang us out to dry if and when it all comes out.'

'I'll tell you what I'm prepared to do for you, Oscar. I'll swing by your nick last thing this afternoon, to talk to you and Joe Barnes, in the same room, at the same time. If you can manage to stay civil to do that.

'Depending on the outcome of that meeting, I'll decide whether or not I should move to get a press conference and make the possible link between the cases public. Over to you.'

Smith threw a 'twat' at the desk phone as he hung up.

He didn't much care if the Det. Sup. heard it or not.

There was only one thing for it. He was going to have to swallow his pride and go and talk to Joe Barnes so they could present a united front when Aird came to see them. If this case did turn out to be a single perpetrator, that would be a nice tasty serious crime for Smith to get his teeth into and head up. It could only be to his career advantage.

Smith went downstairs, tapped briefly on the door of Inspector Joe Barnes' office, but made a point of going in before he was invited to. The knock was a concession, to try to start negotiations off on the right foot.

'Have you got a minute, Joe?'

If Barnes was surprised by the knock, Smith's presence or his attempt to sound polite, he was too professional to show it. He simply nodded for Smith to take a seat.

Barnes was like an advert for some sort of healthy eating magazine. Not as tall as Smith, though not short, he had tightly curling dark auburn hair, piercing green eyes, a sprinkling of freckles and the proverbial washboard stomach. He was probably into all this planking lark, Smith thought, and could probably hold the position for a good half hour at a time.

His starched and ironed uniform shirt dazzled with such whiteness that Smith half wished he had his sunglasses with him.

Sanctimonious bastard, Smith thought to himself at the sight of him. He had a sudden mental image of him standing at the ironing board himself teasing out any hint of a wrinkle in his uniform shirts. Probably not trusting the wife to do it to the right standard. *Prick*.

Chalk and cheese summed the two of them up to perfection. Smith knew he had let himself go, physically, since his Army days, when he'd had to pass periodic fitness tests much more stringent than anything the police service in civvy street had yet come up with. Not to mention ironing his own uniform shirts when his wife had buggered off and left him.

'These missing women. I think we should push again for a public appeal. I know you've tried. Aird is coming in end of play to talk to us both with a view to doing something to move the investigation forward. So the two of us need to present a united front.'

Barnes turned the calm green gaze towards him and let it linger there for several long moments. His look was one of curiosity more than anything. He'd never seen Smith bearing the proverbial olive branch before.

'You weren't remotely interested in mere Mispers when I brought it to your attention right after the first one disappeared, Oscar,' he told him.

'Well, to be fair, young women going off isn't all that unusual,' Smith told him, aware that he sounded on the defensive and trying hard not to. 'But now I've had time to go right through the notes on all four and I can see the similarities, I would say it's a strong possibility that it's the work of one or more persons, working together. And that it's the same ones each time.'

'So if none of them are still alive, which I hope for both our sakes isn't the case, and the public finds out that we didn't take it more seriously from the start, which of the two of us falls on their sword?'

Smith could tell that Barnes was loving this, although he was too professional to gloat openly.

'We've not found any remains yet, so there's still a chance that none of them has come to an untimely end.'

Now Smith realised he was sounding slightly desperate as well as defensive. He had to get his act together to make sure he and Barnes were at least singing off the same hymn sheet, if nothing else, by the time Aird turned up to join them.

It was later than he'd hoped before the Det. Sup. did finally pitch up to talk to them both. Smith had been hoping to get away at a halfway decent time so he could go for a few drinks somewhere, then on for a meal. Maybe he'd pick up a bird along the way. This time he'd be sure to keep his wallet in his inside jacket pocket. The high cost of his time with Lulu still made him seethe with resentment.

Aird, of course, didn't bother to knock. He strode into Joe Barnes' office first then nodded his satisfaction at finding them both together and seemingly having a professional discussion.

'Right, one of you, tell me in succinct detail why I should make a case that we go public with these disappearances being the work of the same person or persons,' he told them, pulling out the spare chair and sitting down.

They were nearly two hours kicking round all the details, the theories, the possibilities and some wilder ideas. Nothing was left without consideration.

By the end of it, Smith was dying for a slash, starving hungry, and increasingly having difficulty holding his concentration. All he really wanted was a drink or several, a nice hot takeaway, and to put his feet up with a purring Clive curled up on his stomach while he watched something mindless on the TV.

But before he switched on the goggle box, he'd phone his Oma. No matter how crap his day had been, she always managed to make him laugh. To lift his spirits up out of his boots and to set him back on his feet. Exactly as she had always done so many times on the ski slopes of their native Germany.

* * *

20:03 – WEDNESDAY EVENING

He could tell, from the moment he walked into the room. His acute sense of smell told him. Hyperosmia, they called it. It was sometimes linked to a medical condition.

In his case it was completely idiopathic. No identifiable cause.

He hadn't always had it. He couldn't remember at all anything like it from his childhood years. He had convinced himself that he could pinpoint the first moment he had been aware of it. The day he had stabbed his father to death. The moment when he'd looked down and seen the blood on his own hands. The metallic stench had been almost overwhelming.

To this day he couldn't explain what had drawn him to dip an experimental tongue into the still warm liquid.

She was curled into a ball of misery in the corner of the room, her knees drawn up to her abdomen, her face wet with tears.

'I'm so sorry I'm late home. There was a departmental meeting and it went on and on.'

He crossed the room in a few short strides and crouched down to ease her gag off. He genuinely didn't like to leave her gagged for such long periods at a time. It was why he always came home at lunchtime, to remove it and allow her to drink.

He didn't consider himself a cruel man. He understood that his proclivities were not considered normal. But then normal was hard to define.

He always tried his best to see that his guests were as comfortable as he could make them.

'I've started my period. I need things. Tampons. Even sanitary towels will do. I need to wash myself, properly.'

Her voice was quiet, dispirited. He could tell that her mouth was very dry and he felt bad about how long she'd had the gag in because he'd been held up by the interminable meeting.

'Yes, I know,' he told her, his voice not unkind.

She looked up at him sharply when he said that.

'Please will you let me go now? I promise I won't say a word. Not to anyone.'

'It's come early, hasn't it?'

His tone was almost conversational as he said it.

'Is it painful? Do you get cramps and pain with it? Would you like me to give you some paracetamol?'

He saw the sudden flash of suspicion in her eyes and hurried to reassure you.

'It's only paracetamol. I can show you the packet. Let you see me take them out of the foil. I'm not trying to drug you or anything. And yes of course you can wash yourself. I'll run you a lovely bath. I have some nice oils to put in it. They smell beautiful. A really strong lemony fragrance.

'I just need you first to promise me faithfully that you won't do anything stupid, like try to scream, or to struggle or anything. I have given you my word that I am going to set you free and this will be the occasion. When you're nice and clean and fresh-smelling, and with something to take away all your pain.

'Do you promise me not to do anything silly? Do you swear on whatever you hold dear?'

A faint glint of hope was back in her eyes at his words. She started to nod, then frowned.

'What about my clothes? I've been wearing them ever since I got here and they're filthy. Especially with this.'

He was brisk and businesslike now. Now that it was finally time to set her free.

'Oh, don't worry about those. I can pop them all in the washer while you have your bath, then I can wrap you up nice and warm in towels and even a blanket while you wait for them to be clean and dry.

'But you have to swear to me that you won't do anything stupid. You are so close to being set free, it would be a tragedy to spoil everything now. I've promised to set you free and that's what I'm going to do. But only if you do exactly as I say.

'I'm afraid I don't have a very forgiving nature. You won't get a second chance to do this.'

She'd thought she'd been frightened and chilled before.

The way he said that made her understand exactly what people meant when they spoke about being so scared their blood seemed to freeze in their veins.

As much as the words themselves, it was the way he smiled at her as he said them. Such a warm, benevolent smile to go with the malevolence of what he was saying.

'I promise, I promise.'

She knew she was babbling but she couldn't help herself. She had to make him trust her. To believe she was telling him the truth. She was so close to possible freedom now she could almost taste it.

She could even convince herself that she wouldn't tell anyone about what had happened to her. She would do anything – anything – just to get out of here and back to her own life.

'Do you want to eat first or have a bath first?'

'A bath, please. Please. I feel horribly dirty. And do you have anything at all I can use until I can get home and find some tampons? What happened to my bag? Have you still got that? There'll be some in there.'

'You don't remember, do you?' he smiled at her again, almost fondly. 'When we first met, in that pub, you'd had rather too much to drink and were making a bit of a spectacle of yourself. I brought you back here so you'd be safe. Then you realised you'd left your bag somewhere, but you didn't want me to leave you here alone while I went to look for it. Although I did offer. You really don't remember?'

She shook her head slightly, frowning. None of it made any sense to her. She had no memory of how she had come to be in this living nightmare. No idea of where she was being held captive. Not even what town she was in.

But getting drunk in a pub in the company of a strange man would have been so out of character for her. She couldn't understand any of it.

'Well, never mind about that now. I'll sort something out for you, don't worry. I'm very good at improvising.

You give me your word you're not going to do anything silly and I'll help you to have a lovely bath to get cleaned up. Then I'll set you free. You have my word.'

She desperately wanted to believe him. She'd always had issues with trust, though. Which was why she couldn't begin to imagine how she'd got herself into this terrible situation.

He must have drugged her. Slipped something into her drink while she wasn't looking. But again that was so unlikely. She was always careful to keep an eye on her drink. Always.

She certainly wasn't about to accept any painkillers from him, despite the bad cramps which were tearing her insides apart. It might well say paracetamol on the packet, but how could she be sure he hadn't tampered with them in some way? Perhaps injected something through the foil with a very fine needle?

She couldn't trust him. She still only half believed that he was going to set her free, but she had to hold on to the slim hope that he was telling the truth. He looked and sounded sincere when he said it. To think otherwise was too depressing.

'Right, then, we're going to go to the bathroom and you're going to remember your promise. Remember, too, that this is your one and only chance. I won't make the offer again.'

He untied her and helped her gently to her feet. She was weak and unsteady, with the long periods of inactivity she'd endured. He put a supportive hand under her arm.

It's going to be all right, she told herself. *It's really happening. He's going to let me go.*

'I'm sorry it's getting a bit late. As I said, I was delayed at work.'

'I don't mind,' she assured him hurriedly.

Now she could almost smell freedom, she didn't want anything at all to delay it.

He parked her on the loo while he set about running

the bath, pouring in some oil from a glass bottle on a nearby shelf. If it did have the scent of lemons, it was too subtle for her to detect.

She couldn't bring herself to use the toilet with him in the room. She had one brief thought of trying to hit him with something to overpower him, then making a run for it.

Almost as if he had read her thoughts, he spoke without looking at her.

'Your shoes are downstairs. I didn't want them to be within your reach. Even sensible shoes like those could be a weapon in the hands of someone determined. I didn't want to take the chance.

'Once I've washed and dried your clothes, I'll bring them back up for you to put on.'

He helped her carefully into the water, which was at the perfect temperature. It felt blissful against her skin, after so many days of squalor. He passed her a flannel and some soap then busied himself rummaging in the airing cupboard in the small bathroom.

'There's a bag of some of those cotton pads in here somewhere. The sort you use for first aid, or for cleaning off make-up, I believe. They'll at least be a temporary fix for you.'

In spite of her constant fear, for days now, weeks, probably, the cradling warmth of the water lapping around her was making her feel more relaxed that she would have imagined possible. Drowsy, even. Her lids were even starting to droop. She couldn't remember when she had last slept properly.

She didn't see him carefully empty the cotton wool pads onto the top of the linen basket. Didn't hear or even feel him move quietly to sit on the edge of the bath next to her. Was aware of nothing until his hands pulled the plastic bag over her head and held it there with powerful hands as she started to struggle and kick, splashing him with water.

'Don't fight it,' he told her quietly. 'You'll soon be free.

The more you struggle, the longer it will take. Just relax. Let go.

'There, now.

'Free.

'Free for ever.'

As soon as she stopped twitching and thrashing, he removed the bag and stood up.

Then he took off all his clothes and climbed carefully over the side of the bath to lie on top of her in the still-warm water.

9.

08:15 – THURSDAY MORNING

If DS Tony Taylor was surprised to discover the DI beavering away at his desk long before most of the team had rolled in to start work, he knew better than to show it. To be fair, he'd half expected it. He knew what the guv was like when there was the chance of a big case and something a bit out of the ordinary.

Smith could shift paperwork, properly done, faster than anyone else Taylor had ever worked with. He'd be up to warp speed now with the prospect of an exciting serial case on his patch.

He looked different, too. He was clearly recently showered and shaved and had drowned himself in a pungent aftershave which Taylor remembered being on every dads' wish list a good decade ago. His shirt was clean and had clearly had a recent close encounter with an iron and he was wearing his Royal Military Police regimental tie, which only appeared for high days and holidays.

The stained and crumpled suit he'd been wearing to work for too long had been replaced with something much smarter which had clearly been dry cleaned within living memory. It was also visibly smaller than his usual one, because the DI was having to make an effort to keep his stomach sucked in, even when he undid the buttons, to stop his belly from protruding.

Smith would die rather than admit to anyone that the sight of Inspector Joe Barnes the previous day, looking like something from a police recruitment advert, had touched a raw nerve in him and made him realise how much he'd let himself go. If the press conference was going to be a goer, and if Smith was going to appear at it, he wanted to look the part.

'What's the plan for today, guv? Any news yet on a press conference?'

'I'm waiting to hear from Aird. If we get an early green light we could be on for later today.'

'Hence the best whistle making an outing?'

Taylor risked a humorous reference to Smith's suit. It was always tricky. It might raise a smile. It could equally risk him getting his head ripped off.

Smith was clearly in a good mood, with the anticipation of a big case and the glory which went with it, as he managed a small chuckle.

'I'm going to be concentrating on getting through all of this shit,' Smith waved a hand at the pile of paperwork on his desk awaiting his attention. Taylor didn't envy him that aspect of his job. Not even for the extra salary which went with the higher rank.

'You brief the team. I want the armed robbery file sewn up as tight as a duck's arse, with no holes or errors anywhere. I want the rest of them concentrating on these disappearances. Get them out there, talking to people the Woodentops wouldn't have thought to speak to. I want to know absolutely everything about each of the missing women. Everything.

'There could well be a tangible link between our victims and I want to know what it is. Cross-referenced against any other Mispers with a remotely similar profile anywhere in the country.

'If and when we have any sort of a suspect in our sights, no matter how remote a possibility, I want Brian to interview them, so make sure he's up to speed on anything and everything we have to date. And keep updating him on anything new which turns up.'

Detective Constable Brian McMahon was the team's secret weapon. Trained and constantly updated in all the latest interview techniques, his best asset was having a face which looked like everybody's best friend. He could ask the most leading of questions in such a seemingly harmless way that unless the person he was questioning had a red hot lawyer present and on full alert, even criminals who would normally know better could fall into the invisible elephant trap.

Mac did most of the interviewing for the team, except when Smith decided to muscle in for the fun of it, and the glory. He didn't have the advantage of Smith's incredible memory, but he was dogged over detail.

They were interrupted by Smith's mobile. He glanced at the screen. The Det. Sup. This looked hopeful.

'Oscar, dig out your best suit. You're on for the press conference mid-afternoon today, so it can hopefully go out on the early evening local news.'

'Already in the office, guv,' Smith told him with the virtuous feeling that, for once, he wasn't bullshitting him. 'Suited, booted and ready for action.'

'I'll come over shortly after lunch and you and Joe and I will get together to sort out how this is going to go. I had to push hard to go public on a possible link, so for god's sake let's not waste this opportunity.

'I want every single minute detail which might indicate any sort of connection. I want the public informed, but the word from on high is definitely don't scare the crap out of them. Balanced and measured.

'And if we blow it with this one, by going too soon, or half-cocked, not only will we risk losing public confidence but the three of us will be publicly putting ourselves on show looking like a right bunch of tits.'

* * *

13:17 – THURSDAY AFTERNOON

He'd called in sick to work, claiming a migraine. It was partly true. He was susceptible to them. It was on his medical records, and he had prescription only medication for it. A certain trigger for his attacks was intense emotion, such as he had felt the previous evening.

It hadn't lasted long, thanks to the tablets, but he'd welcomed the day off. He had an awful lot of cleaning up to do. Luckily he never needed much sleep when he was in such a state of arousal. When it was all over, he would take himself off to bed and probably sleep for twelve straight hours.

He stayed naked for the messiest part of the process. Another useful trick he had discovered. That way there were no soiled clothes to wash. A long soak and scrub under the shower, first hot enough to peel off his skin, then ice cold, finishing with a delicious, sensuously warm trickle.

Before he started, he rearranged the freezer contents to make room. He was obsessive about eat by dates. Couldn't bear the idea of consuming anything which had been in there any longer than was necessary.

The latest one had sadly been too skinny to merit doing much with, despite all his best efforts to feed her up.

But before he began most of his housekeeping tasks, he needed to put a nice lean stew on to cook, so that it had plenty of time to simmer whilst he was busy.

In addition to everything else, he needed to pop to the shops for another tree. There would, as ever, be bones to be buried beneath its roots. He'd heard that the nutrients in them were good for saplings, encouraging strong growth. Certainly his expanding copse at the bottom of his garden seem to be doing well on the source of nutrients he provided for each new addition.

He had considered getting a dog. He didn't know a lot about them, but he understood that they all liked to eat bones. And that as long as they were not cooked, they were good for them. Some of the bigger dogs could apparently reduce bones to something barely recognisable, if given sufficient time to gnaw at them.

He'd even got as far as looking at some breeds online to see what might fit his needs. And of choosing a name for the beast. He favoured Dahmer, but worried if that might be too much of a clue. He doubted it would mean anything to his neighbour, but if she mentioned it to someone else, who knew what might happen as a result.

It was late afternoon by the time he got round to planting the latest tree he'd bought himself. It was an acer, a maple tree. The label on it in the DIY shop where he'd bought it showed beautiful autumn colour in the leaves which had attracted him.

He never used the same place twice for his purchases. Never went to a garden centre. Nor engaged with anyone for advice. Who knew these days who might remember someone picking out trees too frequently.

In these modern times everyone loved to spy on everyone else, he found. After all, the crimes of Dennis Nilsen were only discovered when nosy neighbours complained of smells coming from the drains outside the property.

True to form, as he was patting down the earth firmly around the roots of the acer, he saw a silhouette in the back bedroom of the house next door. One which disappeared rapidly when he paused in his work, stretching his back theatrically, and leaned on the handle of the spade for a moment to look up at the window.

He fiddled about longer than was necessary to give the woman next door time to come trotting down the garden, put whatever it was she used to stand on in place, then peer over the top of the fence at him.

Like some carrion bird looking to see if there were any pickings for it to enjoy, he always thought to himself.

'You've planted another tree, then.'

She should go on some sort of TV quiz programme for stating the bloody obvious, flashed through his mind as he looked up at her and put a neutral smile on his face.

'Yes, that's right,' he told her, amiably enough. 'It's a maple. It will have beautifully colourful leaves in the autumn.'

'Is it foreign?' she asked suspiciously.

Apparently she objected as much to foreign trees as to food from other countries.

'It's a European one,' he told her glibly, although it wasn't, at all. It was Japanese. 'I'm glad I've seen you, though. I know you don't like the smell of my occasional barbecues, but I've just made myself a delicious casserole, with some really lean meat.

'It literally fell off the bone while I was cooking it. I did it with plenty of vegetables and if I say so myself it's delicious. I've already had a little taste. I thought you might like some, for your evening meal, to save you having to cook anything. I know you always enjoy my humble efforts at cookery, and I enjoy sharing my meagre skills.

'I put some aside in a separate casserole for you. You just need to heat it up and it's ready to eat. If you'd like it.'

Her face screwed up in suspicion as she asked again, 'Is it foreign? Like those spare ribs?'

'Oh, no, not at all. I can guarantee you that. It's similar to what you've had before and said you enjoyed. Born, reared and slaughtered in Britain. I'll go and get it for you.

'I've been playing around with the recipe, to get it absolutely spot on. I promise you that you won't ever have tasted anything quite like it in your life.'

10.

16:07 – THURSDAY AFTERNOON

There was a good turnout for the press conference. Better than Smith had expected or hoped. The Press Office had done their job of drumming up interest and getting bums on seats. The local press was well represented, together with local radio and TV reporters.

Sitting right in the centre of the front row was a figure Smith knew well. Don Donovan was older than most of the others present. An old-school freelance hack who was a stringer for many of the nationals. He and Smith had locked horns on several occasions in the past.

One of Donovan's specialities was miscarriages of justice. Rumour had it his obsession was because of something which had happened long ago, either to him in person or to someone very close to him.

He had a master's degree in law from a decent university and was prone to making scathing remarks in magistrates' court when the bench went wrong on points of law and had to be pulled back into line by their clerk. He couldn't get away with the same behaviour as easily in Crown Court, but he felt no such constraint in the lower court.

His was a well-known and respected by-line on criminal

matters. He was also widely suspected of being the acerbic voice behind the excoriating articles on an anonymous website.

He'd had a field day when one of Smith's convictions was overturned on appeal because of procedural irregularities. Smith's team members had had to wade in to restrain the gaffer when he was intent on going round to find the journo and punch his lights out.

Smith was under strict instructions from Aird to say as little as possible, keep all of it civil, and above all, not to let any questions or subtle hints needle him into losing his temper.

Aird sat in the middle, with Barnes on his right hand and Smith on his left. Smith tried not to dwell on the symbolism of the seating. The Det. Sup. would be answering the bulk of the questions and strictly controlling what he turned over to either Smith or Barnes for their input.

A young woman from the Press Office was also present, sitting on the far side of Joe Barnes. Smith fancied her and had tried his luck with no success at all. In fact it was a very definite brush off. He wondered if there was any significance to her sitting as far from him as she could get.

Aird kicked things off by outlining all the information they had to date. He had written notes which he consulted carefully, giving his delivery in his usual measured and deliberate style. Smith would have had it all off pat but he knew he wouldn't be trusted to take centre stage.

The first question came from a young local reporter, keen as mustard and determined to get the angle and the quotes she wanted. Smith was eyeing her up for potential as she spoke. Not his usual style but she might be fun. She looked feisty.

'You said there's a possibility of the cases being linked, Superintendent. How strong a possibility are we talking about?'

Aird's tone was even more measured as he replied to her. It gave him the chance to play about with the techie gadgetry he loved, bringing up a photo of each of the missing women as he spoke about them. The Det. Sup. was in his element with anything like that.

'The young women are all of similar age with physical features in common, in terms of height and hair colour.

'Sally Rogers, aged twenty-four. Medical centre receptionist. No reason known for her to voluntarily disappear off the radar.'

He clicked through to the next image.

'Kathy Morgan, twenty-three. Estate agent. Again no known reason why she might choose to vanish without trace.'

Click.

'Vicky Garcia. The youngest of them, at twenty-one. Beautician. Recently started a new job in a salon. Her dream job, by all accounts, and seemingly happy in her work and her private life.'

Click.

'Gill Burrell, twenty-six. A primary school teacher. Very highly regarded by everyone. No red flags to suggest any reason why she should be absent from her work for any length of time.'

There was an immediate flurry of questions from all corners of the room. Aird indicated a young man from the local press, sitting in the second row.

'The physical resemblance between these women is striking, now we see them all in succession like that. So why was the clearly very strong probability of a link, suggesting possibly the same person or persons involved, if these are abductions, not made public much earlier? Might that have meant that the actual number of potential victims would never have got to four?'

Aird paused to consider before he responded to that one.

'Each individual disappearance was made public as it

happened. The physical similarities might still turn out to be a coincidence. It would have been misguided to issue a warning based entirely on, for instance, hair colour, when that might not be the relevant factor.

'I must stress again that at this stage we do not know for sure that there is a direct link between the four disappearances. Our advice remains the same at all times, for everyone. Be careful when you go out. Make sure someone always knows where you are. Have a mobile phone with you always, and switched on, and think hard about going anywhere with someone you don't know.'

He saw questions forming from various sources as he said that so he cut across, 'And no, we have found no trace of any of the mobile phones these young women had with them. Not so far, although we are continuing to try to track them.'

Don Donovan, in the front row, raised an imperious finger and waggled it to catch Aird's attention. Even the pushiest of the younger news hounds instinctively gave way to him.

'Yes, Don.'

Even Aird sounded if not deferential then more respectful in his tone towards the local legend. Nobody remembered any longer if Donovan's first name was short for something like Donald or was just a nickname based on his surname. His byline had for so long been Don Donovan, and was well known in so many places, it was all anyone ever called him.

'My question is for Inspector Smith, specifically. How many major Misper enquiries have you headed up? I'm assuming that rounding up squaddies who have gone AWOL, back in your Army days, is rather different to dealing with something like this current case.'

Smith opened his mouth to speak then felt Aird's hand land on his thigh under the table and grip it like a vice.

Message received and understood.

Keep your gob shut. I'll handle this.

'Detective Inspector Smith is Senior Investigating Officer on this case, working in close liaison with Inspector Barnes. Both officers have my full support and trust. They are both experienced officers with excellent records.'

'Though not always for sound convictions, in Smith's case.'

It was one of Donovan's famous *sotto voce* remarks, clearly audible to anyone in the room with average hearing.

Smith could do nothing but sit there in furious silence and vow that somehow or another, he would find a way to take the smug prick Donovan down, before too long.

'Superintendent, if these are abductions, are you drawing any conclusions from the fact that they're happening roughly a month apart?'

The question came from a hard-bitten woman sitting behind Donovan, one seat to the left. Smith recognised her as someone whose byline was often to be found on sensationalist nonsense for the tabloids. Just about all they needed.

He tried to avoid rolling his eyes towards the heavens at the thought of lurid headlines.

'SERIAL KIDNAPPER STRIKES WHEN THE MOON IS FULL'

'WOMEN SNATCHED ON MOON CYCLES'

He frowned for a moment at that thought. It conjured up all sorts of strange ideas in his mind. But then serial kidnappers – and killers, if this case had gone that far – were a weird breed. They were often driven by the strangest obsessions.

What if the common denominator for this one was not the superficial resemblance of the missing women, but something based around moon cycles and/or menstrual cycles? he speculated.

It was as far fetched as anything, Smith told himself. But he'd been in policing for long enough to know that the wildest theories were often closest to the truth.

* * *

18:35 – THURSDAY EVENING

'At a press conference today, police announced they are considering that the disappearances of four young women from the area over a period of the past four months may be linked and may be connected to the same person or persons.'

He sat bolt upright as footage of the press conference appeared on his television screen at the start of the local news bulletin. Then he leaned forward with his arms on his thighs, watching every detail. Staring in particular at the three police officers sitting at a long table facing the press and media. One in uniform, with the shoulder pips of an Inspector, the other two in plain clothes.

Some of the questions from the members of the press present were included in the clip. An audible aside from one of the journalists had not been edited out.

'The four missing women are all in their early to mid-twenties and are all natural blondes. All were in regular employment. Enquiries have so far found no reason why any of them should choose to disappear of their own volition.

'None of them has been in touch with friends or families since being reported missing and no trace has been found of any of the mobile phones they were carrying.'

As the newscaster was speaking, photos of the four

women appeared in succession on the screen, together with details of their names, ages, occupations, and where they were from.

He recognised all of them. The photos must be quite recent. He knew their names, sometimes their ages, and where they lived, from their personal possessions. He didn't always know their occupations from what he had found in their things.

He was surprised that the last one had been a teacher. So skinny and frail, so quick to lose her fight. He was surprised the children hadn't eaten her alive before he got to her.

Then he laughed aloud at his own black humour.

'Police are appealing for the public's help in finding the missing women and are urging anyone with any information to phone the number appearing on your screens now.

'Detective Superintendent Murray Aird, leading the press conference, asked anyone who might be able to help with enquiries to ask to speak to the officer in charge, Detective Inspector Oscar Smith, or to make contact with any police station.

'He stressed that if any of the women should be watching this bulletin they should make contact with someone to say where they are and they would face no police action as long as they did so.'

She finished her piece to camera with a backdrop close-up of the three police officers. He concentrated all his attention on the one at the end, on the right. Detective Inspector Oscar Smith. The one they said was the senior officer on the case.

How formidable an adversary would he be, he wondered to himself. They said he was experienced, but that journalist had said something about unsafe convictions, loud enough for all to hear. And what was the reference to the military?

He'd thought the tie looked like a regimental one, or

some sort of a club tie. Dark blue, with two different widths of red stripes. But he had no idea which regiment that might be.

He let the news run to the end, in case there was any update on the press conference. Then he started up his laptop and entered 'Army ties, Regimental ties' in his search engine.

It didn't take much scrolling to find the one he was looking for.

Military Police.

Interesting.

He jotted down the name of the police officer, Detective Inspector Oscar Smith, on the pad he always kept next to the computer. He'd have to do some research into the man who could turn out to be his nemesis if he was not careful.

For now, the press conference had kindly shown him the way forward with his next victim. The police seemed to be focusing on the common denominator being women with blonde hair.

That told him it was time to change his preferences. To go for something completely different to throw them off the scent.

11.

07:59 – FRIDAY MORNING

Oscar Smith was head down at his desk long before any of the other team members rolled in, even Tony Taylor, who was almost always the first one there. The more Smith thought about it, the more he was convinced that there was some other link between the cases, somewhere in the file, and he wanted to find it.

Simply choosing blonde women who looked alike was too obvious to be the only thing. Smith was already getting the feeling that the man behind these abductions – because all his instincts were telling him that these were kidnaps and the work of one man, a loner – was clever.

More than that, he was following some sort of an agenda which, although obvious to him, was so far hidden from anyone else. This needed someone equally clever and with a mind as devious to fathom out what it was all about.

Without being boastful, Smith knew he was well above average intelligence. Various IQ tests throughout his career had told him that. He knew, too, that he found it disconcertingly easy to get inside the head of some truly sick people to work out how they operated. What made them tick.

He could do much of that whilst sitting in his office working on mundane paperwork. He had the ability to compartmentalise his brain that way. But once the full team were in, he wanted to talk to them, to throw around some ideas to see what they came back with.

Smith seldom appeared for morning briefings. He had enough work of his own to do. He much preferred the hands-on front-line policing, but accepted that most of his role these days was administrative.

It never stopped him from leaving his office for a bit of fun whenever he could get away with it. He had the team trained always to provide him with a solid alibi when he needed it. They did it out of fear rather than loyalty but Smith didn't care. As long as the end result was the one he wanted.

'Tony!' he bellowed from his desk, as soon as his DS came into the main office.

He could always tell when it was Taylor. He moved everywhere like a timid little mouse. As if he never knew whether he should be wherever he was. There was no air of authority about him, but in spite of that, he managed to run a good team and get results.

'Yes, guv?'

The tone was as meek as ever as Taylor came into Smith's office looking, as he always did, as if he expected to get ripped limb from limb.

'Let me know when everyone's in and I'll come and say a few words. A few more ideas which have occurred to me about whatever sicko we might be dealing with here.

'I'm pretty sure that we need to do most of our thinking well outside the box for this one. Always assuming all four birds were taken by the same weirdo, which is my gut feeling, we need to think like he's thinking if we're going to get ahead of him and stand any chance of tracing him.'

He saw the pained expression on Taylor's face at his choice of words. The DS was so politically correct it wasn't true. No doubt he expected the gaffer to say 'young ladies' and 'suspect'.

Well, bugger that for a game of toy soldiers, Smith thought to himself.

The team members all managed to roll in more or less on time. DC Dai Evans was still stuffing the last of a bacon sarnie down his fat mouth and had brown sauce on his chin as a result. He visibly jumped to see the DI there waiting for briefing to start and wiped guiltily at his face with the back of his hand at the sight of him. He still remembered the slap round the back of the head, which he hadn't appreciated.

Smith let Tony Taylor kick things off by going through the routine stuff, then he took over.

'Right, our serial kidnapper. Something came up at the press conference yesterday which made me think we need to start looking at all sorts of possible connections, even the far-fetched ones.'

One of the reasons Smith had wanted to be in earlier than usual was to scan the various papers online to see what they'd gone with from the conference the day before.

As he'd feared but half-expected, one or two of the more lurid ones had latched onto the moon phase angle. Putting two and two together from the dates but making seven.

'I know we can't pinpoint with one hundred per cent accuracy exactly when each of these women disappeared, only the point at which they were each last seen or reported missing. But, Tony, I want someone onto plotting moon phases in relation to each disappearance.

'As well as that,' he glared round them all as he said the next bit, making it perfectly clear that he didn't want any smartarse comments, 'I want to know where they were up to on their monthly cycle at the time they were last seen.'

There was a stunned silence. DC Shane Walker risked being the first to speak.

'Fuck, guv, how are we supposed to find that out?'

'You're coppers, aren't you? Figure it out. But here's a clue. Start by checking if any of them were pregnant. Because that would most likely rule out the theory of any link to their cycle.'

'You seriously think there may be something in the monthly cycle stuff then, guv?' Tony Taylor took a chance on the question, fully aware that it was never a good idea to incur the gaffer's wrath, especially in a full team briefing.

'Humour me, Tony,' Smith told him, his tone surprisingly mild. 'We're at ground zero. We have the square root of bugger all to be going on with at the moment. We're potentially dealing with a complete nutter with some weird agenda of his own. So let's out-weird him. Think up all of the craziest motives we can come up with.

'Always assuming he has some sort of a motive and isn't just acting on impulse. Striking when the mood takes him. Because we all know those bastards are the hardest of all to catch.

'With nothing else at all to go on for now, we've nothing to lose and potentially something to gain by exploring every possible avenue. Even the cul-de-sacs.

'But I don't want any of this getting out. Some of the press are already sniffing round the idea for something sensational to print. So anything you happen to dig up comes to me and me only.

'Are we all clear on that? Anyone want me to remind them of the consequences of loose lips on this team?'

All heads were shaken and the team members muttered a 'Clear, guv', almost in unison.

Smith nodded his satisfaction.

'Right, shift your arses and get on with it, then. Debrief at the end of the day and I want something to go on by then.'

* * *

17:49 – FRIDAY AFTERNOON

The most they knew by the end of the day was that if one of the missing women was pregnant, no one in their immediate circle knew anything about it. And in terms of any direct connections between them, nothing had come up despite the concerted effort of all the team members.

They were going to need to crack on over the weekend. The advantage of the press conference was that the public were starting to call in with possible sightings since the appeal had gone out. Smith was relieved it would be the uniform lot fielding those because such an appeal would inevitably bring out the nutters in droves.

There would no doubt be several sightings of Lord Lucan, not to mention the likes of Elvis Presley or Michael Jackson spotted buying cod and chips from a corner shop. Maybe some even more extreme ones. But at least CID wouldn't need to get involved in those unless any had the slightest hint of credibility.

Smith was getting his things together after a final discussion with Taylor, leaving him to sort out rotas for the weekend. Smith fancied a quick drink then home with a takeaway to spend some time talking to his Oma with Clive on his lap once more. That was about as exciting as it got these days, without running the risk of another robbing bitch cleaning him out of cash.

His mobile phone rang just as he was about to grab his raincoat from the hook on the back of the door. The weather was fairly foul outside.

'Oskar, it's Anja. I'm sorry to bother you but your Oma's done it again.'

Anja. The best of all the carers he'd arranged for his grandmother. The one who kept him up to date with what was really happening, not the sanitised version he got from his Oma.

She was also the one he had slept with, last time he'd been over to visit. It was a pleasant enough experience, but neither of them had taken it very seriously.

He groaned quietly as Anja went on speaking.

'She's sacked all of us again and she won't let any of us back into the house. She's bolted all the doors from the inside and there's no way to break in because of the double glazing.'

Smith groaned again, louder this time. He'd paid for the better quality windows himself. It wasn't just the winters which could be harsh in that part of Germany.

'What about the outside cellar door?' he asked her, more in hope than anticipation.

'Oh, she's locked that too, of course. You know what she's like. She's still very nimble on her feet when she needs to be, although she really can't manage on her own, despite what she claims.

'I was going to call the emergency services to break in for us, and then secure the house afterwards, but I'm worried about what the repercussions might be.

'You know what she can get like with strangers in the house. She's quite capable of attacking a police officer with a poker or something like that. Then she would risk being forced to go into care, and I know neither of you would want that. So I thought I'd better ring you for instructions.'

They were speaking in German. He knew Anja spoke very little English so he said, 'Fuck' to himself, quite audibly down the phone, several times.

He remembered, too late, he'd probably said that a few times when the two of them had been in bed together. Her throaty chuckle at hearing him saying it again flooded his mind with sudden memories he could do without at the moment. Too distracting.

'You did right, Anja, thank you. Look, I'd better try to come over, even if it's just for a day. I'm sure I can find a flight if I go to the airport and sleep there until I do, if I need to.

'I'll try ringing her. She'll see the number and know it's me so she might well pick up. But I better come and sort things out. I'll keep you posted when I know what's happening. Thanks, Anja. I know she's not easy and I promise to get there somehow, as soon as I can.'

He opened his office door and shouted again for Tony as he ended the call with Anja, then immediately pulled up his grandmother's number and dialled it. He was pretty sure she wouldn't answer straight away, even if she knew who was calling her. She could be as stubborn as any mule when she was in this frame of mind.

'Tony, look, sorry to drop you in the shit going into a weekend...' words Taylor never imagined he'd hear from the gaffer's lips. Not the apology part, at any rate. 'I have to be somewhere this weekend. It's urgent. There's nothing I can do about it.'

The answerphone clicked in at the other end at that moment and he switched back to German.

'Oma? It's Oskar, and I'm not happy. Anja just phoned me and told me what you did. Oma, pick up the phone. Oma?'

He swore again, this time in German, then hung up.

'It's a... it's a family matter,' Smith told Tony Taylor. 'Only I need you to cover for me, if anyone's looking for me. I wouldn't ask you if I had a choice, and I'll buy you a pint or two as a thank you. Phone me whenever you need to with any updates, but I have to be out of the country and I don't want people to know that, or to know where or why.'

He hated talking about his private life to anyone inside the nick. Especially to Tony, for some reason. They'd never been for a drink together. Never shared any private stuff. Not even chatting aimlessly about the weather over a pint.

From the look on Tony's face, he was as uncomfortable at the mere suggestion as Smith was.

'It's fine, guv, don't sweat it. You go off and do whatever it is you need to. We'll cope, and I'll only call if I have to.'

'Cheers, Tony.'

Smith grabbed his things and hurried on his way, leaving Tony Taylor standing there thinking to himself that that was the first time he could ever remember Smith having thanked him for anything.

Smith rushed home first. Clive the cat would be fine on his own for the weekend, as long as he left him plenty of water and dry food. There was a cat flap so he could come and go as he pleased and he was used to his owner being out a lot.

Smith still got the guilts about it, as he filled up every spare bowl he could find with different dry food flavours.

'I'm sorry about this, you little bugger, so don't look at me like that. I don't need the daggers from you. There's plenty food here to keep you going. Just don't invite any lady friends in and let them eat it all. I'll be home as soon as I can, but you know what Oma gets like. I'll have to sort things out in person. I can't do it over the phone, especially when she won't answer my calls.'

He changed quickly out of the slightly too small good suit. The shirt would do fine, without the tie, and he added chinos and light shoes for the journey. He threw basic necessities into a holdall, grabbed both his passports, then headed to the airport.

He called himself a taxi. He decided he'd better leave his service vehicle at home rather than at the airport in case anything happened to it, or he got delayed returning.

He hadn't been joking about camping out at the airport until he got a flight. Once he knew when he would arrive he could book a hire car the other end for the hour's journey from where he landed to his grandmother's house.

He just hoped that when he arrived he didn't find it under siege by the local police with Oma having taken one of the carers hostage. He wouldn't put it past her.

12.

11:13 SATURDAY MORNING - CET

'Oma? Open the door.' Smith was speaking loudly, thumping his fist on the still locked front door, repeatedly ringing the bell. He'd been calling his grandmother's phone number at the same time but she was so far refusing to answer him.

He knew she was in there, though. He could hear her moving about, just inside the front door.

He'd phoned Anja to let her know when he was on his way from the airport. She'd come over to meet him at the house, although she was supposed to be on a day off.

'Oma, I've just flown over from England to make sure you're all right. I've not had much sleep, I need coffee, and I should be at work, dealing with a serious crime. So open the door. *Bitte.*'

Finally he heard the bolts slide back, saw the door start to open, and his grandmother's face smiled out at him through the crack.

'That's better, Oskar. Never forget to say please and thank you. You get what you want in life when you remember the good manners I taught you.

'It's nice to see you, of course, but there was absolutely no need for you to fly all the way over here. I'm perfectly all right, as you can see.'

She reached out a fragile hand, blue veins standing out clearly through the tissue-thin skin, and gently stroked the side of his face. It was the closest she ever got to any physical show of affection towards him.

She'd been the same with her husband, and with her own son, Smith's stepfather. Always kind and correct but never openly loving. When her son had killed himself, her reaction had been more one of disappointment at his perceived weakness rather than anything else.

An independent, strong-minded woman all her life, until old age had forced her to accept at least some help. Smith had adored her from the moment he'd first met her. He still had no idea to what extent his feelings were reciprocated, if at all.

Apparently her own good manners didn't extend to her acknowledging in any way the presence of the carer, Anja, who spoke quietly to Oskar to say, 'She's not fine. She's wearing exactly what she wore yesterday and I should know because I dressed her. So she's been like that all night. And you know how much she likes to dress correctly in clean clothes every day.'

'Come in, Oskar, come in. I'll make coffee. Although I still have no idea what the fuss is all about,' his grandmother was still speaking to him and only him.

She turned and walked off towards the back of the house, where the kitchen was. The place was far too big for her. Dark, hard to heat, requiring much too much attention. Yet she bitterly fought any attempt to get her to move somewhere more manageable. Just as she refused outright even to consider going into any form of sheltered housing.

Oskar dumped his travel bag on the floor and handed the bag of groceries he'd stopped off to buy on the way to Anja. He knew the carers shopped for his grandmother and saw that she had everything she needed, but he'd bought a few special treats.

'Thanks for meeting me, Anja. I'll pay you for your time, of course. Can you help her make the coffee, and perhaps fix us something to eat from what I bought? The only food on the flight over was disgusting. I'll get the toolbox and take the bolts off the inside of the front door. At least that way she shouldn't be able to lock you out in future.'

It didn't take him long to do the job. He kept glancing anxiously at his phone from time to time, in case there was any word from Tony. He knew he could safely leave him to it. He often did. But he'd be pig sick if there was a massive breakthrough on the case while he was a few hundred miles away, with no flight back available until early the following day.

He put the tools away before he went to join the other two in the kitchen. Anja had almost finished preparing an early lunch for them all from the shopping. His grandmother was now sitting down and looking tired. He wondered if she'd slept at all during the night. Clearly the situation couldn't continue as things were.

He knew she had difficulty getting ready for bed by herself, so he imagined that if she had slept at all, it might have been in her favourite chair. She looked in need of a proper sleep after she'd eaten the meal Anja had put together, which looked good.

Smith wondered with a sudden optimism if Anja was in a hurry to get away. Perhaps if the two of them helped Oma into bed for a snooze, they might be able to make good use of the guest room.

Smith had no plans to sleep there for the night, or at least not much of it. His plane the next day left at sparrows' fart and he wanted to run no risk of missing it. He might even doss down for a couple of hours during the afternoon.

A bit of company might make it even more pleasant. He looked at Anja across the table and gave her what he hoped was his most endearing smile rather than a randy leer.

His hopes weren't the only things which started to rise at the force of the look he got in return. Her lips parted in a sensual smile, the end of her tongue flicked out to run round her lips to moisten them.

Fuck, he'd be in serious trouble if he had to sit there and look at that, with his Oma in the same room, for very much longer.

'Have you had enough to eat, Oma? Why don't you go and have a nice lie down? Anja will help you, I'm sure. You must be tired. I'll still be here when you wake up. We'll have plenty of time to catch up.'

Old his Oma definitely was. Senile she most certainly was not. She looked from her grandson to the carer she tolerated more than any of them. She smiled knowingly.

'I could perhaps do with a nap. I shall take out my hearing aids. Just pull the spare bed away from the wall a little because even if I can't always hear it banging, I can feel the vibrations.'

13

09:13 – SUNDAY MORNING

'Clive? Where are you, you little sod? I'm home. If you've had half as much luck as I have, you'll have done pretty bloody well for yourself, I can tell you,' Smith announced his return home to his cat, wherever the little bastard was hiding himself.

The feline never demeaned himself like a dog by coming bounding to meet his master on his return from anywhere.

Smith dumped his bag carefully on the floor of the cramped hall. He'd used the shopping trip to stock himself up with two bottles of a very good schnapps which was eye-wateringly expensive to buy in UK, when he could even find it.

He headed straight for the kitchen, in need of proper coffee before anything else. The stuff at both the airport and on the flight had been gopping and he needed a hit of the real stuff before he was fully functioning.

It had, as he had hoped, turned into a very lively afternoon. Anja had been more than happy to stay as she was on duty to get his Oma up and dressed the next day anyway. Neither of them had got a lot of sleep but it had been worth it.

Smith had found himself ridiculously uptight at the thought of his Oma on the other side of the wall from them as Anja was not exactly bashful in showing her enjoyment of what they were doing. He'd not really settled until he'd heard the loud, rhythmic and reassuring sounds of his Oma's snores.

It was when both he and Anja realised that he was subconsciously trying to time his slow, deep thrusts to the sound of her snores that first Anja then he had collapsed into helpless laughter like naughty teenagers, which had in turn caused each of them to climax in a shuddering, hysterical convulsion.

Clive was curled up asleep on his favourite chair and didn't even stir when Smith went to put the kettle on. He smiled indulgently at his cat, glad he seemed to have enjoyed himself too. From the look of the feed bowls, Clive had done his usual trick of having a taster nibble of each before settling on his current favourite.

Once he was the right side of some proper coffee, Smith headed for the shower and a change of clothes. He'd effectively gained an hour because of the time zones, so he could still put in nearly a full day to make up for his absence the day before.

He was under no obligation to rock up to work at all hours. Unless they were flat out on a murder case. But it wasn't as if he had a lot else to do with his time.

Tony Taylor was the only one in the main office when Smith went in. He was head down over his computer. He was another one who was completely obsessed with all things techie. He was good at it, too.

He looked up as Smith walked over to his desk and put a carrier bag on it. After long consideration, Smith had decided to buy him a decent bottle of wine as a gesture of gratitude. He'd no idea of his tastes in wine, or even if he knew anything about it, but he'd settled on a good Riesling. Not cheap, and certainly nothing Taylor would find in a UK supermarket.

He'd decided he couldn't face the prospect of an embarrassing hour or so of the two of them trying to make polite conversation over a drink in the pub, as he'd first suggested.

Taylor looked up at him in surprise then took hold of the bag to pull out the bottle inside, looking at the label for all the world as if he knew a bit about wine.

'Blimey, guv, this is very nice. Thank you.'

'Moving swiftly on,' Smith told him, worried it was starting to get a bit gushy, 'what's the latest?'

'Well, guv, I've got everyone out exploring any and all possible connections between the women, and based on the information they input to me, I've started charting any links, to make it easier.'

He leaned over and pulled the nearest chair across for the gaffer with one hand as he deftly opened up some of the stuff he'd been working on.

'We went through all of the usual links, right back from school days and any clubs or activities, as well as addresses where they've all lived at various times in their lives. That drew a blank, so we needed to drill down further. So I started with Sally Rogers, the medical centre receptionist.

'The logical link would be that the other three were on the patient list of that practice. So possibly our suspect was, too, and that was the link between all of them. But no. They aren't now, they never have been.

'Kathy Morgan next, the estate agent. None of the others has recently bought or rented a house through any estate agent, and certainly not hers. Also her firm has a robust policy in place which would prevent a young woman like her going off alone to show a man round any properties.

'However she met our suspect, it wasn't by showing him round a house. Unless, of course, he's working with an accomplice, possibly a female.

'Vicky Garcia, the beautician. None of the other three went to get nails done or anything like that at the salon where she works. There's nothing to show how or where they might be connected. And again, unless our suspect is a woman, that's not a likely link. Unless they went in to ask about a treat for a wife or girlfriend and got chatting to Vicky that way.

'Finally Gill Burrell. One possible way in which the four women's paths might have crossed is through children at the school. None of them have children, not even younger brothers or sisters, so there's no way we can find if they might ever have encountered one another, perhaps at the school gates. Which in turn tends to rule out the possibility of any of them having met our suspect there.

'All of which is pretty depressing news as it tends to suggest that our kidnapper is selecting his victims purely at random, based on some agenda only he knows. And like you've already pointed out, we all know how hard it can be to outsmart someone like that, with no true idea of where they're going to strike next or who their next victim might be.'

14.

15:06 – SUNDAY AFTERNOON

He knew the town well. Knew exactly the sort of places he needed to go to find what he was looking for next. What he wasn't too sure about was the actual protocol of making the first connection. That was going to be a big learning curve for him.

Was it up to him to make first contact? By some sort of a sign, which he didn't know? Or was he supposed to hang around until someone, somehow, magically knew what he was seeking and offered it up?

He didn't want to get it wrong and draw attention to himself, just when it was all going so well. Even better than he'd thought, if he were to be honest with himself. He'd never imagined the police would waste time trying to fathom a link between the victims when he himself knew he was picking them totally at random.

He'd been sure they would concentrate all their efforts from the start on the perpetrator, or whatever they called them in England. He'd heard 'perp' in the American crime shows he sometimes watched on television, but he wasn't sure if it was also in common use in the UK.

He'd been expecting them to do things like use a psychological profiler to tell them what sort of person their suspect might be. He'd been rather looking forward to hearing what some stranger had put together about him. The lack of any such mention following the press conference had left him feeling disappointed.

He'd carefully scanned everything he could find online arising from the press conference. One paper had mentioned a possible link to moon phases, which he thought was quite astute of them, although not correct, of course.

His powers were much greater than being compelled to do something because of some distant orbiting satellite.

But now it was time to shake things up a bit. To break any type of pattern which the police might think they had discerned so far. He was looking forward to it, though with a degree of trepidation because it would take him so far outside his comfort zone.

He started by cruising the pubs. From what he'd heard people at work talk about, he had a rough idea of which ones might provide what he was looking for. He'd thought about looking on the specific streets where he knew the homeless hung out. His cleanliness obsession stopped him. There was no telling what anyone he found on the streets might be carrying.

He didn't want to drink too much, if he had to go from pub to pub until he found what he was seeking. He needed to be fully in control of the situation, all along. He stuck to halves of lager, one in each place he visited, and he always went in the gents. Not only to urinate but to do some window shopping.

He got lucky in the fourth one he visited. There was no one in the toilets when he went in for a slash, but almost as soon as he started, the door opened and a young man walked in. He looked little more than a teenager, with stunning good looks. Darkly curling hair framing a perfect face without a single blemish, with melted chocolate eyes and a sensual mouth.

Best of all, he smelled clean. Wonderfully fragrant. Not like a rough sleeper would smell. The man couldn't stop himself from staring openly at him. And he didn't need to act the part. The young man truly was a head-turner.

The youth had noticed his look towards him. In response, he didn't simply undo his flies to use the urinal. He slowly unbuttoned the denim jeans he was wearing, pushed them provocatively with his thumbs hooked into the waistband, down hips which swayed and circled as he did so. Then got his tackle out of his shorts and balanced it in his hand, all the time looking at the man, a mischievous smile playing round his lips.

It was so blatant that for a moment the man felt gripped by panic. He needed to stay in control, at all times. That was part of the thrill. Yet this boy seemed so worldly, so sure of himself, it made him feel afraid.

On the other hand, he was incredibly beautiful. And young. Very young. So unlike the women in all aspects. The man was frozen in time, unable to tear his gaze away.

The young man ran a provocative tongue round his lips then spoke. His voice was a surprise. Softly spoken, light, with a better accent than the man had expected.

'You like what you see?' he asked teasingly. 'You can look, but you can't touch. Not unless you have money. And I don't come cheap.'

'I have money,' the man said, finding it difficult to speak through a suddenly dry mouth. 'I have plenty of money.'

The boy was urinating now, deliberately waving his cock about as he did so, putting it all on display, making circles of urine on the tiled splashback. He laughed at the words.

'Then what are we waiting for, big boy. Let's go back to your place.'

* * *

15:47 – SUNDAY AFTERNOON

He'd made the youth leave the pub first to wait for him

round the corner. He'd said something, which he hoped sounded convincing, about being nervous of being seen in the company of someone so young and so stunning.

Clearly, though, he couldn't risk being seen to leave with him. The pub was relatively quiet but the young man was the sort people couldn't help but notice. Not worth taking any risks.

He knew there was a possibility that he might change his mind and not be there when he went after him. An even stronger one that he was planning to rob him of all his money as soon as the opportunity arose. He might be in for a bit of a surprise if he tried that.

It was a hopeful start when he rounded the corner and saw the young man, further up the road, leaning against the wall, one booted foot held up and pressed against the brickwork behind him. Even at a distance, to someone who had never considered himself as having any gay tendencies, the pose was distinctly provocative and erotic.

'I thought you might wimp out and leave me standing here,' the youth said with a slow smile as he saw him appear.

He was good. He even managed to look pleased to see him arrive as promised.

'Look, this is a bit embarrassing, but I honestly haven't ever done this before,' he told him as the two of them started to walk, side by side but not too close together.

'With a man, I mean. I'm sure that's what all of your clients say, but it's honestly true in my case. So I've no idea how much I need to pay you. I've got some cash in my wallet but we pass a hole in the wall on the way so I could take out more. I can use my full limit, I'm never overdrawn.'

The young man chuckled.

'Don't worry, ducky, virgins are in safe hands with me. And the cost depends on what you want. You can have anything at all, at a price. Except choking me. I'm really not into that. Ugh, it can get very messy. But anything else.

'Why don't we make a shopping list for you on the way to the cashpoint. Top or bottom?'

'Erm...'

Again the throaty chuckle.

'D'you want to fuck me or do you want me to fuck you?'

'I honestly don't know. This is all so new to me. What I'd really like...I know this might sound stupid and sentimental. I'd like it if it could be like a first date. If we could get to know each other a bit. Perhaps over dinner. At my house. I'm not a bad cook.

'Then maybe we could take a shower together. See where that leads us.

'Then if it's going nicely up to that point, we could go to bed together. And you could show me what to do.

'Could you perhaps stay the night? I'll pay whatever it costs, of course. I just think it would be really nice to wake up in each others' arms. Would that be all right?'

'I told you, you can have whatever you like, if you pay the price. I could stay over, but it will cost you and I'd need to leave early. I have a lecture tomorrow morning at ten.'

He saw the look of surprise on the man's face and laughed out loud.

'I'm a student, at the Uni. Studying modern languages. This is how I pay my tuition fees and all the rest. The only way I can.

'I'm gay. I like sex. A lot. So it makes sense to get paid for doing something I've always enjoyed doing for free. And if I say so myself, I'm rather good at it.

'My name's Marcus, by the way. Is there something you want me to call you?'

'Dennis,' he said, quick as a flash.

He almost kicked himself for his impetuosity. If Marcus was his real name and if he really was a university student, he may well be bright. But hopefully he was too young to think immediately of Scottish serial killer Dennis

Nilsen. There was certainly no flicker of recognition on Marcus's face at the name.

'Well, Dennis, let's go back to your place, via the cashpoint, and see what the rest of the day, and especially the evening, has in store for us.'

15.

17:52 – SUNDAY AFTERNOON

When the team members trooped back into the office at the end of the day, if any of them were surprised to see the gaffer there on a Sunday, none of them was stupid enough to make any comment on his presence. They all simply grunted an acknowledgement.

All of them reported no luck in finding out anything about current significant others of the missing women from the friends and families they'd been speaking to again. None of the four was currently in any type of a settled relationship, unless it was one they were keeping secret from their family and friends, for some reason.

'So if one person has all four of the missing women, has he killed them all?' Smith asked them.

'If so, how and where is he disposing of the bodies, as nothing's come to light yet. Or is he keeping them all alive as hostages for some reason? If so, where? And how is he managing it?'

'Keeping them as sex slaves, guv?' DC Dai Evans suggested. 'He's either trafficked them somewhere, or he's keeping them for himself. Maybe in a cellar, something like that?'

'We're trying to get into our suspect's head, Dai, not to hear you indulge your wildest sexual fantasies,' Smith told him, although his tone was mild enough.

The rest of the team chuckled dutifully at his comment. Always worth staying on the right side of the DI, they all knew, to their cost.

'How do you dispose of one body without trace, let alone four?' Tony Taylor speculated. 'Over a fairly short period of time. If he's dumping bodies, or even bits of bodies, you'd think that in a period of four months, like in this case, something, somewhere, would have come to light by now.

'We can usually rely on a dog walker or a jogger to come across some grisly remains and report the find to us.'

'Dumping them in road foundations, or under a building site?' suggested DC Sean Walsh. 'Maybe our man works on one. Knows exactly when the next load of concrete is going to be dumped, so he gets them in before it arrives.

'He could even be the person who tips it, so he's not going to report seeing a body down the hole, because he put it there.'

'Bit far fetched, that,' Craig Stephens grunted at his oppo.

'The whole case is a bit bloody far fetched, mate,' Walsh told him. 'Four women disappearing off the face of the earth in the space of four months. That takes a bit of doing, does that.'

'Trafficked,' Evans said again, with more conviction this time. 'Someone's snatching them to order and selling them on for the sex trade.'

'Tony, first thing tomorrow, get someone on to checking out any and all major building or road works anywhere on our patch or just off it. Where are we at with similar cases in other areas?'

'Nothing, guv. Nothing with a similar pattern to ours, anyway. So does that tend to suggest that our man is a local? It would be risky coming into another area just to abduct people.'

'And trafficking,' Smith told him, with a nod to Evans.

'We all know of girls being trafficked into the country for the sex trade, but does it go on the other way? After all, these women are all young, blonde, white and attractive. I wouldn't kick any of them out of bed, for sure.'

He saw the face Taylor made at his words but ignored it and carried on.

'So is there a market in some country somewhere for young white women? Not something I'm familiar with, but we all know by now not to be surprised at anything we come across. Get that checked out as well, Tony.

'Right, all of you, piss off back home to do whatever it is you plan to do on a Sunday evening. Let's have all of you back here first thing tomorrow – and that means you, too, Dai – and see if you can come up with some bright ideas for us to run with by then.'

* * *

20:23 – SUNDAY EVENING

'That was a fabulous meal, Dennis, thanks so much. I don't know when I last ate as well as that. That meat was something else. You must have a fantastic butcher. I've never tasted anything like it. You must please let me have your recipe, if it's not an old family secret. Oh, and let me know where you buy your meat.'

Marcus might just have been flattering him as part of his services. But he'd polished off two huge platefuls of one of 'Dennis's' specials. If he had been putting his enjoyment on, he should be studying drama instead of modern languages because it was entirely believable.

'I'm too stuffed to move at the moment, but as soon as I can, I'd better work extra hard to make sure you have as good a time as I've just had, eating that little lot.'

'I use a particular butcher who does all his own slaughtering. It shows through in the flavour, doesn't it?

You clearly have a gourmet's refined palate. I could tell how much you enjoyed each mouthful. To tell the truth, it was rather erotic watching you eat it.

'Would you like some coffee now? I'm afraid we've finished off the wine.'

Marcus picked up the empty wine bottle to study it.

'It was really good, this wine. That's something else I must look out for. I have to say you have very sophisticated tastes, Dennis. And yes, please, some black coffee would be a perfect end to a perfect meal. Thank you.'

Marcus was smiling to himself as he watched the man bustle off to the kitchen, carrying the empty plates. This was going to be easy money. He hadn't been acting, talking about the meal and the wine. They'd both been very good.

And at least the strange Dennis person was clean. Every inch of him. He'd noticed that when he'd knelt in front of him in the shower to take his cock in his mouth.

He leaned back in his chair, stretching languidly like a contented cat. The coffee smells coming from the kitchen were inviting, too. He might just have landed on his feet here. If bashful Dennis could turn into a regular sugar daddy, with plenty of cash, it would be a nicer way to pay his fees than some of the things he'd been doing of late.

Dennis had even insisted on paying him up front. The wad of cash he'd taken out of the machine he'd thrust into Marcus's hands, with the promise of plenty more to come, should it be required.

The taste of the coffee lived up to all his expectations. But the next thing he knew, he woke up on the floor, totally naked, his hands firmly bound, a gag in his mouth, with Dennis sitting on the bed next to him, staring down at him with a clinical fascination.

Marcus's first reaction was panic. He didn't mind the nakedness, at all. He was used to that. It was expected of him. Nor the bondage bit, particularly. That too was okay, it came within the price and he was well used to it.

He didn't like the gag, though. That was a bit too close to the feeling of being choked. He'd experienced that only once and vowed never to again. Not his thing. Not for any amount of money.

He instinctively started to thrash his legs. To make Dennis see to what extent he was unhappy with the way things were going. He hadn't even had chance to set up a safe word. It was usually the first thing he did, before he got down to business, but he'd been enjoying the meal and the wine too much to spoil it with the banalities.

He quickly discovered that his legs were restrained. He sat up and looked at them.

What the fuck?

They were forced apart and held that way by a length of wood. His feet were tied, one to each end, with something like rope stirrups.

That made him feel vulnerable.

Very.

He looked at Dennis again. Noticed for the first time that he was holding another length of wood. Shorter, with a rounded end and a surface so smooth it looked shiny.

'You will be paid for your time, Marcus,' the man told him, his voice calm. Businesslike. 'I'm afraid I need to keep you a little big longer than we had agreed, but I promise you, you will be set free at the end.

'I very much enjoyed our shower together, but I won't be making many physical demands on you during your stay here. All I need is your promise that you will do exactly what I say, at all times. That will mean you will be well looked after, well rewarded, then set free.

'If you scream, or struggle, or try to escape, you will be punished. So let me introduce you to my friend Tickler, who could become your worst nightmare if you don't follow the rules.'

16.

07:32 – MONDAY MORNING

'I've brought you some breakfast. I hope you were comfortable and slept well. I know it's sometimes difficult to get off to sleep in a strange place. Now, I'm going to take off your gag so you can enjoy what I've brought you. But first I need your promise that you're not going to shout and make a fuss when I take it off. Do you understand?'

'Dennis's' tone was all polite concern. A conscientious host, making sure that his guest had the best of everything, to make them feel at home.

'Give me some sign, please. An indication that you've understood and that you won't make a noise or doing anything foolish. I don't want to have to demonstrate Tickler in action so soon in our relationship, so I need to be able to trust you.'

Marcus was curled up inside a duvet on the floor, where he'd managed to sleep, to his own surprise. Whatever the man had put in his coffee was clearly powerful stuff. The sort of thing with a rebound. Once he'd woken up from the initial effects, it hadn't been long before he'd fallen back into a deep sleep which even the image of the man caressing that polished, rounded rod had been unable to prevent.

At least he'd removed the other pole which had held

his legs apart. Now they were simply bound together with soft fabric. Something like a scarf. Apart from the feeling of extreme vulnerability the previous posture had invoked, it would have been impossible to sleep in such an uncomfortable position. Even drugged, he suspected.

His wrists were also tied together with material, then in turn bound to the old-fashioned radiator mounted on the wall, above which curtains were firmly closed. Lying on the floor, he could look up behind the curtains to see that there was also a Venetian blind, pulled down and with the lattes closed.

His mouth was as dry as the bottom of a budgie's cage and a persistent headache thumped away behind his eyes.

This wasn't the first time his work had got him into a tricky situation. It went with the territory, and he knew the risks he was taking. But there was something different about 'Dennis'. A menace about him that he'd not felt before with anyone. He would have to tread very carefully to get himself out of his current predicament.

He didn't for one moment believe that was his real name, either. Few of his clients ever gave him any of their real details. His name really was Marcus and he didn't mind giving it out. He wasn't exactly proud of what he did, but none of it was illegal. Just something which would never appear on any future CV.

For now, he needed to concentrate on finding a way out of his current difficulties. He knew he could be charming, and extremely persuasive. He used both talents to the full to earn the money he needed to pay his fees and to enjoy a decent lifestyle.

He tried to make his eyes as pleading as possible. More than one of the men he'd been with for money had fallen in love with what they called his puppy dog eyes. A couple of them had even wanted to set him up in a nice place where they could enjoy exclusive rights to him, whenever they wanted. One of them had offered him a small fortune for the privilege.

He wasn't into that kind of commitment. He liked his freedom. Loved his student life. He wasn't ready to throw it all away for any price. He shared a decent enough flat with another young man of the same age. It wasn't a relationship, as such, although they slept together when either or both of them was drunk or stoned enough.

He wanted to get back to his own life. To draw a line under this scary encounter, pocket the cash, and get out of here. To do that, he needed first to gain 'Dennis's' trust. He nodded his head as enthusiastically as he could, then lifted his bound hands the scant few inches he could manage and raised both thumbs in the universally understood gesture of approval.

He tried to make his eyes as appealing as a hungry cocker spaniel puppy, as they'd once been described to him.

'Dennis' nodded his satisfaction.

'Good. As long as we understand one another. I'm not a very forgiving person. I don't do second chances. But if you show me I can trust you, you'll find me surprisingly generous.

'Now, I'm going to take off your gag and give you a drink of water first. I know the gag makes your mouth very dry. But only sip it gently and slowly, otherwise you may well make yourself choke, and I know how much you hate that.'

Marcus was no fool. He knew he had to get it right first time. He let the man carefully remove the gag then hold up a chunky earthenware mug to his lip, helping him to take short, careful swallows of water from it, which felt so good to his parched mouth and dry throat.

A mug, he noticed. Not a glass. Much less of a weapon, even if he somehow managed to grab it and smash it.

This man was clever. Which made him even more dangerous.

'There now, I bet that feels better, doesn't it? Now, I wasn't sure what you liked for breakfast. I know you're not a vegetarian and I thought you might have a healthy appetite again this morning, like last night. So I took a chance and made you steak tartare, with an egg. I didn't have quail's eggs in, I'm afraid, but I hope you will like it.'

He lifted a tray down off the bed and put it on the floor between them.

In spite of the fear, Marcus found he was starving hungry, as ever. It looked really good, too. There was literally nothing he wouldn't eat. But first he needed to try to clear up the misunderstandings.

'This looks lovely, Dennis, thank you. But, mate, I think there was a bit of a lack of communication between us about what was on offer. What was included in the price. Something got lost in translation, somehow.'

He was picking his words as carefully as he could. Aware of his vulnerability. The man was watching him, listening to everything he said. Watching his mouth move. Almost as if he were reading his lips. Or perhaps just remembering what that mouth had been doing to him only the night before.

'I thought you said you wanted to wake up in bed with me. That sounded nice. Cosy. I mean, I don't mind the bondage stuff, if that's what turns you on. I didn't like the spread eagle stuff with my legs, to be honest. But I really don't like the gagging bit. I already said. And I need to get going. I told you I had to get to Uni for a lecture this morning.'

For a moment the man looked so contrite Marcus thought he might actually burst into tears.

'I'm so sorry,' he said, a catch in his voice. 'I told you this was all very new to me. I was just enjoying myself so much I might have got a bit carried away. But could we please do it again tonight, and I promise to get it right this time?'

He reached in a pocket and pulled out his wallet. He took out every note in there and put them down on the breakfast tray next to Marcus.

'I'll get more money, I promise. If that's not enough, I can get even more. Please. I'd just really like you to stay for today and tonight. Then if you still want to go, I'll set you free tomorrow. I promise.'

As he spoke, the man was helping his young guest to eat the tartare. In spite of everything, Marcus found it delicious and discovered just how hungry he was.

He finished a mouthful, then said, 'It's the lectures, you see, Dennis. I don't work in the daytime because I go to Uni. I told you that. My studies are important to me. I'm quite happy to come back this evening, and spend the night, for a fee. But no gagging. I'm not into that at all.'

The man effectively silenced him with another forkful of food, although he did it gently.

'The trouble is, Marcus, I have trust issues. Major ones. You say you'll come back, but how do I know that? I've given you the money, so what's to stop you leaving and then I'd never see you again?

'Or if I let you go without paying you, how do I know you won't just write it off to experience and not come back? You can see my quandary, I'm sure.'

Marcus swallowed his mouthful hurriedly, sensing he was losing the argument and desperately needing to be able to pull it back.

'Because I'm a professional. If you make a booking with me, I honour that business arrangement. Just like if you book your car in for servicing, you know the mechanic will be waiting for you and won't have gone off to do something else instead. You can trust me.

'Besides, it's not as if I'm going to tell anyone about this. I don't broadcast how I make my living. I know that if I went into a police station and said things had got out of hand I'd get no help or sympathy there. I'd be told it was my own fault, because of my lifestyle choices.

'And then Marcus isn't a very common name, and it is my real one. You're a clever man. You'd soon find a way to trace me, because you know I'm at the Uni doing

Modern Languages, and that part is true, too.'

'I want to believe you, Marcus, I really do. But I can't. Yet.

'I have to get ready for work now, so have a few more mouthfuls of your breakfast before I go. I'll come back a lunchtime and we can talk some more.

'I know this is hard for you, but please just give me a little bit more time.'

Marcus's appetite left him suddenly at the words. Another half day of being tied up and gagged. He wasn't sure how much more he could take.

He had no mobile phone on him, although he'd had it with him when he'd arrived at the house. It had been in the pocket of his jeans which he'd stripped off for the shower. He'd no idea when his mobile had disappeared from his pocket, but he hadn't consciously noticed its loss until he'd woken up.

He was starting to realise just how perilous a situation he was in.

* * *

09:53 – MONDAY MORNING

'I need progress, Oscar, not a load of old flannel and excuses,' Murray Aird was grumbling down the phone into Smith's ear. 'You knew we were taking a big risk going public. And that the press, plus every man and his dog, would be baying for results in record time when we did.

'So give me something positive. My arse is in line for kicking long before yours, don't forget, if I've nothing constructive to report to the top floor.'

Smith was making his usual gestures at the phone. What did the Det. Sup. expect? That they would have managed to wrap the whole thing up within forty-eight hours of the televised appeal?

Aird knew as well as the rest of them that they would have to wade through endless steaming piles of shit before they got to the one tenuous lead which might take them somewhere.

'We've got Vicky Garcia's ex coming in today, guv. Their split was apparently acrimonious, to say the least. We picked that up from a tip-off after the conference.

'Brian – DC McMahon – will interview him and we'll try to find out if he has any connection at all to the others.'

'But where are the women, Oscar? That's what we need. Even bodies would be better than no news at all. That's what will have the public screaming for our blood. Four young women shouldn't be able to disappear without trace in this day and age.

'The public are always complaining about the number of surveillance cameras. If we're not even able to use them to find high profile Mispers like these, they're going to start questioning even more strongly why we have them at all.

'Find the women, Oscar. Even one of them. I'll even settle for a body or a part of one at this stage. Just give me something we can show the public, so they don't think we're all sitting around here, thumb in bum and mind in neutral.'

'Yes, guv,' Smith told him, with another hand gesture which indicated the opposite.

Aird had called him on his mobile so he didn't even have the satisfaction of slamming his desk phone down, hard.

He'd joined Tony Taylor when he'd briefed the team earlier to make sure every possible angle was being considered. As much as anything, he wanted to cover his own arse if they missed a lead because some minor and seemingly unconnected detail had been passed over.

'What do we know about this bloke...' Smith glanced at the board where the name of Vicky Garcia's ex-boyfriend, Raoul Hunter, was written up... 'Hunter? Any indication of a connection with him and any of the other women?'

'Nothing so far, guv,' Tony told him. 'With a Spanish name like that it was easy enough to track him down. There aren't many on our patch.'

'French,' Smith told him. 'The name's French, of Germanic origin. Although he might never have been further than the Channel ports. Probably one of those names that was trendy when he was born. Named after a footballer or something, no doubt. Anyway, what else do we know about him?'

'It's all hearsay until we actually get to talk to him. We're just going off what Vicky shared with her clients when she was doing their nails. He manages a wine bar where she used to go. They got chatting, he asked her out and it led on from there.

'It got quite serious between them early on in the relationship. They moved in together, stuff like that. But according to what we've been told, he was the jealous type. Gave her a hard time if she so much as looked at another bloke. Always accusing her of seeing other men behind his back.

'They started having blazing rows about it, and in the end Vicky walked out on him. He was furious. He started following her. Stalking her, if you like. She told the women who contacted us that she was afraid of him, so she'd moved back in with her parents to avoid him.'

'So he's an obsessive type? With a tendency towards jealousy? Not unheard of in serial kidnappers, and such cases seldom have a good outcome. How recent is all this?'

'About six months, guv, according to what we've been given so far by her clients,' Taylor told him. 'So it's just possible, if he is our man, that he could be responsible for the other three as well. The timeline would fit, if so. Previous exes he'd also had a falling out with, perhaps?'

'Okay, let's not put the cart before a horse that hasn't even been broken to harness yet. This is all wild speculation at the moment,' Smith said. 'Brian, don't go at the interview with any preconceptions of his connection to any of them, except the relationship we've been told about with Vicky. And check that out carefully, in case the gossip in the beauty salon wasn't accurate. Although the name being unusual is a help there.'

He knew he was teaching his granny to suck eggs. McMahon knew what he was doing, but he didn't want the rest of the team taking their collective foot off the gas too soon and skipping basic groundwork. Too many high profile cases in various places had nearly come unstuck with coppers trying to make connections where there simply weren't any. Or making assumptions not based on any concrete evidence.

'Keep in mind, too, that we only have Vicky's version, second hand, about what happened in the relationship. Did the family mention anything about her experiences with Hunter when they were spoken to?'

Smith was sharp. He didn't miss the looks from the team members, the slight changing of position, the sudden fascination with things on desks.

'Fuck sake, the lot of you. You have asked relatives about former partners, as well as current ones, haven't you? If not, bloody well get back out there and do it. Christ, do you lot remember anything from your training? Get a grip, all of you.'

17.

17:58 – MONDAY EVENING

He was sitting on a bar stool, staring morosely into his half of lager. He was facing a serious moral dilemma, for the first time in his life, as far as he could remember. Things had gone badly when he'd returned to the house at lunchtime to talk further with Marcus, and now he didn't know what to do next.

He'd known the young man wouldn't be happy, having spent the morning once again tied up and gagged. He hadn't expected to be confronted by such anger, though.

Fury, would be a more appropriate word.

He'd apologised profusely when he'd gone upstairs to remove his gag and give him water. But Marcus had been so beside himself he'd been more inclined to rant than to drink.

'I'm sorry. I really am sorry. Look, here's some more money for you. Take it, please. I'm doing this all wrong and I just want it to be right between us. I want to be able to trust you, but I'm finding it so very hard.

'Please just stay for one more night. Please. I did so enjoy our shower together last night. I'll go and get you some more money. Just tell me how much you want.'

'It's not just about the money, Dennis. It's my studies. They're important to me. I don't like missing any lectures.

'And you talk about trust, yet how can I trust you, after

you treat me like this without asking whether it's all right? I told you, almost anything is on offer for a price, but not this.

'I always set up a safe word with clients. A pre-agreed signal that things have gone far enough and they need to stop. I didn't even get chance to do that. And I'm sure you drugged me.'

'I didn't!'

'Dennis' was all wide-eyed innocence now.

'I really didn't. Not drugs, as such. I just wanted you to have a nice sleep, so I could lie awake watching you. You're so beautiful when you're asleep. So innocent and vulnerable. All I gave you was a little antihistamine tablet. Very mild. I thought it would help you to sleep well, and it did.'

It wasn't true. It had been something much stronger than that. Something he knew perfectly well would knock his victims out for hours at a time.

'I'm sorry. Really I am. I got it wrong through being too eager. Please let me try again. Tell me about the safe word. I didn't know about that. Please. I promise to respect it.'

Marcus hesitated. There was bugger all he could do anyway, tied up as he was. The bloke was seriously weird, but he was handing over the cash like there was no tomorrow. If he really was going to let him go afterwards, with the amount of money he'd given him already, plus more, if he stuck to his promise, it would have been worth it.

Maybe if he could string him along until the evening, he might find a way to overpower him and get away, with the money. It was worth a shot, and it wasn't as if he had much choice in the matter, the way things were.

'Okay, just one more night, then I'm leaving. And you will need to pay me more. Double what you've paid already.'

The man was nodding eager agreement. He didn't look

quite as weird now, either. Calmer. More in control.

'The safe word is scissors. Like in rock, paper, scissors. And this is the hand gesture,' he made a cutting motion with his index and middle fingers, 'in case I can't speak at the time, for some reason.

'No more gagging. And no more drugging. Not even antihistamines. If you'll agree to all that, and say it like you mean it, then you can have one more night. But that's it.

'Have we got a deal?'

'Yes! Yes, we have. I'm so sorry I got it wrong and thank you so much for letting me try again to get it right. One more night and you can go free, with all the money.'

But now, sitting at the bar, staring into his drink, he didn't know what to do. He liked Marcus. More than he cared to admit to himself. Not exactly in a physical way, although he had enjoyed their shower together more than he thought he might. Far more than he'd been brought up to believe that he should.

He found himself admiring the young man. So self-assured, so in control of himself. Using his best asset – his exquisite body – to get what he wanted out of life.

And it was just possible that if he let him go, he wouldn't say anything to anyone. If for any reason he did, even if the police came knocking at the door, he could simply say it had been his first time with a male prostitute, he'd got a bit carried away, but he had paid handsomely for his services.

He could give them an artful smile and say, with just the right note of apology in his voice, that things might have gone a bit further than was agreed because he'd been over-eager. Which was why he'd paid double the going rate.

Then he could show them the withdrawal slips from when he'd taken out the maximum allowed from his account on two consecutive days to pay for the young man's services.

He smiled to himself. That was rather clever. He could

see it working.

But then he was taking such a huge risk. If for any reason the police took it more seriously and turned up at the house with a search warrant...

He was so absorbed in his quandary that he took little notice of the large, broad-shouldered man who came in and sat on the high stool next to him, studying the optics behind the bar.

Not until he heard him speak. Then he froze, his lager halfway to his mouth.

'Give me a vodka, please, mate, unless you happen to have a bottle of decent schnapps hidden away under the counter?'

He'd heard that voice before. And when he turned his eyes carefully to expand his field of vision, he recognised the man that went with it.

Detective Inspector Oscar Smith. The man leading the enquiry into the missing women.

18.

18:16 – MONDAY EVENING

The police officer didn't so much as glance at the anonymous man on the stool next to him. Even if he had done so, 'Dennis' knew from bitter experience that even a trained detective would have been hard put to register anything about him.

He was bland. A nothing. Average height, average build. Discreet glasses. Rimless, so they weren't so obvious. Hair an indeterminate shade of brown. Eye colour hard to distinguish because the lenses of the spectacles had various tints to filter out things like sunlight and computer screen glare.

No facial hair, no tattoos, no convenient scars. A nose which was perfectly straight and not prominent. Even his voice had nothing distinctive about it. Quietly spoken. Monotone. Not much light and shade to it. No immediately discernible accent.

Mr Anonymous.

Mr Invisible.

Mr Nobody.

If any potential witness could describe him in the first place, they'd have difficulty picking him out from an equally bland line-up of photos.

Smith was speaking to the man behind the bar now. 'Dennis' carried on taking tiny sips from his lager to make it last. Studiously pretending to ignore what was being said.

'I don't know if you can help me, pal, but I'm looking for a young woman.'

The barman gave a chuckle as he said, 'It's not that sort of a pub, mate.'

Smith smiled in return as he said, 'It's not that sort of a request, either. I met her last week. We seemed to click, but I must have taken her phone number down wrong because I can't get hold of her and I'd like to see her again.

'She's about yay tall,' he held up a hand to indicate height. 'Long blonde hair. Curvy.'

He used both hands to indicate an hourglass figure, although he probably made the waist more defined than it was in his memory.

When he moved his hands to show a full bust, the man serving laughed as he said, 'Oh, you mean Lulu. In which case, you won't have got her number wrong, she won't have given you the right one.

'Let me guess, she couldn't send it to you because her battery was low, or something like that? You're not the first one to fall for that. You won't see her again for weeks and then when you do, what can you prove? She's crafty, is Lulu.

'You can keep looking and you might get lucky and spot her again, but I wouldn't hold your breath.

'Have you tried the Red Lion?'

'I've already asked in there. They've not seen her recently.'

'Where did you meet her?'

'The Crown. They haven't seen her either. Not since I met her there.'

'You'll just have to keep doing the rounds until you bump into her again. But like I said, she's a sly one. She's banned from a few pubs in town for hitting on their clients. Nicking their wallets, sometimes all the cash they have on them.

'Try The Ship. They're not so choosy there so you might run into her.'

Smith was keeping his new wallet inside his jacket now, where he figured it might be a bit safer from the likes of Lulu. He fished it out, took one of his cards out and handed it to the man, who was now wiping glasses and running a cloth round the surface of the bar.

'If you do see her, especially if she comes in here again, give us a call, can you? That's my mobile number on there, so you should be able to get me almost anytime. There's a drink in it for you if you do.'

The barman nodded and put the card down on the counter in front of him as Smith drained his glass, stood up and left the pub.

Then he picked the card up to examine it more closely and laughed aloud, looking at 'Dennis', still sipping his half of lager.

'Oh dear, I wouldn't want to be in Lulu's high heels when he catches up with her,' he told him. 'He's a copper. Detective Inspector. Can you believe it? He must be a bit bloody dozy if Lulu got one over on him that easily and took his money.

'He's a big bloke, though, eh? Looks a bit handy, too. I wouldn't want to be on the wrong side of him. Nor to meet him up an alley on a dark night.'

'Dennis' was still feigning indifference but as the man was addressing him directly, he decided silence would be more suspicious than making some sort of a comment.

'What exactly does she do, this Lulu?'

'She's a pickpocket, you could say. And a bloody good one, by all accounts. It's widely known what she's like, that's why she's barred from some of the better pubs, like the Queen's, and the Royal Oak too.

'But she still finds plenty of places to go and plenty of gullible blokes ready to buy her drinks in the hopes of a shag.'

'If everyone knows, how does she keep getting away with it, without getting caught?' he asked, intrigued, in spite of himself.

It was quiet in the pub. Just one other couple sitting at a table, contemplating one another in bored silence, eating crisps and drinking beer.

'Think about it. Like I said, she's clever. Chooses her targets carefully. She seems to have like a sixth sense to tell the ones who are less likely to make a fuss. Like second sight, if you like.

'I mean, if it's a married man stopping off for a quick one – and I'm not just talking about the drink – on his way back to the trouble and strife, he's hardly going to try explaining how he really lost his wallet, is he? And he almost certainly wouldn't want it to turn into a police matter and him have to turn up in court to explain how he fell for one of the oldest tricks in the book.

'She seems to have made a bad judgement call this time, though, with a copper. And I don't know what you thought of him but I wouldn't fancy having to try explaining myself to a big bastard like him when he's in a bad temper.'

'I didn't notice him really, I'm afraid, to be honest,' 'Dennis' told him in his quiet, colourless voice. 'I've had a bit of tough decision making to do today and I was just trying to decide whether or not I'm doing the right thing.'

The man behind the bar visibly lost all interest in a customer who wasn't up for a bit of gossip and a few laughs.

'Well, good luck with whatever you decide. Another one in there?'

'No, thank you. Now I've made a decision, I'd better go and do something about it.

'Good night, now.'

* * *

18:38 – MONDAY EVENING

He'd taken a big risk. Despite promising not to drug him, he'd managed to secrete one of the ground-up pills into the lunch he'd given Marcus. He'd known he was susceptible to them. He'd only given him half of one the night before and he'd slept like a baby.

This time he'd given him a whole one so he could leave him all afternoon without the gag. He wanted to make a gesture to show he had listened. He needed to get everything back onto a professional transaction, without the anger and the recriminations.

He'd made up his mind what he was going to do. He was going to give Marcus more money – enough to remove all risk of him thinking it was anything other than any of the other business arrangements he made – enjoy another shower with him like the one the night before, and then he would set him free.

The young man was still asleep inside the folded duvet he'd found for him, on the floor of the bedroom when he got home. He looked so peaceful that for a moment 'Dennis' simply sat on the edge of the bed watching him.

He really was stunning, especially asleep and looking innocent and vulnerable. No wonder he could charge the prices he did for his services.

And 'Dennis' fully intended to sample some more. He found himself getting aroused just at the thought of the shower the previous day.

He really wanted to keep him longer. Much longer. But his plans had all been turned on their head by the chance encounter and overheard conversation in the pub. Now he needed the room, and the time, to put an entirely different plan into operation.

He'd have to regard Marcus as a sacrifice he must make to achieve something he'd not even considered previously.

As if he somehow knew he was being watched as he

slept, Marcus stirred, stretched and yawned widely. The dark brown eyes opened and stared up at the man, disorientated for a moment.

He frowned as he took stock of his surroundings.

'How long have I been asleep? Did you give me something again? I told you not to.'

The man smiled down fondly at him.

'No, I didn't give you anything. I think you must just have been tired. Perhaps you study too hard? And look, no gag, as you asked me. And here's some more money.'

He took out his wallet and pulled out a fat handful of banknotes, which he put down carefully on top of the duvet.

'I went into my bank so I could draw out more than I can do from the hole in the wall. I hope that's enough?'

He frowned anxiously as he asked, then hurried on, 'If we can just have one wonderful night together, properly, then you can go free, with all of the money. But I hope I might perhaps be able to contact you again in the future.'

He was busily untying his hands and feet as he spoke. He wasn't worried about Marcus trying to overpower him or anything of the sort. He knew he'd be pleasantly woozy for a bit, at least.

'Would it be all right if we shared a shower first this evening again, before we eat? The food's ready, I just need to heat it up and open the wine. Only I really enjoyed our shower yesterday. Perhaps we could do the same again and then maybe take it a little bit further?'

Once his hands were free, Marcus picked up the money and fanned through it to count it. He didn't want to appear too enthusiastic but it was more than he would have asked for.

If all he had to do now to earn it was give this weird bloke another blow job in the shower, then perhaps let him fuck him, it would be the easiest money he'd ever earned. Especially since he'd obviously taken in the bit about not wanting to be gagged.

'That would be fine. But I really have to leave first thing in the morning. No funny stuff this time. No tying up, or drugging or gagging or anything like that. Or I walk out now and you'll never see me again.'

'I promise. You have my word. I just got carried away last night but I understand the boundaries now. And the safe word. Scissors.'

He made the hand gesture himself as he said it.

'So can we go and have that shower now? Please? There's plenty of hot water. I left the immersion heater on so we can stay in there as long as we want. As long as we need to.'

He guided the young man to the bathroom then watched as he stripped off his clothes, free of inhibitions, and left them in a heap on the floor.

'Dennis' undressed much more demurely, folding his things neatly onto a chair, while Marcus was already under the warm water, soaping himself all over.

Once again he knelt in front of the man and took him in his mouth until 'Dennis' could hardly bear it. He reached down and locked his fingers into the soaking wet dark curls, gently pulling his head away.

'Stop. Please stop. It's too much. And I want to try to…you know. I've never done it before and I want to try to last to enjoy it.

'Can I…would it be all right if I washed you first? Everywhere? I have this phobia, you see. About cleanliness.'

It was far from being the weirdest thing he'd ever been asked for. Marcus was quite happy to stand there patiently while the strange man lifted the shower head down.

It wasn't unpleasant, standing there in the warmth, while 'Dennis' soaped him all over with one hand while the other held the shower and let the water pummel his body.

He closed his eyes and leaned back against the man's body, revelling in the feel of the fine needle jets of water all over him. The sensation against his erogenous zones was strangely erotic and he was feeling something between extreme relaxation and an almost indolent arousal.

It took him longer than it should have to feel the flexible tube of the shower slither round his throat like a slim snake.

His eyes flew open and he tried to twist to look at the man behind him. He opened his mouth to try to say the safe word but terror was setting in as he felt his airway constricting, so that he couldn't speak.

Frantically he lifted a hand, miming the scissor action with his fingers, terrified by how difficult even that small movement was becoming.

'Sssssh, don't fight it. The more you struggle, the harder it will be. Just relax. Let the water carry you on its way.

'Hush, now.

'Hush.'

Marcus's last conscious sensation in life was of the man's erection pressing against him as he slipped to his knees in the shower tray and everything went black.

19

08:53 – TUESDAY MORNING

Smith was in early again the following day. He wanted a catch-up with Tony before he briefed the team, and he was hoping for encouraging updates. Smith had been out for most of the previous day, at a meeting for inspectors and chief inspectors. One of the reasons he'd headed straight to the pub as soon as he got out. Not just to find Lulu.

The meeting had been at the divisional headquarters building and had consisted of an executive officer virtually reading to the assembled underlings from a new set of regulations which they would have been able to read and assimilate themselves in a couple of hours from a detailed email. Or in Smith's case, probably less than that.

He hated such gatherings with a passion, viewing them as a total waste of everyone's time. They had a habit of turning into contests to see who could piss highest up the wall. Promotion-hungry officers all wanting to catch the attention of the higher ranks, whilst fighting over the creep's prize.

But he'd attended, though not with good grace. Been seen in the right places. Asked a couple of pertinent questions to get noticed, then avoided the mingling and flesh-pressing at the end like the plague. He'd disappeared as soon as he decently could to start another round of pubs on the trail of the so far elusive Lulu.

He called Tony into his office the next morning while

the others were getting themselves organised. He could see at once that his DS had something to get off his chest. Either that or he was suffering from a serious bout of constipation or haemorrhoids. Or possibly both.

'Guv, the Det. Sup. phoned me while you were up at HQ. Something he wanted to run past me.'

Smith correctly interpreted Taylor's verbal shorthand. It meant that Aird had had what he considered to be a brilliant idea. One which he knew Smith would fight tooth and nail against. So he'd sneaked the idea in to the DS first and left it to him to put it to his gaffer.

'Not interested,' Smith told him.

'You haven't heard it yet, guv.'

'I'm psychic,' Smith sniped back, with more than a note of sarcasm. 'Seriously, Tony, when did you ever know the Det. Sup. come up with an idea any better than anything we could? And if he's put you up to telling me about it, I instinctively know I'm not going to like it.'

Seeing Tony getting his stubborn look on, Smith sighed and said, 'Go on, then, tell me about this brilliant idea, but make it quick.'

'He thinks we should have another officer on this case. One with good Misper experience. He's got one lined up for us, ready to come on board later today.'

'And the "but" is?'

'It's a woman, guv.'

Seeing the look on Smith's face, Tony hurried on.

'I think he has a point, though. We're coming at this case from the point of view of blokes. We can try all the "thinking outside the box" stuff. Talk to the women in our lives for ideas. But at the end of the day, none of us can think like a woman would, faced with circumstances like these abductions, if that's what they are.

'Like I said, I spoke to my wife and daughter about it and they both said the same thing. Why are the women going off with whoever the abductor is? Most women these days are too wary even to think of doing that. Not with a complete stranger, on their own.

'We've not found any link between the four women to suggest their paths ever crossed anywhere. So there's no reason, from what we have so far, to think they might each have known the abductor, even from a perfectly innocent setting.'

'Tony, I go out on the pull. Often. Round the pubs and clubs. Yes, I get the brush-off sometimes, but you might be surprised about how often I don't. And of all the things I show them, my warrant card isn't one of them.'

He wasn't about to admit to his sergeant that he wasn't averse to picking up two at a time for a threesome, if they felt happier in pairs. Nor how badly the last encounter had panned out. He preferred to dwell on the positives, and there were some.

'Guv, should we not give it a try? He's offering us a very experienced DS who could come and join the team this afternoon. What if we at least let her come and talk to us? See what we've got? Then give us any input she might have.'

Smith smirked at him.

'She's welcome to see what I've got and depending on what she's like, I may have a bit of inputting to do myself.'

Tony didn't get innuendo at all. He was one of the most literal people Smith had ever encountered. But he could read the lewd look on the guv's face and he visibly grimaced at it. He hoped the gaffer wouldn't be crass enough to talk like that when DS Mitchell came to join them later on, but he knew there was no guarantee.

Seeing his expression, Smith told him, 'All right, give Aird a bell and get him to send her over. I'll at least listen to anything she might have to propose.'

He couldn't resist a broad wink at Tony as he said that, then he went on, 'Right, tell the rest of them to get fell in and let's have a bit of an update. I'll just grab a coffee.'

DC Brian McMahon took centre stage, to feed back everything he'd gleaned from interviewing their only potential suspect to date, Raoul Hunter, ex-boyfriend of Vicky Garcia.

'Unless he's a bloody good actor, I'm inclined to believe him when he says he hasn't seen Vicky since they split up. He admits it all got a bit messy between them and accepts that was all down to him for being too jealous and possessive.

'He said he didn't know she was missing until we got in touch with him. Apparently he never watches the TV news and he's not on any social media anywhere. He voluntarily showed me his phone and he certainly doesn't have any such apps on it.

'It's hard checking his alibi as we really don't have any kind of a time frame for when Vicky disappeared exactly. Although she's lived with her parents since the break-up, she's always been independent, they told us, and does sometimes go and stay with a friend for a couple of days. She didn't always let them know but as they said, she's an adult, she has her own life to lead.

'It was only when she hadn't shown up at work for two days, which was completely out of character, that the salon got in touch with the parents and she was reported as missing. No trace anywhere of her mobile phone.

'I asked Hunter about his whereabouts for the whole of that time period and they've been checked out.

'Since he was dumped by Vicky, he's been taking every extra hour going at work. He's taken in a lodger, someone who works at the same place as him. Craig spoke to the lodger and he's confirmed that whenever Hunter's not at work he's in his room, asleep or brooding.

'I also showed him the photos of the other three women. Again, unless he is a bloody good actor, there was no flicker of recognition. He admitted it was quite possible any one of them, or even all of them, might have been in the bar at some time. He could even have served one or more. But the faces meant nothing specific to him.

'He hadn't even seen anything about the press

conference. It was his flatmate who told him that Vicky was missing as he'd seen it on telly and knew he used to go out with her.'

'What about any independent evidence of a connection to the other three, as a former boyfriend of any of them?' Smith asked. 'Have you finally got your arses in gear to check that, at least?'

'Nothing, guv,' Tony replied. 'None of the relatives and friends we've spoken to know anything about Hunter at all.'

'So we're back to the main question – how and where is our abductor meeting and selecting their victims?'

'Hopefully when DS Mitchell arrives later today, she might have some valuable input, with some lines which haven't occurred to us yet, as mere men,' Tony told him, with a wry smile.

* * *

09:27 – TUESDAY MORNING

He'd had to call in sick again, blaming another migraine. He didn't like to push his luck, although he knew the management would turn a blind eye. He was very good at his job. He saved a lot of money through sniffing out the benefit frauds, and the proof to sanction them. He seemed to have a sixth sense for it.

Besides, his militant tendencies were hardly a secret in the workplace. They knew full well he'd have them straight in front of an industrial tribunal if they attempted to make any waves.

He had so much to do, and none of it was planned for now. There wasn't as much room in the freezer as he would have liked, so he'd have to do some sorting out and possibly some improvisation. And that would include a trip to another DIY store to select a new tree. Not to mention all the cooking he would need to do once he'd finished the butchering.

He was genuinely full of regret about Marcus. He'd admired him so much, both for his physical attraction and for his determination to get what he wanted out of life. He really wished he could have let him go, but it was a big and a reckless risk to take.

At least his wallet was now bulging with cash from gathering up all the notes and stuffing them back into it. He needed that for the next stage of his plan.

He experimented with the size and weight of it in his rear trouser pocket. It was almost too full to fit in there. He couldn't risk it falling out and spoiling his plans, so he took some of the money out and hid it at the bottom of his obsessively neat sock drawer.

That made it much easier to take out of his pocket without it snagging, which would never do.

He smiled at himself in the mirror above the chest of drawers where he kept his clothes. Proud of the way he had dealt with things almost going so wrong, but being now back on track.

He went round the house carefully closing all the blinds and curtains in every room. The neighbours were well used to seeing that. He never opened the ones in the front bedroom. Nobody ever commented. It was not that sort of a neighbourhood. Had any of them done so, his cover story was perfect. Those crippling migraines, which sometimes kept him off work. They left him intolerant to any light at all when they hit with their full might.

Next he stripped off all of his clothes and left them folded neatly on the chair in the bathroom. He slipped his feet into waterproof clogs then went down to the garage, accessed from a door in the kitchen at the rear of the house. There he got the plastic sheeting down from the top storage shelf and spread it over the floor.

He lifted up the lid of the freezer, took out what he could reasonably cook over the next few days. Then he started to assemble all the power tools he would need.

'Dennis' was surprisingly strong. Even he didn't know why as he never did any sort of physical exercise or training which might explain it. He'd always been wiry, even as a small boy, and that, coupled with a fierce determination never to lose at anything, had made him powerful in a deceptive way.

Marcus's inert weight had presented no problems to him in moving it downstairs and through the connecting door to the garage. Marcus's once glorious face had gone puffy and blue around the lips with the strangulation but even that didn't disguise the good looks.

He found it harder than for any of the others, even his own parents, to make the first cut with the electric saw. He had to steel himself to start the first slice in the throat, to hold the vibrating saw steady as it bit through into the spine, stopping it at the precise moment the head separated from the rest of the body, before the blade chewed up the sheeting or caused damage on the concrete floor beneath.

He was getting to be a dab hand at it, after so much practice.

He didn't consider himself a sentimental man, but for some reason he simply couldn't bring himself to open the skull and extract the brain as he usually did. It somehow felt like a violation of its beauty.

Instead he wrapped it in a clear plastic bag, untouched, and found a corner for it in the freezer. He'd bought himself the biggest chest freezer which would fit in the garage, after his mother had joined her husband in the old one, highlighting how little room there was.

The whole thing had been incredibly easy. His parents had had few friends. No one appeared to notice their absence much. One or two had asked about his mother at the beginning but had seemed satisfied that she'd gone to look after a relative who lived up north somewhere unspecified. Even those people had stopped asking after a time.

The house was perfect for his needs, too. The mortgage had long since been paid off, so 'Dennis' had few outgoings. His father had bought the place cheap years before, because of the railway. What had once been a busy branch line ran past the bottom of the garden, set down in a steep cutting, which did little to muffle the noise.

So many services had been cut that it was now much quieter, especially since an ambitious tree-planting scheme all along the embankment, had helped to screen out some of the sound.

The gardens were narrow but long, and because of the cutting, the likelihood of anyone coming snooping around the properties that way was slim. And there was plenty of space for 'Dennis's' own tree collection, which was growing nicely.

He was just tamping down the earth round his latest addition at the end of the afternoon when he heard the familiar scrabbling sounds on the other side of the fence. Then the weasel face of his neighbour peered over the top.

'Planting another tree, then?'

'That's right,' he told her with a pleasant smile. 'I thought I'd been planting more for autumn colour and I wondered if you might appreciate having a splash of spring blossoms to enjoy looking at from your window. So it's a flowering cherry tree.'

'Oh. Thank you. That's very thoughtful of you.'

He could tell how much of an effort it was for her to say that. The words almost seemed to choke her. Something he'd often been tempted to do, but he made it a rule never to do anything as stupid or as obvious on his own doorstep.

'I'm glad I've seen you. I've been doing some more cooking today. Casseroles. And as usual, I got carried away and made far too much.

'I wondered if you might like some? I'm particularly pleased with this batch. The meat is very young and tender.'

20.

13:42 – TUESDAY AFTERNOON

Two o'clock was when Detective Sergeant Jody Mitchell was due to join the team. It was almost twenty minutes before the appointed time when, after a brief knock on the gaffer's door, Tony Taylor stood aside to let his new colleague go in first.

Smith had just crammed the best part of half a takeaway hamburger into his mouth, which put him at a distinct disadvantage. Especially when he realised there was ketchup and mustard trickling down his chin from both corners of his mouth to land with a splat onto his tie. Not the regimental one, luckily enough, but still.

'Sorry to catch you in the middle of your lunch, Oscar,' DS Mitchell told him.

Chewing and swallowing as fast as he could so he wasn't at any more of a disadvantage, Smith thought how much that rankled with him. Pun intended. He'd left the Army years ago but he still found it hard to get used to the increasing informality within the police out here in the civilian world.

He confessed to himself that he missed the stricter rank structure which had seen others lower down the ladder than him snapping to attention in his presence, calling him 'sir' every time they spoke, and saluting him when he was wearing his red beret.

He grabbed the couple of paper napkins which had come with his burger and tried to make himself more presentable by rubbing and mopping at the escaping mustard mix. All the time he was doing so, he was eyeing up the first woman to join his team, even on a temporary basis.

She was medium height, sporty build, wearing well-tailored trousers with a powder blue jumper in a soft knit which looked like Cashmere. Striking red hair cut short. An expensive cut, he could tell. A sprinkling of freckles. Eyes the colour of forget-me-nots. Just as well, as they stopped her looking like Joe Barnes' love-child.

Tony was fussing about finding chairs, placing them opposite the gaffer. Smith had finally emptied his mouth. He didn't offer a handshake. Wouldn't have done even if his paws hadn't been covered in grease and sauce. It wasn't his style in the workplace. Nor even a word of welcome.

'I understand you've got experience in cases like ours, DS Mitchell,' he told her, hoping his formality might set the boundaries. 'So you're going to be able to point out what we're missing.'

'Not necessarily, Oscar,' she told him, deliberately ignoring his broad hint on modes of address.

She sat down and crossed one leg over the other. She looked cool, calm and totally in control.

'I'm sure, from what Tony has been telling me, that you and your team have gone over all the basics for any Misper case. What I'm here for is to look over what you have so far and to give you a woman's perspective on it. Particularly in relation to where and how your perpetrator might be meeting the women.

'What I intend to do first is to go through all of the case notes to date, looking for anything which jumps out at me. To see if I can start to build a profile of whoever is behind these disappearances.'

Smith was already starting to feel hostile towards her. The mere mention of profiling was enough to ratchet it up several notches. He had yet to be convinced by that load of old bollocks.

'I'm assuming you have some sort of a debrief at the end of the day? If so, I want to use that to go over anything I might have picked up and suggest further lines of enquiry worth exploring.

'I have to feed back to Murray Aird at the end of the day about how long my presence here is likely to be useful, so I'll need as much information as I can, so he and I can decide on that.

'So, Tony, if you can find me a quiet desk and show me where the loos and the coffee are, I can go and make a start.'

She barely nodded at Smith as she swept out of his office, Tony Taylor trotting in her wake like a devoted little doggy.

Smith was left sitting there feeling he'd been effectively sidelined from his own enquiry and wondering if DS Mitchell was the Det. Sup.'s ultimate revenge on him.

* * *

17:58 – TUESDAY EVENING

'Right, well, having gone through all of the notes to date, including those from the interview of Raoul Hunter, I can tell you a few things about our suspect which are more likely to be accurate than not,' DS Jody Mitchell told the assembled team members at the end of the day, all of them sitting there apparently hanging on to her every word.

'As I've already told Oscar, I don't have a magic crystal ball to look into and tell you exactly who your perpetrator is. But I can confidently predict a few things about who the person is likely to be. What type of person they are. Which should in turn save some time in going off half-cocked in the wrong direction.'

Smith was leaning against the wall in the background, arms folded, looking truculent. He didn't miss the looks of surprise from his officers to hear this newcomer refer to the gaffer by his first name. Even Tony Taylor didn't do that. Not in his presence, at any rate.

'The first thing I can say with some confidence is that whether or not Raoul Hunter abducted Vicky Garcia, I don't see him as a likely suspect for the three other cases.'

'What makes you say that?' Smith asked, interested, in spite of himself.

'He clearly has anger management issues. Seemingly directed at his ex for perceived cheating on her part. He might well be capable of assaulting her, possibly even killing her, in the heat of an argument. He could conceivably kidnap and keep her somewhere, although that's unlikely as he appears to go nowhere but work and the flat he shares with someone.

'But with a person with that kind of low flashpoint, it would be unusual for him to be able to charm four complete strangers enough to go off with him.

'Apologies for the sexist stereotyping, guys, but you might think that a charming man could easily seduce four women on four separate occasions into going somewhere with them, never to be seen again.

'We women know how unlikely that is in this day and age. For one thing, we tell one another about such characters, to warn one another. Not just when we meet up, but also on social media. Think of the hashtag Me Too movement.

'You've already had two of Vicky's clients come forward to say she'd talked to them about Hunter. There's a good chance that she talked to others, too, who may not, for instance, have seen the appeal for information about her and the other women.

'You could do worse than getting hold of the list of Vicky's clients and asking all of them if she ever said anything to them. There's just a chance that by doing that you might find a connection which hasn't yet come to light.'

She was looking at Tony Taylor as she spoke, more or less blanking Smith once more.

'You also need to find out if any of the others had ever mentioned anything about having met or seen someone who made them feel uncomfortable. And for that you need to get access to all of their social media, for a start.'

'Fair play, Sarge, that's the sort of stuff us blokes don't always think about,' Dai Evans told her.

'You're talking a shitload of man hours,' Smith put in, thinking about having to balance his budget to cover the additional time involved.

Mitchell gave him a hard look as she corrected him.

'Personnel hours, Oscar. And they're your headache, not mine. Mr Aird asked me to come in to take a look and make some suggestions from a woman's point of view, which is what I'm doing. It's up to you whether you take any action on my recommendations. But if you want to have any chance of finding any of these women alive, I would suggest you give it serious consideration.'

More than one of the team had to lower their head to hide a smirk to hear the gaffer getting soundly told off by a woman of a lower rank, who was addressing him by his first name in front of his team in the process.

'So now let me tell you a bit about the type of person I think you need to be looking for as the suspect. And this is not guesswork. Nor is it the so-called female intuition. It's based on a good few years working on Misper cases, and getting some decent results.

'It's more likely than not that the person you're looking for is a man working on his own. The tricky thing is he's likely to be someone easily overlooked. He'll be bland, ordinary, probably polite but in an almost shy way. The kind of person who would be easily overlooked in a crowd.

'He's likely to live a normal life, with nothing about him or it to send up red flags. He probably lives alone, possibly with elderly and/or disabled parents. One at least. He'll be reasonably intelligent and articulate. He may hold down a fairly responsible job requiring some skills. But he's very likely to be a loner. Possibly shy and socially awkward.'

'Right or left-handed?' Smith couldn't resist asking with a note of sarcasm.

Mitchell turned her gaze towards him and regarded him as if he were something she might encounter as a museum exhibit. Faint curiosity rather than any real interest. Yet again, some of his team members looked down at their desks to hide mouths which were twitching at the corners.

'I'm aware that some find the whole concept of profiling hard to accept. In this context, I would just like to remind you of a few things about serial killers, like Dennis Nilsen, for instance. Ex-Army, a former Met Police officer, later civil servant. Nobody had any inkling about his other life.'

'So you reckon our bloke is killing the women, Sarge?' DC Sean Walsh asked her. 'He's not holding them somewhere, or selling them on for something?'

'Sean, is it?' she asked him. 'You've been watching too much crime fiction on telly, I think. It's very rare indeed for a serial kidnapper to keep more than one victim alive and imprisoned at a time. The only exception would be, of course, where ransom demands were being made, and there haven't been any in any of these cases. Unless anyone is keeping that part secret, out of fear, but again that's highly improbable.

'As for selling them on, there'd be more of a market if we were talking young girls. These are all reasonably good-looking women, at first glance of a similar type superficially. But there's not much of a market in adults going out of the country. Coming in is a different thing altogether.

'The odds are against our victims, I'm afraid. It's more likely than not that he's killing them.'

She was doing a good job, Smith was forced to concede to himself. He'd better sharpen up his act and start behaving like an SIO who knew what he was doing if he wanted to come out on top of this one. Something which the latent caveman within him couldn't resist.

He straightened up, unfolded his arms and took a step forward.

'So why aren't we finding any bodies, or even any body parts? How is he disposing of them?'

'Don't forget that this is likely to be the original Invisible Man. A person no one notices. And someone clever. He'd be just the sort who, when digging his allotment and being asked by someone what he's planting, would make a joke of saying something like it was his next door neighbour because they always played their music too loud.

'The best way of putting someone off a trail is to tell them something so close to the truth that they wouldn't believe it.'

'So we're looking for someone with an allotment?' Dai Evans queried.

'Not necessarily. That was just an example for illustrative purposes. It could be anything. Perhaps he takes a boat out to sea to fish and drops body parts over the side. If anyone should happen to see him, he'll say he's putting down bait to attract the fish.

'I can't stress enough that he's likely to be clever. Resourceful. Able to think fast on his feet.'

'And this bit about the monthly intervals?' DC Craig Stephens asked. 'Could there really be something there? Moon phases, or women's stuff or something.'

It wasn't quite an eye roll but Mitchell did look up at the ceiling for a moment before replying.

'Based on my experience to date, plus a lot of research on the subject, a link to moon phases is unlikely in the extreme. Unless we're dealing with a serious psychotic who thinks they're a vampire or a werewolf or some such. If that were the case, it would be more probable than not that there were some signs of such behavioural deviance in their daily life.

'Menstrual cycles, however, is a far more likely explanation. And it may be nothing more than a man who knows nothing about such things and has some phobia or revulsion at the mere idea. So once his victims start their period, he has an irresistible urge to get rid of them.

'Don't forget, this person is quite likely a loner who may have very little sexual experience. Quite possibly an only child, who won't have had female siblings, so no knowledge of such things that way. There's also a distinct possibility of older parents, as I've said, so it won't have arisen there, at an age when he would know much about it.'

She turned and looked at Smith as she said, 'I'm going to suggest to Mr Aird that I stay on a bit longer with this case and that we also look at bringing in another couple of female officers. I think there's nothing to be lost in trying to map the menstrual cycles of all four missing women and I think that's something which might be better handled by other females for the necessary questioning. You could perhaps liaise with Uniform to see if we can borrow a couple of PCs.'

Smith didn't like that. Not one bit. She'd been with them five minutes and now it was 'we' and she was handing out instructions to him as well as to the others. Time for him to exert a bit of Alpha male authority.

'Tony, you speak to Joe Barnes and get him to lend us some bi...,' he so nearly said birds as he would normally do but decided against it, 'a couple of female officers to work with us on this. DS Mitchell, you work with Tony to oversee anything and everything that comes in, then both of you feedback the main highlights to me, at least once a day.

'And DS Mitchell, I want your full report on everything you've told us and your reasoning behind it all on my desk first thing tomorrow.'

'I've already emailed it to you, Oscar. Check your inbox,' she told him calmly.

Smith went back to his office to get his things, leaving the door open so he could listen out for any sniggering behind his back. He'd already shut down his computer and he wasn't about to boot it up again now.

He was not best pleased. He felt he'd walked into an elephant trap and made himself look like a proper pillock. He needed to get a grip of things.

But for now, he was intent on doing another bit of a pub crawl in search of the elusive Lulu. And heaven help her if he found her when he was in a mood like this.

He was at least halfway down the stairs before he heard the sounds of laughter from the main office.

21.

18:12 – TUESDAY EVENING

He was once again nursing half a lager at a bar in a pub. One of the advantages of not currently having a house guest was that he could stay out as long as he chose, although he seldom had more than a couple of halves when he had the car.

The last thing in the world he wanted to happen was for him to draw any police attention his way, for anything. That would never do.

He'd avoided The Ship, as the inspector had been told to try there next. He knew he was good at blending into the background and had the sort of appearance most people found hard to describe.

Mr Anonymous.

Mr Faceless.

Mr Forgettable.

But he suspected a police officer would be wary of coincidences, and seeing him again so soon might just trigger a memory, even if only a subliminal one.

He couldn't afford to take that chance.

He needed to find Lulu before the officer did.

* * *

20:05 – TUESDAY EVENING

Smith was in his armchair with his feet on the raised rest, Clive as usual sitting on his midriff. The cat was attentively watching the hand holding a fork which moved regularly from the plate on the side table to the mouth.

Smith had the phone to his ear and was talking to his grandmother, between mouthfuls. He had to pay a higher rate to get the carers to go in last thing on their evening rounds to put her to bed. She refused point blank to be packed off early like a child, as she was always complaining.

She would have preferred to stay up until at least midnight as she had always been a night owl. The best compromise he'd been able to make for her was for the night carer to arrive between nine-thirty and ten local time, which gave him up to half an hour to chat, as he did almost every evening.

He'd dumped his jacket on the back of a dining chair and thrown his tie on the table. His shoes were in the hall where he'd left them when he came in, but he'd not yet bothered to change out of his work things.

'What are you eating tonight, Oskar? And don't make so much noise about it. Keep your mouth closed while you chew. It's deafening.'

He swallowed before replying. There was certainly not much wrong with her hearing when it suited her.

'A Chinese takeaway. Kung Pao chicken.'

'It's probably made from cats, not chicken at all. I hope you're not eating it in front of your cat. That would be too much like cannibalism.'

'It's chicken, Oma. From a good shop. Reputable. They've never had the health inspectors in and I would hear about it if they did. The shop is on my patch. Besides, Clive wouldn't care, the greedy little sod. He'd probably eat another cat happily enough, if there was nothing else.'

'You should cook for yourself, Oskar. You're perfectly capable.'

'I've only just got home from work, Oma. If I started cooking now, I'd fall asleep before I managed to eat anything.'

'Then get yourself a woman, like I keep telling you. You obviously have what it takes. Anja hasn't stopped moping around ever since you went back home.'

He swallowed a hasty mouthful and pushed Clive's experimental paw away from his plate before he replied.

'Funny you should say that. My boss has given me a female officer on my team. The first one ever.'

'Are you sleeping with her? Can she cook?'

Smith laughed.

'She only joined the team this afternoon. And I have no idea whether she can cook. She doesn't seem to approve of me.'

His grandmother gave a loud snort down the phone.

'Then she's a fool. Or a lesbian. Probably both.

'Anyway, why do you need a woman? Why can't you solve the case? You're good at it.'

'My superintendent thinks we need the input of a woman on a case where all the missing persons are women.'

She gave a sound like a tut but made no further comment.

'Anyway, are you all right, Oma? Are things any better?'

'Most of the carers are still complete fools. But since your visit, Anja has been much improved. You'd better come and see her again soon.'

He could clearly picture the mischievous smile on her face as she said that. He chuckled to himself.

'Goodnight, Oma. I love you.'

'Goodnight, Oskar. Make me proud once more.'

22.

08:59 – WEDNESDAY MORNING

Smith had just got off the phone with the Det. Sup. when there was a light knock on his door and Tony Taylor came in. Aird had phoned to confirm that he'd had a long talk with DS Mitchell and was happy for her to stay with Smith's team, at least for the time being, to see if she could help them to move forward.

Mitchell was already in and working at the desk she'd been assigned when Smith had arrived, earlier than his usual time. He couldn't prevent a stab of resentment that she had beaten him to it. He realised he was probably being petty but he found he couldn't help himself.

He didn't so much as acknowledge her as he headed for his office, with a brief detour to the coffee machine. It wasn't much of a gesture, but one he couldn't resist.

It was totally lost on her, though. She seemed unaware of his presence in the room, head down at the computer in front of her.

'Guv, I spoke to Joe Barnes last night and he's lending us two of his officers,' Taylor told him. 'They'll join us for the usual team briefing then Jody will explain to them in detail what she needs them to do. They're going to try to check out the missing women's monthly cycles, just in case there is some bizarre correlation there.

'Uniform also had another Mispers reported late

yesterday afternoon. Here's the details.'

Taylor had a print-out with him which he put on the gaffer's desk. As ever, Smith hadn't invited him to sit down. He simply left him standing there like a spare part.

Smith scanned the page, which had a colour photo on it. A young man, dark-haired and dark-eyed, strikingly good looking.

Smith looked up, frowning.

'Tony, are you shitting me?'

He brandished the page in a large hand as he went on, 'This is a bloke, in case you hadn't noticed. Missing two days. On what planet do you see any link between this and our missing women?'

Tony had expected a reaction like that. He stood his ground, though, digging his heels in.

'Guv, this young man, Marcus Campbell, is a very good university student. Never missed a single lecture. Takes his studies extremely seriously. His flatmate, Daniel, reported him missing when he hadn't seen him since Sunday and found out he hadn't been in for any of his lectures.

'It's completely out of character. Especially as he's off the radar. Mobile phone not connecting, no sign of him anywhere. Daniel's rung round all his friends. Everyone he can think of. Nobody's seen him since the weekend.'

'So he's found a girlfriend. He's shagging himself senseless somewhere and funnily enough, phoning a friend or doing some studying is the last thing on his mind.'

'He's gay, guv.'

'A boyfriend, then. In between shagging they're getting pissed or stoned or both and generally having a good time. Seriously, Tony, if the police got involved every time a student skipped lectures for two days, we'd never bloody get anything done.'

He was just about to toss the sheet of paper back at Taylor when the DS told him, 'Marcus pays his way through uni by working as a male prostitute, guv. He's ultra careful about who he goes with. He always stays in contact with his flatmate. Always. He's his safety back-up.

'Forty-eight hours without being in touch is their pre-arranged signal that something has gone seriously wrong. And he's not the type to cry wolf by messing about. Far too intelligent for that.'

Reluctantly, Smith lifted the sheet back up and studied it more closely.

'Still a bloke though. And dark hair. Not much in common with our missing women.'

He frowned for a moment, then said, 'Maybe that's the point? Perhaps our man saw the press conference and has decided to try throwing us off the trail by changing his MO completely.'

'Jody and I were just saying the same thing, guv. So should we at least consider the possibility of a connection with our existing Mispers?'

Smith stood up from his desk and started heading out into the main office, Tony following at his heels.

'We can't afford to ignore it. If we do and there is a connection, we're going to look like a bunch of totally incompetent pillocks. But we're not going public on this one yet. It's still possible he'll turn up, hung over, still stoned, and feeling a bit of a dickhead for worrying everyone.'

The team members were waiting for Taylor and the gaffer to join them. There were two young women with them. They were the officers on loan from the uniformed branch but were wearing civvies. Smith had no idea of their names and no one seemed inclined to introduce them.

Tony had put the photo of Marcus up on the board with those of the four missing women and pointed to it now as he started to speak.

'We need to keep trying to find where our suspect is meeting the women, and possibly this young man, Marcus Campbell, if he is connected to the case.

'He's only been out of contact since Sunday but it is so

totally out of character for him that it's a red flag and we should strongly consider the possibility that something has happened to him. It might, of course, not be connected to the others, but it's something we need to keep in mind.

'Carry on asking round the pubs, bars, restaurants, anywhere else you might think of. But remember all of you, this is serious work. I expect it done properly. It's no excuse to go on the piss,' he told them.

'Sports venues, too,' Mitchell put in. 'There's nothing I've seen mentioned in the notes but that might simply be that no one's asked the right questions so far. But it's a possibility that our women might have been into something like yoga, Pilates. Swimming, perhaps.'

'So could our abductor be someone who teaches something like that?' Taylor asked her.

She frowned.

'I'm not dismissing anything at all at this stage. We can't afford to. But I would say it's unlikely. There'd be gossip. People would be sure to get suspicious if four people from the same class or group stopped coming to the sessions over a period of four months, especially at roughly monthly intervals. Too big a coincidence. People would notice, and they would talk. Especially if any of them happened to see on TV or anywhere about them being missing.

'Also it's statistically far more probable that this abductor is quiet, shy, withdrawn. Used to blending into the background and using that to his advantage. So not usually the type to be prancing about in tight Lycra in front of a load of women. But as I said, we need to consider any and every angle so we don't overlook the obvious.

'Trish, Maggie and I,' she nodded towards the two officers who'd just joined them, 'will be going to talk more to any women known to be friends or acquaintances of our Mispers, so we can ask about anything like that at the same time.

'I have to warn you, though, that our worst possible

nightmare will be if there is no logical connection to be found anywhere. Random abductions with no apparent pre-planning, by a loner who is pretty much anonymous, are the hardest of all to solve. Again, I cite Dennis Nilsen as evidence of that assertion.'

'Dai's drawn up a list of all the pubs and bars in town,' Tony Taylor began, before laughter interrupted him.

'I bet you did that from memory, eh, Dai?' Sean Walsh asked him.

Taylor ignored them and carried on.

'I've divided them up between you. Remember the no drinking on duty rule or I might just order random breath tests on some of you when you get back in. Especially any who come back empty-handed. This is work, and I want some results.

'I'll stay here and coordinate, so if any of you gets a sniff of anything at all, I want to know about it straight away. I don't want any time wasted if there's something concrete to go off. If there is, I'll pull you back in and reassign.

'If not we'll regroup here at close of play and see what, if anything, we've come up with between us. And there better be something to show for it. Anything.'

'In case any of you are unwise enough to ignore Tony's words of warning, let me just tell you that I might be out and about a bit myself today,' Smith told them all. 'Once I've shifted the day's paperwork, I might fancy a trip round some of the city's finest hostelries, to see what I might be able to come up with.'

'So heaven help you if I come into a place where you're having a swift bevy thinking no one will know. And not just low alcohol. Alcohol free only on duty.'

Not that he hadn't been known to have a sneaky glass or two when he was officially on duty, but the team members didn't need to know that.

'Tony, copy me in on who's going where.'

Smith wasn't about to say so but he wanted to try a few

more pubs himself for a different reason to the others. He was still hoping to get a lead on Lulu and he might as well do it on work time with the excuse of checking up on the team.

***

12:35 – WEDNESDAY MIDDAY

He didn't like coming back to an empty house. He felt the loneliness the minute he walked through the door. It was bad enough at lunchtime. But the long evenings stretching in front of him with no guest upstairs waiting for him were intolerable.

He liked to think of himself as the nurturing type. He loved making and serving such delicious and nutritious food to his guests. He even enjoyed seeing the greedy glint in the eyes of his neighbour whenever he handed her another casserole over the top of the fence.

He must give her some more and get the other dishes back from her. The freezer was full to the top and he needed to make room for the next one. From the description the police officer had given of her in the pub, she might be bulky.

He could do with a second freezer but he couldn't take the risk. He couldn't collect one himself in his small car, clearly, so he would have to get it delivered. It would be just his luck if the delivery driver and mate were the nosy talkative type and commented on bringing him another one when he already had a maximum sized chest freezer in the garage.

He could spin them some yarn about the old one being unreliable and him needing to empty and defrost it before he could get it taken away. But that was just the sort of thing which could stick in people's minds.

Far safer for him if he remained what he always was.

Mr Anonymous.

When it had only been his father, that first time, he'd managed with the modest family-sized one they'd had. He'd had no intention, back then, of doing it again. But then his mother had forced him into it. Unplanned, and against his will. Now he found that he couldn't stop.

He missed Marcus most of all. Even in such a brief encounter, he'd made the most profound impact on him of any of them.

He'd kept his clothes. Took them to bed with him at night, hugging them close to drink in the scent of him which still lingered, while his tears flowed down to soak the fabric.

He had no idea why.

Perhaps he was gay?

He'd never considered that before. Not even when he was young and his hormones were raging out of control.

Perhaps he should try again with another young man. Although they might not be so easy to encounter as the women had always been. They had seen nothing at all about him to raise their anxiety levels.

Mr Anonymous.

Mr Invisible.

Mr Nobody.

Men might be different. Unless he went after the most vulnerable, like the homeless.

But then there was the hygiene issue. He shuddered at the mere thought. That's why Marcus had been the perfect choice. So clean and fragrant. Even before those decadent showers they had shared.

He opened the door of the fridge; time to make himself some lunch.

He lifted out a plate with a piece of fresh liver on it.

Brought the plate up high to his face and sniffed at it.

Put out an experimental tongue until it made contact with the offal, cold and inert.

He ran a hand over it, caressing the contours.

Then he picked it up, flaccid and helpless in the hand which held it.

The hand which, without conscious thought on his part, brought it up to his mouth. Slipped the end of it inside.

He felt himself harden almost instantaneously. Such a strong erection that the sensation was almost painful.

He let the organ slide over his tongue until it seemed to touch the back of his throat, making him gag immediately.

Was he subconsciously punishing himself for choking Marcus, he wondered.

Marcus.

The feeling of loss was acute.

He wished he could have kept him for longer. Much longer. Enjoying the sensations.

But then he'd seen that policeman in the bar. It was like a sign to him. It showed him exactly what he needed to do next.

He needed to find Lulu.

And soon.

But first he put the frying pan on the hob and switched it on.

23.

18:15 – WEDNESDAY EVENING

There was a depressing lack of progress to report at the end of the day. All four women had disappeared after leaving work. None of them had said anything to friends or family about going anywhere on their way home, but all of them would frequently go shopping first, or meet friends for a drink or a coffee.

Tony Taylor had used his office time to go over CCTV footage in the vicinity of all four workplaces. It had been done before but in the absence of anything else it was worth another shot.

'People get the wrong idea from the rubbish crime drama stuff on TV,' he grumbled at the debrief. 'Everything gets conveniently solved by one flickering image that could be anyone. They don't know the reality about how many of the cameras don't even work. Nor how quickly stuff is recorded over. So there's nothing to report on that score for any of them, not even Marcus, and he's recent enough for the tapes not to have been reused, in theory.'

'Time to consider a re-enactment, Oscar?' Mitchell asked Smith.

He was beginning to wish he'd not let her see how much it irritated him, her calling him by his first name in front of the team. It seemed to make her more inclined to do it. Although that might be him projecting his own petty behaviour onto her, he conceded to himself.

'Hard to do one when we don't have any idea of where they went,' he told her.

'We know roughly when they left work for the last time, and we can get a pretty good idea of what they were wearing from the statements we have,' she countered.

'It might we worth doing one with a lookalike of one of them coming out of their workplace. Perhaps shots of her turning in either direction. It might just jog a memory somewhere.

'Maybe the most recent one, Gill Burrell. She might be the most fresh in people's memories. And let's factor in accurately the weather at the time. That might in turn throw something up. If it was pouring down, for instance, even the most cautious of them might perhaps have accepted a lift from someone they at least knew by sight.

'What have we got to lose by trying? We're having a spectacular lack of success so far, so isn't anything worth a shot for now?'

Smith would need clearance from higher up to justify the cost of doing it. That was only going to draw even more attention to what Mitchell had accurately described as their abject failure to come up with anything concrete to date.

He was saved from answering by one of the PCs starting to say something.

'With the menstrual thing in mind, guv, I talked to Vicky Garcia's mum at length. Vicky had just finished her period when she disappeared, if that does turn out to be significant at all. Regular as clockwork, her mum said, so there was a pattern there, if anyone was looking out for such things.'

'Gill Burrell, on the other hand,' the other PC put in, 'was anything but regular. She'd suffered a lot with eating disorders as a teenager, which can sometimes cause periods to stop altogether, although they might come back if they stabilise their eating habits.

'Hers had come back recently but very sporadically. Her health generally isn't good. She has a lot of food intolerances and is obsessively vegan. All of which combined has tended to leave her underweight. Her flatmate had no idea when she last had a period and said even Gill had no idea when the next one would happen.'

'There's a religious thing about menstruating women being unclean, isn't there? Torah? Old Testament? Something like that,' Smith speculated. 'So is that what we're dealing with here? Some sort of religious nutter?'

'Anything is possible,' Mitchell conceded. 'But then how would an abductor know where they were up to in their cycle? I suppose someone like *Rain Man* could get away with asking such an intensely personal question on a first encounter, but as chat-up lines go, there are better.'

Once again Smith noticed some of his team looking down in sudden concentration at the DS's tone to the gaffer. He asked another question, as much as anything to make it look as if he was still in charge of this enquiry.

'How did the women travel to and from work? If it was by public transport, could that be where they met our abductor?'

'Should we not be considering Marcus in all of this, guv? How he travelled? All that sort of thing?' Tony Taylor asked him.

'When he had his period?' Smith sniped at him with heavy sarcasm. 'You're not selling any connection to me, Tony. Come up with something concrete which links him to the women and I might take the theory more seriously.

'The kidnapper might just have taken him to throw us off his scent but at the moment I don't see any link, so chuck it back to the Flatfoots. Tell them it's more one for them.'

There was an uncomfortable silence. The two young PCs from downstairs looked angry at that. One of them flushed red from her neck up. For an awkward moment,

Tony Taylor looked as if he might just say something. But proving the saying about discretion being the better part of valour, he stayed quiet. Even Mitchell seemed at a loss for words.

'Back to the women,' Smith ploughed on, undeterred. 'Tell me how they all travelled to and from work. I assume we know that, from the early information on the disappearances.

'Let's for god's sake give ourselves something we can be working on. Even if it means some of you hopping on buses or trams or whatever, armed with photos. Start with the last one. With Gill Burrell. Did she drive?'

The first PC spoke up again.

'No, guv. Never learned, never had a licence. She had some anxiety issues and suffered from panic attacks. She also walked everywhere. Obsessively. Power-walked, you could say. That was a hangover from the eating disorders. She used to exercise all the time to keep her weight right down.'

Smith frowned.

'So how would someone with all her sort of issues get taken in enough by a stranger to go off with him? Or am I missing the point here, being a mere man?'

He knew it sounded snarky but he couldn't help himself.

Mitchell replied as if speaking to someone particularly slow on the uptake.

'As I've already said, Oscar, this man most likely won't be perceived as any kind of a threat. He'll be shy, probably. Or at least will appear to be so. Quiet. Nothing about him to raise suspicions.

'And let's not overlook the possibility that, although we've not yet found the links, he might well be known to our Mispers in some way. Someone bland, who they might have encountered somewhere then immediately forgotten about.

'He's not obligingly walking about with a sign round his

neck announcing him as a serial kidnapper and possibly killer. It's very important that we keep that in mind.

'I would suggest Gill Burrell might be the ideal one to start with, in a reconstruction. Someone walking like that, fast and purposeful, might have stuck in someone's subconscious memory without them actually realising it, until they see something similar.

'And I would suggest, Oscar, in the strongest possible terms, that we look at putting out a statement saying we're seriously concerned about the current whereabouts of Marcus Campbell, even if we don't publicly link him to the other Mispers at this stage. Making an appeal to him directly that if he is safe and well somewhere, to at least let us know because he's been reported as missing and we need to know if he genuinely is or not.

'Because if it gets out in public that we appear to have refused to take his disappearance seriously, possibly because he's a male prostitute, we are going to be hung out to dry in the press and media. Especially if it comes out at a later date that our delay in linking him to the others may have had fatal consequences.

'If the women are being killed within a month of capture, for whatever reason, there's a chance that Marcus too would be killed within that time frame. And it would seem probable that they are only being kept for a month, because that would seem to be when our suspect goes on the prowl for his next victim.'

Smith made a pretence, at least, of listening to her and considering her suggestion before he said, 'Like I said, let's leave the Marcus case with the Plods for now. We don't want to start a full-scale panic by making the public think no-one's safe. Let's concentrate on the young blonde female profile for the moment, unless something else comes up.'

If he noticed the various bristling reactions at his turn of phrase, and not just from the uniform officers, he showed no signs of having done so.

'Tony, you bat it back to Joe Barnes and tell him we don't see a link to our cases at this stage, but make sure he knows to update us if anything changes. Especially if Marcus turns up somewhere, totally shagged out and with the mother of all hangovers, which I reckon might well still be the case.

'Plan for tomorrow, then, is to find out how, when and where our victims met our abductor. Thinking caps on tonight and let's have some more bright ideas of how to do that to start the day off with tomorrow morning.'

He went back to his office to shut down his computer and gather his things together. He might as well try a couple more pubs before he went home, looking for Lulu. He'd drawn a total blank everywhere on his foray out earlier in the day.

He smiled to himself, thinking that the phrase, *Looking for Lulu*, would make a good title for some TV cop show of an obsessive policeman hunting a city for the tart who'd robbed him. He wondered fleetingly who would play him.

He'd left his door ajar, ready to leave. He heard it flung wide open with enough force to make it nearly jump off its hinges. He turned in surprise to see DS Mitchell slamming it shut in such apparent fury the racket must have been heard halfway round the station.

'I know Tony won't say anything, Oscar, but I bloody well will. It's totally out of order to talk about Plods, Flatfeet and Woodentops at all, and especially when we have officers from Uniform joining us to help out.'

'Calm down, dear,' he replied, deliberately at his most annoying. 'It's just an expression. Words. Perfectly harmless.'

'Not harmless at all, and don't tell me to calm down, you patronising bastard.'

He studied her in surprise. She actually looked quite sexy, as angry as she was. He wondered what she would be like to shag.

He opened his mouth to reply but she wasn't finished

with him yet.

'It's the twenty-first century, in case you hadn't noticed, Oscar. You seem to be living in some sort of permanent re-run of *The Sweeney* or something like that. It's not acceptable. I'm more than capable of speaking up, but you need to bear in mind that not everyone will tackle you to your face, like I will. One of these days, someone is going to report you to higher authorities for your behaviour, and you will be called to account. And about bloody time, too.

'You're misogynist, you're racist and you're totally disrespectful to officers from Uniform. It's high time someone challenged you on it. How would you like it if we all referred to you as a Monkey in public?'

Now that really did surprise him. Most non-military types had no idea that Monkey was derogatory slang for the army's Military Police, known more frequently as the Red Caps. He wondered if she was an army brat, like himself, born into the military. Or in his case, adopted into it. Maybe she'd married into the forces, although she didn't wear a ring.

He decided it was time to assert himself and fight back.

'While we're on the subject of respect, DS Mitchell, I am your superior officer. At work, you should be calling me sir, or guv at the very least. Not addressing me by my first name.'

'No, you're not,' she snapped back, eyes flashing. 'You hold one rank senior to me. That in no way makes you superior, despite what you may believe. This isn't the Army. I'm under no obligation to call you sir. You're not my boss – I would refuse to work with you, for one thing, other than in an advisory role as I am now.

'Respect has to be earned and if you want to get it from me, you've got a long way to go. I know you have a good clean-up rate, although I dread to think how. But if you and I are going to work together to get the right result on this one, you are going to have to start behaving like a modern police officer who's at least read PACE, for a start. Not to mention one who's learned and believes that all police officers are equal.'

With that, she turned on her heel and left the office, leaving Smith standing staring after her, bemused.

Time to go and resume his *Looking for Lulu*, and she'd better hope today wasn't the day he finally caught up with her. After that broadside, he was in the mood to teach a woman a lesson.

* * *

18:36 – WEDNESDAY EVENING

It was a big city, with a lot of pubs, bars and clubs. Looking for one busty blonde with a fondness for picking pockets was the proverbial needle in a haystack job. Smith was leaving his card everywhere he looked for her but so far the answer wherever he went was the same. Knew her, knew what she was like, seen her before, but not recently.

He knew that if he had any sort of a relationship with the uniformed branch, he could have asked a quiet question in a discreet ear and got the answer he needed in no time. But he'd never gone out of his way to form any kind of a working relationship with that lot and it was too late even to try now.

It was a throwback to his Army days. Officers and Other Ranks seldom mixed outside the workplace, where the ORs saluted the officers and called them sir or ma'am all the time.

For Smith, it would have gone totally against the grain to give any of the officers in uniform the satisfaction of discovering how he'd made a total pillock of himself by getting robbed by a hooker. It would be grist to the station's gossip mill. He'd never live it down, nor hear the end of it. He wanted to sort it out himself, on the quiet.

So far, he was having no luck at all.

'Of all of the gin joints in all the towns...,' 'Dennis' thought to himself from his high stool perch when he glanced towards the door of The Plough to see the distinctive big frame of the police officer come in from the cold and wet outside and head straight for the bar in search of a drink and to ask his questions.

'Lulu? Nah, mate, not seen her in here for a while. Have you tried The Crown?'

It was a rerun of the conversation he'd heard before, more or less. This time the man behind the bar suggested a few more pub names, including a few 'Dennis' hadn't heard of. He hadn't been to all that many of the pubs in the city, so that was no surprise.

'She's like the invisible woman,' the officer grumbled. 'I've been trying to find her for days. Give me a ring if you do see her, will you?'

'That depends on what you're going to do to her, mate. Nicked your wallet, did she? We all know what she's like. But as long as she's no trouble in here, we tend to leave her alone. She makes the punters she picks up buy her a few drinks before they go off to get at it, so you could say she's not that bad for business.

'And no offence, but you're built like a brick shithouse. If you're planning on knocking her about a bit, I don't want to be any part of that.'

Smith jabbed a finger at his card, where he'd put it down on the counter in front of the man.

'I don't need to thump her, pal, I'm a police officer. I'm going to arrest the thieving little bitch for robbing me. That's what I'm after her for. Sounds like it's about time someone did. So bell me, right? You wouldn't want me to think you were deliberately withholding information from a police officer, would you?

'Now I'll take a vodka, the best you have. And there'll be a drink in it for you if you help me find this Lulu.'

'Try The Wheatsheaf,' the man told him as he put the

drink in front of Smith, who reached for it immediately. 'She sometimes goes in there and as far as I know she's not been barred there. At least not yet.'

Smith didn't even glance towards the man at the end of the bar, with his half of lager. He might possibly have caught a glimpse of him in his peripheral vision, but he showed no evidence of having registered him as he tossed back his vodka and threw a note on the table which just about covered the drink and a small tip.

Mr Anonymous.

Mr Invisible.

Mr Nobody.

'Dennis' glanced over his shoulder as he heard the outer door swing open, letting in cold air, as the officer went on his way.

Now, at least, he had the name of another possible pub to try. He also knew to avoid it for the time being. Even someone as faceless as he was risked being clocked on a third time encounter.

24.

10:07 – THURSDAY MORNING

'Oscar, have you seen the online editions this morning?' Detective Superintendent Murray Aird's voice in his ear, sounding far from amused, never augured well as a start to the day for Smith.

Especially as he hadn't seen them, so whatever shit had hit the fan, he knew nothing about it.

Smith was in his office. He was frantically searching online for some clue as to what had put the Det. Sup. into what was clearly a black mood from the moment he'd seen whatever the headlines were all about.

'Not yet, guv, I've just been briefing the team on the direction we need to go in on our Mispers case.'

'And does that include briefing them about finding Marcus Campbell?'

His tone gave Smith a premonition of impending doom. At the same moment his scrolling finger found the first of the lurid headlines.

'Where is missing rent boy Marcus?'
'No police hunt for young gay man'
'Police appeal about missing women but no mention of Marcus'

They got worse as he carried on flicking through them. Every article had the good-looking face of the young man, smiling seductively into the camera, big and bold under the headlines.

Unsurprisingly one article, one of the most savage, had the byline of Don Donovan on it.

Shit.

'And what the bloody hell is all this stuff supposedly from an unnamed police source?'

Aird must have been seething. Smith seldom heard him swear all that much, even mildly.

Smith's eyes had found that line and he was scan-reading it.

'A police source close to the enquiry said that the disappearance of Marcus Campbell, 21, had been brought to the attention of the officer leading the investigation into four young women, missing from the same area.

'Detective Inspector Oscar Smith (pictured) has ruled out any connection between missing Marcus and the four women. No public appeal has been made about his disappearance.

'Campbell's flat mate, Daniel Holmes, 22, said he reported the disappearance to the police who promised to pass the details over to the Serious Crime Team. But an officer with connections to that team told this newspaper that because Marcus is a young university student, openly gay, and using his body as a means to pay his fees, Inspector Smith had dismissed any suggestion of him having been kidnapped or being at any risk.

'He allegedly told other officers that Marcus had probably found a new boyfriend and was busy getting drunk and stoned with him.'

'Who the hell has been speaking to the press?' Smith demanded.

'Never mind who the mole is, Oscar. That's the least of your worries. If you've said the half of what is alleged, it's hard to see how even your friend in high places is going to protect you from the fall-out from this one.

'The top floor are in meltdown. Get yourself up to HQ, now. Put the blues on if you have to but get here fast. I can't promise there won't be a lynch mob waiting for you. You don't need me to tell you how catastrophic this is for public relations and public confidence in the police.

'Just get here.'

Aird rang off abruptly.

'Tony!' Smith bellowed at the top of his voice.

Rule Number One. When you got kicked from above, kick the next person down the line immediately, even harder.

Tony Taylor looked even more nervous than usual when he crept into Smith's office.

'Guv?'

'Have you seen all the shit in the press?'

Taylor didn't need to answer. His expression said it all.

'I've been summoned to HQ. God knows how long I'll be, but when I get back, I want to know whose loose lips have been flapping to the gutter press.'

'Guv, I really don't want to get involved in this. Wouldn't it be better simply to ignore it all and get on with finding the missing women, and Marcus as well? That's what's going to restore public faith in us, after all.'

Smith looked at him searchingly. Taylor held his gaze.

Had the worm finally turned? Had Taylor grown a pair, at long last? Enough to do something to shake things up?

But then probably not. He'd be unlikely to do anything which would make their already difficult job even harder than it was by turning the public against them. No matter how big an axe he had to grind with his gaffer.

Smith would have put money on Taylor knowing, or at least guessing, who was behind the leak, though. Come what may, Smith was determined to find out.

Then God help them. The consequences would not be pretty.

* * *

10:47 – THURSDAY MORNING

It didn't help to defuse the situation or improve Smith's mood that he got stuck in a major snarl-up of stationery traffic from which there was no escape. Not even the blue lights, the occasional trill from the siren or a flash of his warrant card at anyone he saw could find him a way through.

Aird was on the phone to him seemingly every couple of minutes demanding to know where he was. It was only when he checked the situation for himself that he conceded there was nothing Smith could do for the moment.

Eventually a uniformed officer came over to Smith's car.

'Inspector Smith? HQ have asked me to find you a way out of this mess. Can you manage to do a u-ey here, sir? Then we can get you on your way. There's been a Majax up ahead and it's not pretty. But if you can at least turn round, we can get you through and on your way via the back roads.'

It was the ultimate irony for Smith. He was in the mood to kill anyone in uniform who crossed his path. Yet now here he was, totally reliant on one to get him out of his current impasse and on his way. Although why he should be in a hurry to go and get a bollocking, at the least, he wasn't sure.

'Three inches yet, sir. That's it now. Whoa. Now forward on a hard lock and you should do it. Good luck.'

The tyres squealed as Smith let the Ford have its head as soon as there was a bit of clear road. He hated to be late for anything. Even to get to somewhere he didn't want to be. That was his military training, deeply ingrained and hard to shake off.

Once he'd arrived at HQ and parked, he sprinted across the car park, took the stairs two at a time, and exploded into the Det. Sup.'s office, still trying to get his breath back.

Aird was sitting waiting for him, flanked by two executive officers, with the young woman from the Press Office sitting to one side.

From the faces and the atmosphere as he entered the room, he could tell he had no allies there and that his head was well and truly on the block. No sign of his good friend and supporter from the top floor, whom he had been hoping to see present. He would probably keep well out of the way for now. Smith just hoped he wouldn't let him down, if push came to shove. Knowing what Smith did about him, there was a good chance he would come out on the right side in a crisis.

When it came to that particular executive officer, Smith knew where the bodies were buried, as the saying went. And the man knew he knew.

To make matters worse, one of the senior officers present was one whose disapproval of Smith was written all over his face whenever they met. Smith's unwritten but open secret 'no women, no suntans on the team' policy was never going to sit well with an Asian officer who had clawed his way up through the ranks by sheer determination.

'Sit down, Oscar,' Aird told him stiffly. 'Unfortunate about the RTC but at least we know that was genuine and beyond your control.'

Nothing like setting the tone from the start, Smith thought to himself. This was clearly going to be a 'guilty until proven innocent' occasion. He wondered if he should insist on having a Federation rep present but decided he might just as well throw up his hands and admit to everything as do that.

Let them set out their stall with what, if anything they had against him. Apart from some lurid gutter press headlines. He could deal with those easily enough.

'Perhaps you could begin by reassuring us that you haven't simply brushed the case of this young man to one side on the basis of any form of prejudice against him because of his sexuality or anything else.'

'Not remotely, guv,' Smith told him. 'It was a balanced decision based on his case having no identifiable links to the enquiry into the missing women at all.

'Setting aside him being gay, all of the other presumed victims are female. He's not. He's only been missing for two days. Right after a weekend, and he's a student. Students are sometimes known for going on benders when they're not in lectures.

'There's also the fact that he's a male prostitute. Nothing wrong with that, of course. He's not breaking any laws, if he's chosen to do that. But it doesn't fit with the profile of the missing women. We have a doctor's receptionist, an estate agent, a beautician and a teacher. In other words, all in perfectly normal employment. No link there at all.

'I took the view that after only two days of him not showing up or contacting anyone, it would be wrong to treat this as a confirmed Misper yet. Nor to publicly link it at this stage to the other cases, which might lead to unnecessary public fear.'

He sat back slightly in his seat, looking from one of the three officers to the other, feeling sure of himself so far.

Khan, the Asian officer spoke first. He didn't seem to share Smith's conviction.

'Yet the newspaper has Marcus's lecturers saying he's an exemplary student who has never missed a single lecture since he started there. And his flatmate saying the same.

'I assume your team has at least made some enquiries and found out the same information. So in those circumstances surely we should be taking this disappearance more seriously?'

'I've never said we shouldn't be taking it seriously,' Smith countered. 'Neither on or off the record. I've simply said that I don't see it as helpful at this stage to link Marcus's disappearance to those of the women.'

'Whatever the rationale behind it was, these articles are a PR disaster which we really don't need now,' Aird said.

He was still very much chairing the meeting, despite the presence of the heavyweights from up in the gods.

'The purpose of this meeting is not scapegoating. It's to come up with some sort of plan for damage limitation.

'In the face of all this bad press, what we need to do, before anyone leaves here this morning, is to come up with a plan between us to show the public that we can be trusted to investigate any case with no prejudice towards anyone. Certainly not any potential victim.

'So, ideas, anyone? Anything?'

25.

13:28 – THURSDAY AFTERNOON

'Dennis' was sitting at his dining table with the television on, tuned to a twenty-four hour news channel. It was for the company as much as anything. He was enjoying a bowl of Marcus. He shouldn't have been, he knew, because he liked to stick to his own strict rules on stock rotation.

He'd initially been wary. After his father, he'd convinced himself to avoid males of the species, thinking they would all taste as strong and rank as he had done.

He couldn't have been more wrong. Even the nosy neighbour had complimented him on the latest creation. She'd deliberately been looking out for him so she could return the dish and drop unsubtle hints about how that had been the best one so far and to remember her if he was going to the same butcher again soon.

He'd had to put her off the trail a bit at that, telling her it was someone right outside the city, a longish drive away, and he went seldom because of the journey. But he had promised her some more when he could spare it, despite the feelings of jealousy of having to share anything of Marcus with her.

He could probably get away with fobbing her off with one of the others, he thought. Number Three had always been his favourite. But that was before Marcus.

He literally jumped in his seat, his heart suddenly

thumping against his chest when, as the thought was running through his mind, a photograph of the young man appeared on his television screen, smiling straight at him.

He'd been filtering out the words, looking idly at the moving images as he ate, with not much interest in what was going on.

Now he picked up the remote to make the soundtrack louder.

'A police spokesman said the investigation into the disappearance of twenty-one-year old university student Marcus Campbell, who has not been seen since leaving his flat on Sunday, is still ongoing.

'They said there was no reason at this stage to link his disappearance to those of four young women, Sally Rogers, twenty-four, Kathy Morgan, twenty-three, Vicky Garcia, twenty-one and Gill Burrell, twenty-six, who have all been reported as missing from their homes in the city over an approximately four-month period.

'Those disappearances are being investigated by Detective Inspector Oscar Smith...'

Another photograph appeared on the screen. There was no mistaking the broad shoulders and chiselled jaw of the man 'Dennis' had seen trawling the bars in search of a woman called Lulu.

'...who was not available for comment. A statement issued by the force's press office said that Inspector Smith is an experienced officer who has successfully worked on missing person enquiries before with excellent results, and who has the full confidence and backing of senior officers.'

'Dennis' frowned at that as he turned the volume back down. The bulletin was moving to something which didn't interest him in the slightest.

That statement had sounded to him like doublespeak of Orwellian proportions. Such a public declaration of confidence could so often mean the exact opposite. Perhaps Smith's time as Senior Investigating Officer on the case could be coming to an end, in the absence of any results.

He didn't want that to happen. Not yet.

He wanted to see if Smith was a worthy opponent for him. And for that he needed him to be kept on the case for longer.

More importantly, he needed to find the elusive Lulu, before Smith did.

* * *

15:05 – THURSDAY AFTERNOON

Smith had been at HQ for most of the morning, getting grilled like a kipper. It was lucky for him he had such an exceptional memory and could field any and all questions with factually accurate details without the need of notes.

Khan had done his whole career in the uniformed branch. He'd never worked serious crime. Another reason it irritated Smith to be interrogated by this man on how he ran his enquiries when he'd never headed anything similar himself.

Khan was a nitty-gritty details man. He was clearly waiting to pounce on any inaccuracy, no matter how small, which Smith might let slip. He would have a long wait.

Aird and the other executive officer had at least done the same sort of work as Smith. Aird had enjoyed a bit of celebrity status for heading a successful enquiry into a serial paedophile who had killed one of his victims and was now serving a life sentence.

At the end of an intense couple of hours, Aird surprised Smith by coming down more or less on his side, although it felt like a case of damning with faint praise.

'I think, on balance, Oscar, that it was right initially not to publicly link Marcus to the women. There's still a chance that the cases aren't connected, and a slim chance he might yet resurface, safe and sound. Although given his careful arrangements about staying in touch with his flatmate, he doesn't seem like the sort who would cause such anxiety if he had a choice.

'Your mistake, and therefore collectively ours, was not to put out some sort of a statement about Marcus as soon as Uniform handed the details over to you. We'll rectify that now. I'll sort that out and get it issued without delay.

'Oscar, you need to get back to your team and get us some progress on this case. Soon. And factor Marcus in as at least a possible fifth victim to date.'

Smith was seething on the drive back to his own nick. He stopped for a coffee and something to eat on the way since he'd not been offered so much as a glass of water at HQ.

He wasn't comfortable with working under public scrutiny like this. He'd not had experience of that in the military setting. But out here in the civilian world there was so much of the accountability bullshit to deal with. Trial by media of everything the police did and didn't do.

He'd been determined enough before all this shit to catch whoever this serial kidnapper and possible killer was. It would be a good tick on the books for him.

Now it had become intensely personal. An obsession. He'd be all over the team like a rash until they had the bastard behind bars.

At the same time he was determined to find out who the mole on the team was, and heaven help them when he did.

Only Tony Taylor was in the main office when Smith got back, still in the blackest of moods.

'Progress?' Smith demanded.

'Nothing as yet, guv. We've been trying to piece together the last known movements of the four women.'

Taylor jutted out a defiant chin as he added, 'And I'm factoring in Marcus's last known movements as well, just in case there is a link.'

'Was it you, Tony?' Smith asked him suspiciously. 'Did you talk to the press?'

Taylor held his gaze.

'No, it wasn't. And I honestly don't know who it was. It was a daft bloody thing to do because it doesn't help anyone and it reflects badly on the rest of us, who didn't agree with you about Marcus, guv. But I can see how someone might have felt driven to do it.'

Seeing Smith open his mouth to speak again, Taylor hurried on, 'But it happened, and there's nothing we can do about it now, except crack on with the case until we get a result and possibly find at least one of the Mispers still alive.

'So, what about a reconstruction? Are we on for that?'

Smith had, at least, found time to talk to Aird before he left about the idea of a re-enactment of the last known movements of the fourth missing woman, the teacher, Gill Burrell. The Det. Sup. had taken the view that the more they were seen to be doing to get on top of the case, the better it would be for public confidence.

'That's a goer. Can you set it up? Have we got enough info to do it accurately?'

'We have, guv. We know the route Gill Burrell walked to go home from work, and we know roughly the time she left the school the last time she was seen there. We can at least show that and it might jog a few memories. We don't know if she stopped anywhere on the way home, but it might hopefully make someone remember something.

'Maggie, PC Davis, has a superficial resemblance to Gill Burrell. She's the right height, at least, and she can wear a blonde wig. She's not as slim, but Gill Burrell always wore loose-fitting clothing to hide her figure, so that might be all right.

'Maggie's gone to the school to talk to her colleagues to

learn the way she walked so she reproduces it as close as she can. This power-walking stuff she always did. That's bound to be distinctive and might strike someone on the reconstruction.

'Oh, and it was pouring down, cold and windy on the day she was last seen, so that does possibly increase the chance that she might have accepted a lift from someone.'

Smith parked a buttock on the edge of Taylor's desk. Sometimes, between the two of them, they'd kicked things around and come up with something not far from what actually happened. Perhaps they could do the same on this one.

'With all her anxiety issues, who would she happily get in a car with? We have checked out all her neighbours carefully, haven't we?'

'We have, guv, the whole road she lives in. Plus any known friends, of which she had few. Nothing. Total blank.'

'Mitchell could be wrong, of course. She's convinced it's a man, working alone. What if it isn't? What if he has a woman helping him with the abductions?'

'Or what if he has a child in the car with him? Gill Burrell is a primary school teacher. The presence of a small child would probably reassure her,' Taylor suggested.

'We need to get this bastard, Tony. It's a few weeks since Gill Burrell disappeared so it's likely he's either stalking his next victim, or he has them already and they've not yet been reported missing for some reason.'

Smith stood up and headed for his office. Taylor looked at his departing back and thought, *'Or he's changed his pattern to taunt us after the press conference, and Marcus is his next victim, you arrogant sod. And because you refused to even consider the possibility of a link, that young man is in serious danger.'*

26.

20:15 – THURSDAY EVENING

'Dennis' was on his fourth pub of the evening and starting to give up hope of ever finding the elusive Lulu. He was drinking lager shandy, a half in each pub, because he had the car with him and needed to be able to drive, without drawing any attention to himself.

He knew it was a long shot. Realised he was starting to get obsessive about his plan, and that could lead him to lower his guard and make a mistake. He kept telling himself just one more pub. One more night of looking. Then he would stop.

He'd finished his drink, got off the bar stool and was heading towards the door when it opened and a young blonde woman walked in.

He knew who she was the moment he saw her. The detective's description had been a good one, but it wasn't just the impressive bosom that she flaunted as she headed towards him. It was the calculating way she was eyeing him up and down as a potential target.

He wasn't surprised to see the dismissal in her eyes, which then started to sweep the room for a more likely punter. He would have to take the initiative.

'Hello,' he said, putting all the pleasure he could manage into that one little word.

He saw her gaze returning to his now smiling face.

Recalculating. Scanning it for something she might recognise.

Finding nothing.

Mr Anonymous.

'You're Lauren's friend, aren't you? I haven't seen you for ages. I'm so sorry, I can't remember your name.'

'Lulu,' she told him, still eyeing him up appraisingly for potential.

She so obviously found him still wanting. He was going to have to do something, unsubtle though it might be, or she was going to walk past him and the opportunity would be gone for ever.

He pulled his wallet out of his back pocket, still stuffed full with most of the notes he'd given to Marcus, then reclaimed.

Her gaze locked on it like a heat-seeking missile, barely listening as he went on, 'I was actually just leaving, but now I've bumped into you, would you like to have a quick drink? I haven't heard from Lauren for ages. I was just wondering how she was and what she was up to.'

'I've not seen her for a while either,' she told him, not having a clue who Lauren was, nor having any memory at all of ever having seen this bland and uninteresting-looking man before.

His wallet was interesting, though. Anything which bulged like that was always sure to get her attention.

'I was supposed to be meeting someone but I'm horribly late so it looks like he gave up on me. So, yes, please, I'd love a drink. A vodka and cranberry, if that's all right. And I'm really sorry but I've forgotten your name, too. It must be ages since we last met.'

'Oh, it is, so I quite understand that you forgot all about me. Dennis. My name's Dennis. Why don't you grab a seat somewhere and I'll bring the drinks over?'

He found his hand was trembling slightly in anticipation as he got their drinks from the bar and took them over to the table she'd found for them. He couldn't believe his luck. It had seemed so improbable that he would find her at all. Let alone before the policeman, Smith. And he clearly had done, because she was looking so unconcerned, not to mention eyeing up his wallet with greedy eyes, that Smith couldn't yet have caught up with her.

He made inconsequential small talk for a while. She dropped increasingly unsubtle hints that she was available for something more than a cosy chat.

Eventually 'Dennis' cleared his throat awkwardly, as if embarrassed, then said, 'Look, I know this is a bit forward of me as you don't really know me. But my wife, Myra, is away at the moment and I don't like eating on my own. I'm not a bad cook, if I do say so myself, and I've got rather a good casserole in the oven.

'I wondered if you might like to come and have some supper with me? If there's nowhere else you need to be? Oh,' he went on hurriedly, as if the thought had just occurred to him, 'as long as you're not a vegetarian or anything. It's a meat casserole, but the meat is rather good. I get it from a specialist butcher. I can confidently say you won't have tasted anything like it before.'

She ran a lascivious tongue round her lips, batting her eyelids at him, as she said, 'Oh, I love the feel of real meat in my mouth.'

She was beginning to wonder if he was gay because he didn't appear to be picking up on any of her less than subtle signals. She didn't mind that. All she was interested in was getting her hands on that nice, big, fat wallet. That was more of a turn-on for Lulu than any man.

'There's just one thing. Myra is a very jealous woman and she has her spies everywhere, so we need to be careful. We often drink in here together.'

He was amused by his own wit at bringing in another serial killer's name. He was fairly sure that neither Dennis nor Myra would mean anything to Lulu. Whatever her attributes might be, he was already certain that her intellect wasn't one of her best.

'Would you mind very much going and waiting for me outside, so we aren't seen to leave together? I promise I will come and find you but I honestly don't dare risk being seen to leave with you. If you go out and turn left, then take the first road on the left, my car is just down there. I'd be really grateful. I will follow you, honestly, in about five minutes. It's safer that way.'

She was looking at him carefully, weighing up whether or not she could trust him to come after her, as he said he would. She wasn't remotely interested in him as a person. Nor in whatever kind of a jealous cow his wife was. All she wanted to do was to get her hands on that overstuffed wallet. It was a long time since she'd so much as seen anything as bulging as that. She decided it was worth the risk.

He came out to join her not many minutes later. She was already looking considerably more drunk than she should do after one vodka. But of course, that was not all she'd had, although she had no idea of what he'd slipped into the drink he'd brought back to her from the bar.

They'd made some of the so-called date drugs instantly colour a drink now so they would show up. But not all of them. If you knew where to look, you could still find things just as effective which left no visual trace and had no taste to alert suspicions.

Drunk as she was, she still tried to manoeuvre herself round to his right-hand side as they walked, where the wallet sat provocatively in his back pocket.

He made a careful show of positioning himself on her right. To anyone watching, a chivalrous type who put himself between the traffic and his lady friend. Old fashioned good manners.

It was a very wobbly, giggling Lulu whom Dennis helped, carefully and gently, into the front passenger seat of his car. Then he positioned the seat belt between the magnificent breasts which strained at the fabric of the low-cut blouse she was wearing, and clicked it safely closed.

She was already half asleep by the time he moved round and got into the driving seat, feeling an elation like nothing he could remember before.

He'd done it.

He'd found her.

Lulu.

Before the detective had done.

'Now the games can really begin, Detective Inspector Oscar Smith,' he said aloud, aware that Lulu was long past hearing or understanding anything he said.

* * *

21:47 – THURSDAY EVENING

'Hello, Oma, are you in bed?' Smith asked her, hastily swallowing a piece of fish batter when she answered the call more quickly than he had anticipated. They were an hour ahead in Germany and with luck the night carer would have been and settled her by this time of night.

'No, Oskar, I'm at a night club, playing roulette,' she bit back with withering sarcasm which made him laugh. Typical Oma.

'When I've finished at the tables I might pick up a young man by flaunting my winnings and go dancing. After that you can use your imagination as to what will happen next.'

'All right, I get the point. Stupid question. But are you all right?'

'Of course I'm all right. I never get to do anything to make me anything other than all right, so I just continue to exist.

'But what about you? You're not all right, are you? I can hear it in your voice.'

She could tell. Hundreds of miles apart and she could

always tell his mood. She should have been a police officer. She would have been outstanding in interviews, with that intuition of hers. Smith had learned from being a very small boy that there was no point at all in trying to lie to his Oma. She always knew.

'I'm just tired. It's been a long day. Not much progress and a lot of pressure to make some.'

She made that scoffing noise she was so good at. Somewhere between a tut and a snort.

'It's more than that, Oskar, even if you won't admit it to yourself. You're doubting your own ability. I can hear that in your voice, too. Like the time when I took you to the top of your very first black run and you were convinced you weren't ready. Not good enough.'

He remembered that so well. As soon as he'd got off the ski lift and seen what lay ahead of him, he had literally frozen to the spot, convinced it was beyond his capabilities.

'What did I tell you then?'

'You said if I didn't trust myself I should trust you to know better than I did what I was capable of and what I wasn't. And that you would never do anything to put me in danger.'

'Exactly so!' she said with a note of triumph. 'And you did it, didn't you? A little cautiously to begin with, then like a true professional as we got going.

'You've been promoted to a responsible role and you're starting to doubt your ability to succeed at it because you haven't solved a case in two seconds flat. Skiing isn't like that and nor is life, Oskar.

'How many times did I have to pick you up out of the snow, wipe your tears and remind you to remember the basics? Start with the simple steps, the basic turns, until you grow in confidence.

'What's holding you back?'

'I'm trying to find a connection between a perpetrator and four – no, possibly five – missing people. But I can't.

Which means I have no real suspect at this stage.'

'Back to basics, Oskar,' she repeated. 'What would Poirot do? He'd sit and use the little grey cells. You're probably rushing round like a bull at a gate which is going to see you flat on your face in a drift once more.'

He laughed at that. Poirot was a rare entity in that Oma admired him without question. She spent a lot of her time reading and rereading the Agatha Christie books with the little Belgian detective, both in German and in English. She claimed the intellectual stimulation was good for her own little grey cells.

'Take a step back from it all and think. You're at the top of a black run focusing only on the gradient and how frightening it looks. Use your intelligence. Remember your training. Make some sort of a plan. Write it all down and analyse it.

'You can do this, Oskar. I know you can.'

Clive the cat stood up and started rubbing his head against the underside of Smith's chin, his purrs loud enough even for his Oma to hear when the cat got close to the phone.

'Your cat agrees with me,' she said firmly, as if the opinion of a feline clinched the matter. 'Come and see me soon, Oskar, to tell me you've solved the case. Anja will be pleased to see you again.'

There was a hint of mischief in her voice as she said that.

'Goodnight, Oma,' he told her firmly. 'I love you.'

'Goodnight, Oskar. Remember you've faced worse black runs than this in Garmisch. You can do this. Make me proud.'

* * *

22:19 – THURSDAY EVENING

Lulu woke with the mother and father of all hangovers,

and no recollection of where she was or how she'd got there. It took her some time to prise reluctant eyelids apart. While she tried, she attempted to move her tongue, to bring some much needed moisture to parched lips and a dry throat.

That's when she discovered the cloth in her mouth, biting into the corners of her lips, making it hard to swallow or to do anything to relieve the dehydrated feeling.

What the fuck?

She opened her eyes to take stock. The first thing she noticed was that she was totally naked and sitting on a towel on a carpeted floor.

Next she saw that her two wrists were tied firmly together, then in turn lashed to one of those old fashioned radiators under a window over which the curtains were firmly closed.

She started to struggle at that point. She'd been with some kinky beggars in her time, trying to get her hands on their wallets, but this was way beyond that and she wasn't having any of it.

She tried to thrash her legs, to get some purchase to do something about her predicament. That's when she managed to bring her eyes into focus and saw that they, too, were tied. Only they were bound to a piece of wood which held them a couple of feet apart or more, leaving her unable to move them independently.

It was both extremely uncomfortable, putting the muscles of her hips and buttocks into spasm, and left her feeling exposed and vulnerable.

A voice from behind her started to speak.

'Don't struggle. It won't achieve anything and will only increase your discomfort.'

She twisted and craned her neck to look over the bed, which was behind her, to the man standing there watching her, no emotion at all showing on his bland face. A face she didn't even recognise.

She tried to say something. To register her protest.

This wasn't how it was meant to go. When she went back with a mark to their house, it was usually a quick wham, bam, thank you mate, for the nice fat wallet I pocketed while you were busy fondling my tits. You've had your jollies, now I'm out of here.

It wasn't meant to finish up like this. Although her friends were always warning her of the risks she was taking. She laughed at them. Showed them instead how much cash she was making at it. Far more than her meagre wages, working in a seedy club, getting her bum pawed by dirty old men who didn't even leave her a tip.

He was speaking again. His voice quiet and pleasant, as if talking to a welcome guest.

'I'm Dennis. You won't remember that because you were very drunk when you agreed to come back to my house for a meal. I left you to sleep it off. The gag was just a precaution in case you became hysterical and frightened the neighbours into calling the police.

'I removed your clothes to keep them clean, in case you became unwell or incontinent because of the amount you'd had to drink.

'You're quite safe here, for now, and I have got a lovely hot meal for us both in the oven. I just need to make sure that you understand the rules very clearly before I remove the gag so that you can eat what I've prepared for us.

'You staying silent is the most important rule of all. You may speak, of course. But you must never shout or scream. I don't like people breaking the rules and I'm not a forgiving man.

'You're quite safe with me. I don't plan to touch you. No offence meant, but you're not really to my taste. A bit too much...'

He made a graphic gesture with his hands in front of his chest.

'But it is vital that you understand that there are consequences for any breach of the rules. And where I find administering punishment distasteful myself, I pass the task over to a friend.

'Before you meet him, I want you to understand and to remember that I've brought you here for your own safety.

'You think you're clever, no doubt, picking up strange men and stealing all their cash. But you've recently made a big mistake. A very bad mistake. Because one of the men you robbed is a policeman. I've seen him. A big man, who looks to have a short fuse. And he's been going round all the pubs and bars looking for you.

'So whatever you think about the situation you now find yourself in, believe me, you're safer here than out there where Detective Inspector Smith will eventually catch up to you.

'Safer as long as you remember the rules, that is.'

He reached for something on the bed then moved to stand in front of her, by her feet. He held up a piece of round-ended wood in one hand as he spoke again.

'So now let me introduce you to that friend. This is Tickler. I hope for your sake that you won't have occasion to meet him too often during your stay here.'

27.

08:08 – FRIDAY MORNING

Tony Taylor could tell straight away that the gaffer hadn't slept. He was still in the same clothes as the day before and clearly hadn't shaved or showered. For once, after a night like that, he didn't stink of booze. He looked surprisingly alert.

Taylor had found him already in his office first thing, before anyone else was in. He knew he'd left work the day before so he must have come in much earlier than usual. There were already three empty espresso cups on his desk. He must be pinging.

He'd expected to find him hungover, in a foul mood carried over from the day before. Ready to rip the head off the first person who crossed his path. Instead he found him strangely relaxed. There was even an air of excited anticipation about him, although that might simply have been the caffeine hit.

'Ah, Tony, I'm glad I've caught you before you briefed the team. I've been up all night, going back to basics, as a person older and far wiser than I am reminded me to do.

'Pull up a chair and I'll show you what I've been working on.'

Blimey, Taylor thought to himself, *who are you and what have you done with the gaffer?*

He tried not to let his expression betray what he was

thinking. He'd never seen Smith like this before. If that was what three espressos before breakfast could do to him, he'd willingly start paying his coffee tab himself, just to see the improvement.

Smith had shoved things aside on his desk to make room for some sort of a chart he appeared to be working on. At first glance it looked like various A4 computer print-outs roughly stuck together with sticky tape. There was a spider's web of different coloured lines overlaying it all.

'It occurred to me that we're coming at this whole case arse about face. We've looked for connections between the women and not found any. We've looked for common ground between them where they could have met their abductor and not found anything there either.

'We've convinced ourselves that these women are too smart to go off with someone they don't know. But we're overlooking the obvious.

'Have you ever done any skiing, Tony?'

The abrupt change of subject left Taylor wondering whether the gaffer had in fact had too much caffeine to start the day.

'I haven't. Not the sporty type at all, apart from watching a bit of rugby on telly from time to time.'

'Well, I have. I used to do a lot of it. My grandmother taught me. She was very good. Competition standard, and she taught me well.'

This isn't the gaffer, Tony thought. It looks like him and sounds like him but all this "sit down, Tony" and bonding over sports isn't him at all. I wonder if he's taking something.

'You might be doing up to forty miles an hour downhill on a black run,' Smith went on. 'Mistakes at that speed can be serious. Sometimes even fatal. So you learn to do very quick risk assessments, to avoid trouble.

'But any experienced skier will tell you, your biggest enemy is failing to spot the real danger. The one you look at and think everything is fine, then it turns out to be the worst part of the run. The part then brings you crashing down and, if you're very lucky, leaves you with nothing but bad bruising to teach you a lesson.'

Taylor frowned, not sure he was following what the gaffer was on about.

'You're saying the victims are failing to identify the danger in the abductor?'

'Exactly! Mitchell is probably right when she says he'll turn out to be somebody bland, anonymous. They might pass him in the street or somewhere so often without noticing him that when he finally makes contact with them, they see him as harmless.

'They'll probably know they've seen him somewhere before, but can't remember where. And most importantly, they'll know that nothing untoward happened to them from those encounters. Therefore no perceived risk involved.

'They look at him and they see only soft white powder snow. They don't see the black jagged rocks just below the surface, which is where the true danger lies.'

All the skiing metaphors were a bit lost on Tony, but he got the gist of what the gaffer was saying.

'So you mean they might all have seen him before without registering it, but in a setting which only goes to emphasise how harmless he is?'

'Yes! That's it, precisely.'

Smith's eyes were bright, the dilated pupils making them look darker than usual. Whether he was right or not in his ideas, he looked manic about them.

'We've been concentrating on them actually having met. In a pub, at the gym, that sort of thing. But it may be much more subtle than that.

'You know the feeling. Someone passes you in the street and says hello like they know you. You can't for the life of you place them but you reply in case it's someone you do know but have forgotten.

'The next time you see them you say hello first because

you feel like you should and then it becomes a thing. You have no idea who they are but you've convinced yourself you must know them so you always greet them.'

'But guv, doesn't that make our job even harder? If they've never even met properly, just passed one another in the street, or on a bus or something? How the heck are we going to pick up on a link like that? It's not even possible.'

'That's why I've been up all night with the coloured pens. We know this is a big city. With a lot of pubs and bars and other likely meeting places, right?

'But what if you stop looking for meeting places and look instead at crossing places?'

He swivelled the sheet of printouts towards Taylor, who could see large red circles dotted about. He peered at them for a moment, trying to get his bearings.

'I'm trying not to be negative here, guv, but how the heck do we go about identifying when, how and where people may have passed one another in the street?'

'Tony, you're missing the point here,' Smith told him, his tone surprisingly patient and devoid of any of its usual sarcasm.

'You've gone over CCTV, but starting with all the obvious places. Nothing wrong with that. But factoring in the theory of our abductor being bland and anonymous, I've stopped looking at the bare rock and started looking for the powdery snow which hides the danger beneath instead.

'We need to be checking out CCTV from within these red circles. There's bound to be some, and hopefully some of it will still be current.'

'Guv, stating the obvious here, but that is a hell of a lot of personnel hours. And no guarantee of a result at the end of it.'

Smith carefully folded up his work of art and handed it to Taylor as he said, 'Look on the bright side, Tony. I stayed up all night doing the donkey work for you. Imagine if you had that to do as well.'

* * *

08:26 – FRIDAY MORNING

'I wasn't sure what you might like for your breakfast, but you do need to eat something. You hardly ate enough for a little sparrow last night and you need to keep your strength up. This is some nice oatmeal broth. I thought you might enjoy that.

'Now, I'm going to have to remove your gag, of course, so that you can have a drink of water first, then eat, so I need to remind you again about not shouting or screaming. I hope I made it clear enough to you what the penalties are for doing that.'

She was lying half on the towel, which was bloodstained. There was pain when she moved. Internal pain.

He'd thrown a light blanket over her at some point the evening before but her thrashing in the night meant it was covering little of her.

There was raw fear in her eyes as he moved nearer to her. Real terror. Of all the bad situations she'd got herself into in the past, this was the worst, by far.

'Before I take off the gag, you have to give me a sign that you understand and agree that you must not scream. Ever. Remember that you now know without a doubt what will happen any time you do. Nod your head to show you accept the terms.'

She nodded. Quick, jerky movements she could scarcely control. She'd have done anything at that moment to get rid of the gag and not to face what she had experienced the previous night.

'That's very good. But remember, you only get one chance. I'm trying to keep you safe, from the police officer who's trying to find you. You must understand that. He would treat you far worse than I ever will. I don't think it's just an arrest he has on his mind.

'But I'll protect you. Keep you safely hidden here until it all blows over. Then I'll set you free. You have my word on that.'

He's insane, she told herself. *Completely fucking mad. He actually believes what he says. How can he think what he did to me last night is in any way normal? Or that he's somehow helping or protecting me?*

She was still nodding her head frantically. Like one of those stupid toy dogs you used to see on the parcel shelf of cars. Right now she would do anything at all to get him to remove the gag, untie her and let her put her clothes back on.

He moved closer still, putting down the tray of food he had brought upstairs with him. She tried not to flinch at his presence, yet couldn't stop her eyes desperately looking everywhere for sight of that awful wooden pole.

What had he called it? Tinker?

She'd done some things in her short life to earn a bit of money. But nothing like that. Never.

It was not just the pain he'd inflicted, although that had been bad. It was the utter humiliation and degradation of it. Especially his clinical detachment whilst it was going on.

She couldn't think of anything she wouldn't willingly offer him to make sure he never did that to her again.

Stay quiet, she told herself. *That's what he said. Don't shout, don't scream, and everything will be all right. He'd promised.*

He was crouching in front of her now as she used all her will power not to shrink away from him. With the gag in her mouth she couldn't produce anything like a smile of compliance. She did her best to express with her eyes that she understood and agreed not to make a sound.

Not a scream.

Not a shout.

Not a... *oh god please don't let him do that again. Please,*

please, please.

He was almost gentle as he undid the piece of cloth and carefully took it out of her mouth, smiling at her, like a fond parent whose child had just shown good behaviour.

'That's very good. You'll have to stay here for a while, of course. Until the policeman gets tired of looking and forgets about you.'

'But if you keep me here I'll lose my job,' she couldn't stop herself from blurting, alarmed at how trembly and unlike her usual bubbling confidence her voice sounded.

He frowned slightly at that, but his tone stayed patient and reasonable.

'If I let you go now and Inspector Smith finds you, at the very least he's going to get you sent to prison. So then you'd not only lose your job but you'd find it very hard to get another one when you came out, of course.

'And I don't imagine prison is a very nice place to be. You hear such awful things about what can happen to people in there. Especially young and vulnerable ones.

'No, you're much safer here, with me. As long as you remember the rules.'

She was scanning his face. Trying for the life of her to think who he was, where she'd picked him up.

There was nothing distinctive about him at all. A face which would easily be lost in a crowd. Even the eyes behind the glasses were more grey than anything else. The original invisible man who would never stand out in a crowd.

No wonder she'd considered him an easy target and gone with him. There was nothing about him to indicate what sort of a madman he clearly was.

How could she ever describe him accurately to the police, if she got out of there alive, she wondered.

Then she corrected herself.

When.

When she got out of there alive.

Because she was going to.

Of course she was.

Then her only nightmare would be if the big, beefy policeman caught up with her, bent on revenge.

But surely nothing he would do to her could be worse than what she'd been through at the hands of this complete maniac last night.

Could it?

28.

10:37 – FRIDAY MORNING

Detective Sergeant Jody Mitchell and Police Constable Maggie Davis were out of the office working on the reconstruction of the fourth missing woman, Gill Burrell's, last known movements, from her leaving the school where she worked.

Once they had all the details they needed, they'd sourced suitable clothing, as close as possible to what the woman had been wearing when last seen. Then, working in liaison with the press office, they'd filmed sequences of PC Davis reproducing the distinctive power walk and heading away from the school. Two sequences of film, one of her going in each direction, as they had no firm information on which way she went.

All that was known was that she had not arrived back at the terraced house she shared with a friend.

When there was no phone call and no answer on her mobile phone, the friend had phoned her colleagues and discovered she'd missed school, which was totally out of character. That was when she'd contacted the police to express her concern.

If everything went well with the filming, they could hopefully get it out in time for the early evening local news, at least, and for the first online editions of the papers.

Teachers in the school were doing their best to divert the curious attention of any pupils who spotted what was going on. As much as anything, Mitchell was anxious that no child should catch a sudden glimpse of someone who looked like their former teacher, whom they hadn't seen for a month or so now. If they ran out to investigate, it might cause upset when they realised it was someone simply dressed and walking like her.

Once they were finished and Davis had changed back into her own clothes for the drive back to the station, she risked a question.

She didn't know Mitchell well, hadn't worked with her before, but she seemed all right. Approachable. Not up herself, like some CID officers could be. Smith, for one.

'Sarge, who do you think went to the press about the case? About Marcus, specifically?'

Mitchell was driving, concentrating on the road and the traffic, which was heavy, even at that time of day.

'I'm assuming it wasn't you then, Maggie,' she said dryly. 'Since you're asking me about it. And there's no need for the rank thing outside the office. Jody is fine.'

'It wasn't me, no, but I can't say I entirely blame whoever it was. DI Smith is a bit special, isn't he?'

Mitchell turned off into a side road, clearly knowing all the short cuts to avoid the worst of the snarl-ups. She said nothing while she weaved through parked cars on the narrow street until she was back onto a larger road when traffic was moving more freely.

'If I have a problem with the DI I'll confront him with it in person. If it's serious enough, I will take it to the appropriate authorities. What I don't do, and don't tolerate, is gossip behind anyone's back. Especially about a senior officer.

'On the other hand, if you or anyone else working on this case has a problem with him, or any other officer on the team, you can always come to me in complete confidence and I'll deal with it.

'Would I ever go to the press without first going through the right channels? No, never, whatever the provocation. Do I approve of whoever did that? No, not at all. So if you do happen to find out who it was, you might warn them to keep their head well down around me.'

* * *

18:03 – FRIDAY EVENING

'We're in for a heavy weekend, everyone, so brace yourself and forget about whatever plans you had with your nearest and dearest,' Tony Taylor told the team members when they got together to debrief at the end of the day.

'Thanks to the guv's idea, we now have a load more CCTV which needs checking for any sign of our missing women, or of Marcus.

'We also have a lot of locations where it is just possible their paths could have crossed, with each other and possibly with their abductor. Not just pubs and bars, but now also things like a library, off-licences, coffee shops, small supermarkets. Plus a lot of offices and administrative buildings.

'And that, of course, might be the missing link as to where our women met their abductor, if he works somewhere like that and they'd been in for something or another they couldn't do online.'

'Bloody hell, Sarge, that's a lot of legwork,' DC Dai Evans grumbled.

'Stop moaning, Dai,' Smith told him. 'You're being asked to spend your weekend going round the pubs, which is what we all know you do with your free time anyway.

'Tony, I'm happy to do a bit of pub-crawling myself this weekend. I've got nothing else planned. Put me down for a few, and make sure everyone knows which ones, because there's no point at all in any of us doubling up on locations.

'And Dai, that's not to say I might not be popping up somewhere unexpectedly that's not on my own list. So heaven help you if I catch you drinking on duty.'

He needed Tony to allocate pubs for the team members. It wouldn't do for any of them to come into a pub where he was asking about Lulu. He was even more determined to find her, the longer she eluded him. She'd soon hear word that the police were cruising all the watering holes in the city asking questions, even if not directly related to her, so she'd be likely to give most of them a miss for now. He didn't want her disappearing into the woodwork before he'd exacted his revenge for her having robbed him.

'I'll make a start on the way home now, Tony, so if you're not in a tearing hurry, let's look at the list and I'll take two or three for this evening. On the off chance that I get lucky with any of the women – or Marcus,' he glared round at the team members as he said that, daring any of them to comment on his change of stance about the young man's disappearance, 'I'll give you a bell straight away.'

Taylor was trying not to stare. The gaffer, not only being civil but volunteering for work. Perhaps he was having some sort of a born again moment. He wasn't going to knock it, though.

The chart stuff he'd come up with had been a bit of a breakthrough. When the team had gone out checking all the sites he'd drawn circles round, there were all sorts of potential places they might not have thought of. A specialist deli on a street corner, with good food cheaper than in the bigger chains. A second-hand bookshop which might encourage people in for a browse on the way home from work. All of them would have to be checked, with officers going door to door with the photos of the missing people.

Dai was right. It was a lot of legwork. But if they didn't do it and it later turned out they'd missed a vital lead which had led to unnecessary deaths, the consequences didn't bear thinking about.

'Dennis' was just coming out of the office, later than he'd planned, when he spotted the distinctive big, heavy figure striding up the road towards him.

Marching suited the action better. There was definitely something martial about the way the man moved and carried himself.

For a moment 'Dennis' froze, trying not to stare at him, averting his eyes so as not to attract attention, whilst all the time wondering how Smith had found him. How he had left a trail which had brought him here.

His mouth went dry, his heart thudding painfully. Keeping his eyes averted, he fumbled in his pockets. A man checking he had his car keys on him before he shut the office door at the end of the working day.

As he was doing that, the police officer had drawn level with him then strode on past without the slightest pause nor even a glance in his direction.

'Dennis's' hyperosmia hit him with a full frontal assault of smells as the man passed by. Sweat, strong aftershave, a whiff of cat, and the nutty scent of some strong alcoholic spirit, tempered by the aroma of harsh coffee.

Then all sensation disappeared with the man himself, leaving 'Dennis' feeling the wobbles and tremors of the sudden adrenaline rush.

If ever he needed proof positive that he was anonymous and easily forgotten, there it was. In a city which was home to hundreds of thousands of people, the detective had twice been in touching distance of the man he should be hunting, without so much as registering his presence.

It left 'Dennis' feeling elated.

No longer Mr Invisible but Mr Invincible.

29.

09:46 – MONDAY MORNING

Smith was wading through all the bumf which had landed on his desk over the weekend. He knew most of it would be crap that he could either junk or pass on, but he had to check every single piece in case he missed anything vital.

He left Tony Taylor to brief the team and go over any new leads the weekend's intensive efforts might possibly have thrown up. He knew Taylor would come and find him to bring him up to speed on anything he needed to know about.

He'd not had a lot of success with *Looking for Lulu – the movie*, as he was now mentally calling it. Even in such a big city with so many people, it was still surprising he hadn't found so much as a sniff of her.

'Has she gone missing now?' one of the servers he'd spoken to had asked him. 'Like these women on TV? Mind you, we're all noticing that fewer women seem to be going out on their own now, with a stalker on the loose. Have you not caught that nutter yet?'

'Not missing in the same sense. I'm simply trying to find her in connection with ongoing enquiries into theft of property.'

The man had smiled at him knowingly.

'Oh, she nicked your wallet, did she? Well, she's not been in here for ages. She's barred because of her tricks like that. If you go in enough pubs around the city, you'll eventually run into her again, no doubt.'

He'd done slightly better with the photos of the missing women, and Marcus. A couple of places he visited knew the young man by sight. One had seen him recently but the girl who told him that couldn't add anything about who he had been with, and particularly who he might have left with.

'It gets mad in here of an evening. I don't even get time to go for a wee sometimes. I'm sure that's against some sort of laws or rules or something.'

He'd decided, while he was out, to see if he could find Dai Evans in one of the places he was on the list to visit. He might as well check up on him. He was the most likely one of the team to be either skiving or having a sneaky drink on duty.

He'd found him propping up a bar talking to the man behind it, with what looked suspiciously like a half of lager on the counter in front of him.

Smith picked it up and sniffed at it, without a word of greeting.

'Alcohol-free, guv,' Evans told him indignantly. 'Ask Jimmy if you don't believe me.'

The alibi confirmed and having established that Evans had nothing of substance to report, Smith turned and headed for the door.

He'd heard Evans' comment of 'wanker' clearly enough, directed towards his parting back. He'd hesitated for a brief moment, tempted to go back, drag the DC outside by the neck and teach him a valuable lesson. Then he'd decided it wasn't worth it. Not just now. The last thing he needed, with a major enquiry not making the progress he'd hoped for, was some bastard with a mobile phone to start filming two police officers having a punch-up outside a pub.

'We made a bit of progress over the weekend, guv. Your red circles threw up a couple of slight connections between two of the women. There's a coffee bar cum sandwich place here,' he had part of Smith's poster with him, which he put on the desk. He jabbed a finger at a point near to the centre of one of the red rings Smith had drawn.

The gaffer hadn't asked him to sit down today. He was clearly back to normal now he'd slept a bit and had a shower, which was evident from the way he was turned out.

'Gill Burrell often stopped there on her way home for a drink. It's just over halfway and that power-walking stuff must make you thirsty, I imagine. They remember her well enough because she only ever drank mineral water and never had anything to eat.'

'CCTV?'

Taylor shook his head.

'They have a camera but it's just for show. A deterrent. It hasn't worked in ages. Nobody could remember seeing Gill Burrell with anyone else at any time, but they're going to ask other staff, the ones who weren't working over the weekend, to see if any of them can add anything.

'We also got a positive on Kathy Morgan, the estate agent, who often popped in there for her lunch. It's only a short walk from where her office is. She would often be with other people, not a loner like Gill.'

'Make my day and tell me we have a full, detailed description of some weird bloke who was hanging round the two of them, preferably with a large sign round his neck proclaiming "serial kidnapper".'

'Sadly, no can do, guv. The young lady Sean spoke to in there made a very good point. It's the sort of place where they get the lonely and the loners dropping in frequently. Their prices are better than the big chains, it's nice and clean and always warm and welcoming.

'She said they often see people on their own, especially older ones, who go in and make one cup of tea or coffee last an hour or more. So unless our kidnapper is a lonely pensioner who's picking people up to take home just for the company...'

'We'll have to ask Mitchell about that,' Smith couldn't resist saying, with thinly disguised scorn. 'She's the ace profiler. Anything else of any value?'

Taylor had another sheet of paper with him which he put on the desk in front of the gaffer.

'Not good news, guv. We have another Misper. Another young woman with long blonde hair, so a definite possible link, I would say. So should we release the details?'

Smith's heart kicked hard against the inside of his ribs, like an angry mule. He didn't risk reaching for the page because he knew an adrenaline dump like that would have given him the tremors.

The face looking up at him from the top of his desk was Lulu's. No doubt about it.

Shit.

Bugger.

And fuck, for good measure, he thought.

'Louisa-Marie Anderson. Known as Lulu. Twenty. Works part-time in a sleazy bar. Bit of waitressing, bit of stripping, some pole-dancing. That sort of stuff. Shares a very small bed-sit with two other young women. They've not seen her since Friday and that's out of character.

'The one who reported it says the two of them are worried about her because of her lifestyle. They've been telling her how dangerous it is.'

Smith decided his best bet was to spread a bit of his usual cynicism.

'None of our other victims did anything like that, so she probably was at no more risk from our suspect than the next woman. Besides, lot of birds work in bars and clubs quite safely.'

Taylor didn't waste time pointing out that missing Marcus had worked as a male prostitute. He said instead, 'The problem with this one, guv, is that she was known to be light-fingered. She'd often go off with blokes happily enough, maybe even sleep with them, but pick their pockets while they were at it, if they were stupid enough to fall for that old trick.'

Yeah, rub it in why don't you, you sanctimonious bastard.

Smith's inner voice was so loud that for a moment he couldn't understand why Taylor clearly hadn't heard it.

'Well, yes, fair enough, that might put her at more of a risk, I suppose. But still, she's only been gone the weekend. She may simply have found herself a sugar daddy.'

'Boss,' Taylor explained patiently, 'her friend pointed out that weekends are her biggest earners in the club. When she's more likely to pick up the decent tips. She wouldn't gamble on losing those to go off with someone, no matter how much cash they had, in case it didn't work out.

'Well, she might go off with them, she'd done that enough times. But once she'd got her hands on all the money they had with them, she'd be out of there.'

As Smith knew to his cost.

Now he faced a real dilemma. If it somehow came out that he himself had been one of her victims, and that he had been searching for her, he'd be off the case. And if he refused to release details of her disappearance because of the implications for himself, and she did turn out to be another kidnap, potentially murder victim, he'd be facing disciplinary action for gross misconduct.

He had no choice.

'Let's release the details,' he told Taylor. 'Hopefully if she's holed up in bed with some rich bloke drinking champers and eating caviar, it might just guilt her into contacting someone, if she sees herself on telly.'

Smith couldn't remember the last time he'd been obliged to say a prayer. At some sort of church parade or another in his military days. Before that, not since his school years.

As he picked up the phone to inform the Det. Sup. and to arrange with the press office to get a statement out about Lulu having joined the ranks of their other Mispers, he was fervently praying that once the news broke, it didn't start jamming police switchboards all round the city with bar staff phoning up to report that a big copper called Smith had been cruising all the drinking establishments looking for Lulu, long before she was reported missing.

30.

15:49 – MONDAY AFTERNOON

For once Smith was glad of a shitload of paperwork as an excuse for him to stay shut in his office in case the crap was about to hit the fan. He only ventured out for coffee when he could hear that there was next to no one in the main office.

He was hoping for any sort of a positive outcome. Top banana would be Lulu herself seeing the news bulletin and making contact with her mates, to let them know she was fine and just spending time with a wealthy bloke.

The longer the day went on, the more he was hoping he'd got away with it. Until his office door opened without a knock first and Inspector Joe Barnes, of all people, strode in.

Barnes pulled out the spare chair and sat down without being invited, folding his arms and looking businesslike.

'This is a courtesy call, Oscar. I'm not obliged to tell you, but I will, anyway. No sooner had the news gone out about this latest missing woman than we started getting calls from people who work in various pubs around town.'

Smith tried hard to control his face. Not to show any inkling that he knew what was coming. He had a fleeting flash through his brain. The director of *Looking for Lulu* telling the actor playing the police officer to twitch an eye or have a muscle spasm in his face, so the audience would know he was hiding something.

'They're all saying the same thing. You've been cruising the city for days now, before this Louisa-Marie, known as Lulu, went missing. Looking for her, asking questions about her. You've even been leaving your card and asking anyone who sees her to contact you direct. Which is how it got back to us so quickly. Unless, of course, you have a doppelgänger who has somehow managed to clone your cards.

'Now, what you get up to outside work is none of my business. Unless and until it starts to reflect on the service in a bad way. And just at the moment, I'm struggling to come up with an innocent explanation for this. Not to mention how we handle damage limitation if any of it gets out in public, which it's bound to do.

'I have, of course, had to pass the info on to the next level. I had no choice in that. But I thought I'd at least come and tell you about it first, in case you need to get your story straight.'

Smith didn't think his day could get any worse. Having to thank Joe Barnes for anything meant that it did.

Barnes stood up to go.

'I'm not judging you on this, Oscar. There may be a perfectly innocent explanation for it all. If there is, I hope you can get it sorted out quickly. Stuff like this in the middle of a major case the public are now following all the time is the last thing you need.'

'Yeah, thanks for the heads-up, at least. I appreciate it,' was the best he could manage through clenched teeth, while in his mind saying, *'thanks for stating the bleeding obvious, you twat.'*

Something like this required espresso, and plenty of it. Hopefully most of the team would be out and he wouldn't have to run the gauntlet of any knowing looks. News like this would be round the station like wildfire in no time flat.

Only Tony was in the main office and he barely raised his head as Smith helped himself to two cups of espresso and headed back to the relative sanctuary, for now, of his office. He wondered where and how the first contact from the upper echelons would be made.

He didn't have long to wait for the answer. Once again, the door to his office opened without a knock. This time it was the Det. Sup. who strode in. His expression was usually hard to read. This time his face was set in firm lines.

Oscar had time for a fleeting thought that bloody Edith on reception wasn't getting any more lifts from him. Never mind any more expensive boxes of chocolates for her mother, when she'd once again failed to warn him of the impending arrival of a Det. Sup. with a face like thunder.

'Oscar,' he said, by way of greeting, sitting down opposite Smith, 'I think you could say the proverbial has well and truly hit the fan, where you're concerned. You've heard, I take it?'

It was pointless denying that he had. Aird wouldn't have believed him, even if he'd tried that. The station was full of jungle drums. It was unlikely that anyone from the newest probationer right up to the top ranks within it had not yet heard the news.

'It's true I've been looking all round town for Lulu, guv. I had a one-night stand with her, I'm not denying it, and the robbing little bitch lifted my wallet and all my cash. I just wanted to find her and put the frighteners on her a bit. She's well known for it, apparently.

'I didn't expect to get my money back, but I wanted to warn her off doing it again on the patch. I didn't have anything to do with her disappearance, though. I never caught up to her.'

'Right, well, we'll need to check your movements, and where you live for any sign of her, for form's sake, if nothing else. And clearly you can't go on having anything at all to do with this case until she turns up.

'Take some leave. Go and lie on a beach or climb a mountain, or whatever it is you do by way of relaxation.

Better still, you've got family in Germany, haven't you?'

'My grandmother, guv.'

'Well, not wishing any ill on the lady, but I think she might just have taken a bad turn, don't you? So you'll need to fly out and see her. Get your things together.

'You'll need to leave your service vehicle here, of course, and turn in the keys. I'll get someone to drive you home and at the same time they'd better have at least a cursory look round your place. And don't worry, I'll pick someone who knows to keep schtum about everything.'

Seeing the expression on Smith's face, he went on, 'It's form, Oscar. You know that as well as I do. We'd look like a bunch of incompetent imbeciles if all the time you had the poor lass tied up in your spare bedroom, or whatever, and we never even checked.'

Smith stood up, his turn to have a face like thunder.

'I'd better go and tell Tony, do a hand over of some sort.'

'Absolutely not. You have no further contact with anyone in the station. Not by any form at all. I will liaise with you and keep you informed of anything you need to know. I'll tell Tony, and Joe Barnes. Explain you've had to go to Germany suddenly for a family crisis. But you contact no one until you hear from me further. Is that crystal clear?'

'Am I being suspended, then?' Smith asked him.

'Don't be a pillock, Oscar. Of course you're not. Too much paperwork, for one thing. You can hang on to your warrant card and your ID pass, as long as you don't use either of them until further notice. You're just being advised to go and see your granny for a few days, until all of this blows over. Nothing more than that.

'Unless, of course, the officer who drives you home finds this young woman in your house, in one state or another. Then you might have some serious explaining to do.'

***

20:36 – MONDAY EVENING

Don Donovan was waiting, reading his paper and sipping his Parma violet gin and tonic. He was the only person who could get away with sitting in such an old-school spit and sawdust rough pub as this was, drinking such a concoction. The pub bought it in specially for him. He was a frequent customer, and certainly the only one ever to ask for it.

Detective Constable Dai Evans was late, as he always was. Donovan suspected Evans was afraid to find himself alone in the pub, waiting for the journalist to turn up. The only coppers welcome within these dirty walls were those in the company of Don Donovan. He was revered by all those who drank within. More than one of them owed their restored liberty to the dogged determination of the man to right wrongs in miscarriages of justice.

When Evans finally arrived, he went straight to the bar and ordered a pint of Guinness, on Donovan's tab. It was a gesture he insisted on sticking to, to enable him to say with a clear conscience that he had never been given so much as a free drink by the journalist, if anyone ever found out what he'd been up to.

He didn't even like Guinness. He simply felt it might help him to blend into the surroundings more in such a place. Although realistically, he knew that he was safe only as long as he was under Donovan's protection.

'Late again, Dai,' Donovan greeted him, a slight note of rebuke in his strangely high-pitched voice. 'I hope you've got something worthwhile for me?'

'You can say that again,' Evans told him smugly, raising his glass towards Donovan with a '*Iechyd da.*'

From Evans' usual accent, Donovan knew any links to the land of his fathers were tenuous, if they existed at all. At least he didn't say *sláinte*.

The journalist waited patiently while the officer went through his usual ritual. Taking a swallow, making a supposedly appreciative 'aaaahh' sound, then wiping the creamy head from his upper lip.

'Right,' he said, rubbing his hands in a 'down to business' manner. 'You know there's this other woman gone missing? Louisa-Marie, known as Lulu?

'It only turns out that the SIO on the case, the one and only Detective Inspector Bastard-face Smith, has been trawling the bars of the city looking for her, and for some time before she disappeared.'

Evans smirked at his companion, clearly pleased with himself and looking for some sort of a reaction. Donovan was a past master at the deadpan expression. He simply said quietly, 'Go on.'

Evans appeared to deflate slightly at the lack of enthusiasm so he pulled out what he hoped was the ace in his poker hand.

'Well, now said DI Smith has suddenly disappeared off, apparently to Germany, on so-called compassionate leave to visit some relative none of us who work with him have ever heard about. And any of us who work with him can tell you he doesn't have a compassionate bone anywhere in his miserable body.

'He hit me once, at work. Round the back of the head.'

So that was it, Donovan thought to himself.

Evans wasn't man enough to have done anything about that for himself, so instead he was spreading gossip about the SIO which may or may not be reliable. It might be safe enough for one of his innuendo-filled pieces on his own website, but he was going to need a lot more than that to do anything for the papers.

'Are you saying Smith has been suspended?'

Evans shifted in his seat.

'Well, no, not officially suspended. Sent on leave might be nearer the mark. And he wasn't allowed to go home in his service vehicle. He had to leave that at the nick and be driven home. The driver was told to have a quick shufti round his gaff to see if he had Lulu there, as a prisoner, or maybe even as a body.'

'And was she there?'

'Well, no, but...'

A lot of the time Evans was as much use as a spare prick at a wedding. Occasionally, he came up with the goods. It was just possible that there was something behind this, but Donovan needed to check it out from a more reliable source before he went with it.

Always best to go as far up the ladder as he could, even if he got nothing but a 'no comment'. The fact that he even asked questions would rattle a few cages.

'Right, Dai, *diolch yn fawr*,' Donovan liked to throw in Welsh words of his own, ones he'd learned on a brief visit there many moons ago. It was his way of showing Evans that he wasn't taken in by any of his pretence.

'I need to go and get started on writing this up. You stay and finish your pint.'

He said it every time, for the devilment. He loved watching the man squirm at the very idea of being left without his protector in what he clearly viewed as the enemy's front line.

Evans was chugging his stout down as fast as he could swallow, before heading for the door in unseemly haste.

Donovan chuckled to himself as he got out his telephone and called up a saved number.

'Good evening, Murray,' he said as soon as Detective Superintendent Aird answered the phone. 'Sorry to bother you when you're probably relaxing at home.

'Certain information has come my way from a hopefully reliable source and I wanted to give you the chance to confirm or deny it, before it goes to press.'

31.

09:52 – TUESDAY MORNING

Smith woke to the unmistakeable smell of a cat's arse planted on his face and what felt like the work of a deranged acupuncturist; dozens of red-hot needles stabbing him in his chest. The percussion section of a major orchestra appeared to have taken up residence in his skull, where they were practising *Fanfare for the Common Man*.

His tongue seemed to have been glued to the roof of his mouth, while the same demented sadist responsible for the rest of his suffering had been sandpapering his eyeballs.

His chances of being able to speak to tell Clive to piss off and leave him to die in peace were slim at best. He opted for lifting a weak hand, picking the cat up as carefully as he could, then dropping him unceremoniously over the edge of the bed.

He lay as still as he could manage for the moment, trying to piece together fragmented memories to explain his current state. It had clearly involved a very large quantity of alcohol.

Lulu, becoming the latest reported Misper.

Not good news.

Bar staff phoning in to say he'd been looking for her.

Worse news.

Being driven home from the nick by PC Martin Hancock, who was under orders to search his home for any signs of the missing Lulu.

Much worse news.

The look on Hancock's face as he went from room to room, in what looked like a student squat after the wildest kind of party, would remain forever burned into Smith's brain, no matter what state he was in.

Smith risked a wry smile when the satisfying memory of Clive registering his disapproval of the intruder by spraying his leg with rank *eau de* tomcat popped into his head.

Aird had told Hancock firmly, in front of Smith, that everything he saw and did when escorting the DI home and checking the premises was to be kept strictly confidential.

Smith could tell by the man's face that he couldn't wait to tell everyone in the nick about the kind of solitary squalor the DI lived in, in his grubby little flat, with only a smelly cat for company.

At some point Smith was going to have to get his arse out of bed and head for the bathroom. He needed a piss, if nothing else. But then what was he going to do with himself for the rest of the day? And all of the empty days which lay ahead until Lulu was found and he was cleared of any involvement in her disappearance?

Assuming that would eventually happen.

He'd been ordered to take leave, pack himself off to Germany or wherever he fancied, and to have no contact with anyone on his team.

Like he would even consider doing that.

He still had his warrant card. He was not officially suspended. He was still a serving police officer, and a bloody good one, when he put his mind to it.

There was one certain way to clear his name of any involvement in the disappearance of Lulu. He was going to have to find her, hopefully alive, and solve the case himself, without access to any of the usual resources, nor anyone to help him in his task.

But first, he was going to have to lever himself up out of his pit and get his arse under the shower. That and fill himself up with some strong coffee so he might once again be fit to function.

* * *

10:39 – TUESDAY MORNING

It took him far longer than it should have done to get himself clean, presentable, and looking halfway human. He'd caught sight of himself in the bathroom mirror whilst showering and had been shocked by what he saw.

He knew he'd let himself go a bit from his military days, with the Annual Fitness Tests always there as a reminder that he could be on active service at short notice.

No amount of sucking in his midriff made the spectacle in the mirror look anything other than what it was – a pen-pushing bastard who'd stopped taking proper care of himself to a disgraceful degree. No wonder he wasn't on top of his game.

Any self-respecting serial kidnapper or killer would know from looking at him that they would be able to run rings round this blobby creature. And he'd put himself on show looking like that, at the press conference. Thinking that a clean shirt and a military tie would disguise the fact of how combat unfit he was and how his good suit was straining at the seams on him.

Then the realisation hit him, harder than the jet of ice-cold water he'd just inflicted upon himself as a final wake-up call.

That was what this was all about. Whoever their suspect was, he'd started to play games with him ever since seeing on television who his adversary was.

That was when his pattern had changed completely. Smith had been resistant to the idea that Marcus could be another victim, but now it all made sense.

Having seen that the police were basing their investigations on the victims being young blonde women, he'd suddenly switched to taking a dark-haired young man.

Then when he'd somehow found out that Smith was out and about *Looking for Lulu*, he'd taken her as well, leaving Smith firmly implicated.

So whoever this suspect was, he wanted to play mind games, did he? Well, Smith was well up for that. The body might not yet be battle-ready but the mind was as good as ever. Or at least he hoped it was.

He towelled himself roughly dry then dressed in scruff order. Before he did anything else, he was going to sort out the total shit-heap he was living in. It was no way to exist and certainly no place to do the kind of work he needed to.

He spent all of the rest of the morning cleaning up, and it left him with a stack of bin bags outside his back door. He didn't currently have his own vehicle. He'd got used to using his service one. He'd left his own previous car to fall into such a state of disrepair that it had spectacularly failed its MOT test and been carted off to the great car park in the sky.

There was plenty of public transport for him to get about on, when he didn't want to walk, but he could hardly take bin bags to the tip on the bus. He'd put them to one side outside the back door for now and would sort something out when he had the time.

Next up on the agenda was to cram his blubber into his old running gear and go out to pound the pavements. He reckoned the 1.2 mile Army fitness test distance might kill him, in his current state, but he needed to set the bar high.

He took some cash and a folded up carrier bag, though left his wallet behind, so he could pick up some basic supplies on his way back. He would need to eat, sensibly, and he wasn't planning on leaving the flat until he had made some sort of breakthrough on the case.

He had to admit to himself that it was better for morale to come back into a clean, uncluttered environment which now had a fragrance more of lemon than cat piss. And it was a bloody sight easier to lay out paperwork and scribblings on his small dining table without the usual clutter.

He could have done with the maps with circles which on he'd given to Tony Taylor. He'd just have to spend some time reproducing them. It might make him think of something else which had so far eluded him.

He'd taken to mentally referring to the suspect as 'Harold', after Dr. Shipman, Britain's most prolific serial killer, although he was still hoping that at least some of the six Mispers might yet be found alive.

If Harold had deliberately set him up as a suspect in the disappearance of Lulu, that must mean he'd been aware of Smith looking for her, long before it became public knowledge. The most likely explanation for that was that he had been in one of the pubs where Smith was asking about her and giving out his card. That put bar staff he'd spoken to at the top of the list, followed by anyone within earshot when he'd been talking to them.

He'd ask Tony to get the team to check out staff in the bars he'd been in, for starters. He knew a lot had already been questioned about the other missing women, but not specifically about Lulu.

Then he remembered he was not currently supposed to ask Tony anything.

Bugger.

He didn't want to put him in a compromising position by trying to call him and having him block the call. He certainly couldn't risk going back to any of the pubs himself to ask more questions. If that got back to the Det. Sup. he would be risking disciplinary action, which didn't help anyone.

Shit.

He'd have to fall back on a skill he hadn't used in a long time, so he hoped it was still functioning. He did, at least, feel more alert after his run. Knackered, yes, but mentally fitter than he could remember feeling for a long time.

Part of his memory skills involved subliminal face recognition. He could see people without consciously seeing them and if he concentrated hard enough afterwards he could occasionally produce face recognition to rival that of a basic computer programme.

It had come in useful in some of the places he'd served with the Military Police, where remembering a face could often be a literal life-saver.

The trouble was, of all the faces he had seen whilst he was cruising the pubs on his *Looking for Lulu* mission, he was setting himself the almost impossible task of picking out one from his memory banks who stood out, but not in any distinctive sort of way.

What had Mitchell said about him? That he'd be bland, ordinary, the kind of person who would be easily overlooked in a crowd, which wasn't going to make his task any easier.

And what was it his Oma had told him? Use his little grey cells. A lot of this he could do simply by concentrating and eliminating information which would take him nowhere, in all probability.

If Harold had seen him asking about Lulu and decided to use her to taunt him with, there was a chance he would not have gone back to anywhere he'd met and possibly abducted one of his earlier victims. He would know there would be a slight risk someone working there might have seen him talking to one of the missing women and if asked by the police about the women, they might remember the connection.

Which meant Smith needed to concentrate his thoughts

on any pubs he'd been too where the earlier questioning had produced no positive sightings of the other four women.

Time to test his memory to see if it could still oblige him with total recall when he needed it to. First for the names of the pubs he could leave off his list for now, then those where he'd been asking his questions. Then finally some glimpse of anyone, no matter how fleeting, who could possibly have been their bland, anonymous abductor, watching him, listening to his questions about Lulu.

After that, he could route his runs past all the right places, searching every face he encountered for an elusive match.

He was so engrossed in his task that he started at the sound of his mobile phone ringing, more so when he realised it was already late afternoon. It gave him a jolt of unpleasant anticipation. When it couldn't be work, it was inevitably news from Germany, of the sort he didn't want to hear.

There was no caller name displayed and he wasn't expecting anyone so he answered curtly with 'Schmidt.'

'Is that you, guv?' Taylor asked. 'It's Tony here.'

Smith couldn't remember ever having been so pleased to hear the hesitant voice of his DS.

'Tony!' he tried not to gush. 'I didn't recognise the number and I wasn't expecting you to call. Haven't you been warned off all contact with me on pain of death?'

Taylor gave a short chuckle.

'I have, guv, which is why this is a burner phone. I wanted to make sure you were okay.'

Smith was touched by his words. He'd never thought of their working relationship as particularly close, never mind any personal one. He must make an effort to be nicer to him once he was back at work. Perhaps take him for the occasional drink of an evening. He felt he owed him that much, at least.

'I'm fine, thanks for asking. Just doing a bit of detective work of my own from home to pass the time.'

'That's good, guv.'

Smith could tell Taylor had more to say and was plucking up the courage to do so. That didn't bode well.

'What I also wanted to say, to give you a heads-up, if you like, is that the Det. Sup. did a press conference this afternoon. It's going out on the local news later this evening. He's announced that you're off the case because you're on compassionate leave and that he's taking over temporarily as SIO.

'I thought if you saw that on telly without advance warning...'

'Thanks, Tony, I appreciate it.'

Smith's tone was much more terse now. He was trying to talk with his teeth well and truly gritted.

That was an unusual move. A mere change of SIO didn't usually merit a further press conference. There was clearly a hidden agenda there somewhere.

'Well, good luck, guv. I'll try to keep in touch as and when I can.'

Two men shouted loudly at their television screens at more or less the same time when the local news followed the main evening national news later that evening.

'Pompous lying bastard!'

Smith's yell, at the sight of the Det. Sup. doing a piece to camera, was so loud that Clive the cat, who had been curled up asleep on his stomach, teleported himself vertically into the air, fur and tail fluffed up, hissing and spitting, and ready to do battle with whoever the enemy might be.

'We hope to have more news about our six missing persons shortly. Detective Inspector Smith, who was leading the enquiry, has had to take sudden compassionate leave. So pending his return, I will be overseeing the operation in an acting role of Senior Investigating Officer.'

'And I bet you're revelling in it all, you twat,' Smith shouted at the face filling his TV screen.

Surprisingly, the news, instead of sinking him into some black despair, galvanised his resolve that he would be the one to find the breakthrough that was needed to solve the case.

His determination clearly showed through in his voice. As soon as he phoned his grandmother and started to speak, she told him, 'Now that is the sound of my Oskar at the top of a black run which he knows is his for the taking.'

The Det. Sup.'s announcement had a similar effect on 'Dennis' as he sat downstairs in his lounge, watching the same footage as Smith.

'No!! No, no, no, that's not supposed to happen.

'Bring him back.

'Bring him back!'

His outburst was more howls of anguish than an angry shout.

Upstairs in the front bedroom, with the blinds down and the curtains firmly closed, Lulu curled herself up into the corner at the sound. Whatever had upset the man might not bode well for her.

She drew her knees towards her chest and buried her face against her bound hands, tears flowing down over them as she whimpered quietly to herself.

'Please let me go.

'I don't want to be here.

'Let me go home.

'Please.'

32.

09:42 – WEDNESDAY MORNING

Smith was breathing hard and dripping with sweat when he let himself back into his newly clean flat after his morning run. He'd kept it up for a lot further than the day before but he'd paced himself at a steady jog so he didn't tire too quickly.

As well as allowing him to scan every face he passed for anyone he might recognise, the running gave him time to put his brain to work on theories. It was what he was good at.

There was no point going near pubs early in the day, and he'd already decided it wouldn't be a good idea to be seen near any at any time in his current circumstances. But he picked his route to include things like office buildings where he might spot a face he'd seen before, someone going in to start work for the day.

There was no lightning bolt of recognition. No sudden 'gotcha' moment which would have merited a thought bubble in a cartoon. The main lesson of the morning was that he was not even as unfit as he thought he was. He was much, much worse. He had a lot of work ahead of him.

The first thing he did when he staggered back home, wondering if he was about to suffer a cardiac arrest and therefore who would call the ambulance, and how long would it take to arrive, was to head for the kitchen sink and gulp down two glasses of cold water.

It tasted like piss, which it probably was, recycled and hopefully much diluted, though probably with equally polluted river water, and he knew it was not a good idea anyway. He'd have preferred bottled mineral water, but without a car at his disposal, he didn't fancy lugging that back to the flat. Especially after a run which had nearly left him on his knees.

He must look into home deliveries, now he wouldn't be embarrassed to open the door of the flat to anyone who rang the bell. It would save him time, apart from anything.

He sat down at the table, leaning back in his chair and closing his eyes. If he sat in the armchair he'd probably fall asleep. This way he could recall all the images he could summon, let them play through his mind, until he could sift out the one which might lead him somewhere.

Tony Taylor had had a long briefing with the Det. Sup. early on, before the rest of the team arrived. Tony was running things, as before, Aird had been quick to assure him, but he wanted to keep a finger on the pulse because it was him who would be paraded in front of the cameras, not Tony, to explain himself if progress was slow.

'As long as we don't find any bodies or body parts, there's a chance our victims are still alive somewhere,' Aird was telling him. 'I know you know all this, Tony, I'm not teaching you to suck eggs, just summing up for my own benefit.

'So what's your plan going forward?'

'Logically, if we concentrated on the most recent disappearances, any details people may have noticed are freshest in their minds,' Tony began, then hurried on, 'That doesn't mean we should give up on the earlier ones, like Sally Rogers, though, sir.'

Taylor had a lot of respect for Aird so he accorded him the courtesy. It indicated a difference in his attitude to him than to the gaffer.

'In a sense the last two, Marcus and Lulu, are completely different to the others, in their lifestyle. Not the same sort of thing at all. If it is all the work of one abductor, he's changed his signature considerably. It would help us if we knew why.'

'Any thoughts on that?'

'I did have one, sir. You might not like it, though.'

'Try me anyway.'

'Well, Marcus disappeared very soon after the first press conference, when you and the gaffer were on TV linking the four missing blonde-haired women for the first time officially in public.

'So supposing our kidnapper saw that and decided to change his MO to shake things up a bit? Give us the runaround?'

'That's possible, but does it get us anywhere, in reality?'

'I've been talking to Jody Mitchell about it. The significant factor is that we only found out after it was announced that Lulu was missing that the gaffer had been looking for her. Now, I'm taking it as a given that you weren't connected to Lulu, sir, and I know Joe Barnes isn't either.

'Which means the only one of the three of you who appeared at that press conference with any connection to her turned out to be the gaffer.

'So what if our man, and Jody is pretty certain it is a man working alone, took her in order to send a message to the DI? Part of some strange game he has going with him, for whatever reason.'

Aird was already ahead of him. He was no pen-pusher. He was a good copper, with excellent intuition. And he never tried to pass the buck or to blame others for his failings.

'So me taking him out of the equation very publicly is going to have had an impact on our kidnapper. And possibly not in a good way. Assuming Lulu was alive when I did that, have my actions now put a young woman's life

12:27 – WEDNESDAY AFTERNOON

'Hello, I hope you've had a good morning. I'm back from work for my lunch now so I'll make us something nice to eat. I'll take you to the bathroom first. I expect you might like to freshen yourself up a bit.

'Have you been crying?'

His voice was so caring, so totally normal, that it scared her more than anything. He sounded like a considerate husband, back from the office and offering to prepare a meal for the wife he worshipped.

He crouched down in front of her, smiling pleasantly all the time.

'Now, I'm going to take your gag off, of course, so you can wash your face and then come downstairs and eat with me, as a special treat. But first of all, I need to remind you of the rules. You have remembered, haven't you?'

She nodded frantically. She knew exactly what he meant. The trouble was, she was now so scared and so out of control of herself that she had a horrible feeling that as soon as he took the gag off she wouldn't be able to stop herself from screaming her lungs out.

He was chatting away to her as he removed the gag, untied her from the radiator and helped her to her feet. She was unsteady, from the position she'd been in all morning. Pins and needles radiating down one leg, so she could barely feel the foot at the end of it.

'The neighbour was keeping an eye out for me coming home. She wants more of my home cooking, no doubt. She's always on the scrounge for some. She's quite greedy, I think.

'She keeps asking me where I get the meat from. Which butcher I use. But that's my special secret. I'm not going to share it with anyone. Certainly not the nosy old woman next door.'

He'd be sure to give her some more, though. A few dishes of it. He needed to make some room in the freezer, and soon. He hadn't expected Marcus to end up there as quickly as he had. And now there was this Lulu, too, to consider, and she wasn't small.

'Right, come on, I'll take you to the bathroom. But just remember what I told you about staying quiet.'

It was the extremes of his behaviour which frightened her the most. Hearing him raging at the television last night. Knowing what he was capable of doing with that Tinker thing. Yet hearing him now, speaking to her as if their relationship was completely normal.

She got as far as the bathroom. As far as sitting on the toilet with his gentle help. She'd managed to keep quiet and compliant. Until she saw him standing there, smiling fondly at her, as she tried to have a wee.

Then she lost it.

She opened her mouth wide, sucked in a lungful of air, and started to scream.

He was across the small room in seconds. One surprisingly strong hand clamped over her mouth and her nostrils, stifling her, pushing her head right back. The other hand tightened around the back of her neck.

His face was close to hers now, his lips against her ear.

With a terrifying realisation, she knew without a doubt that the right amount of pressure in the position she was in would snap her neck like a stick.

'Sssshhh, hush now. You mustn't make a sound. I told you. I warned you. So now you have to pay the price.'

* * *

18:32 – WEDNESDAY EVENING

Smith had adjourned to his armchair in front of the TV in time to watch the early evening news. He didn't expect to see reports of any further developments in the case yet, but if there were any, hearing about them on the news was, for now, possibly his only way of knowing.

There was nothing at all happening in the big wide world which was holding his attention, and sitting down, with his feet up on the raised extended part of the recliner, was making him realise just how tired he was after all the unaccustomed physical exercise.

The prawn salad baguette he'd brought back with him for lunch was but a distant memory. He was hungry again but sat a while longer, promising himself he'd watch the local news then stir himself and make something decent for his evening meal.

Eating sensibly was going to be part of his new regime to get himself into some sort of fitting shape for a police officer with a good record on results. He would draw the line at giving up the coffee, though, or even cutting it down. His system was so used to the strong stuff by now that it didn't seem to affect his ability to sleep.

At some point he must have started to drop off because all of a sudden he snapped awake with a grunt and the feeling of something hard sticking into the back of his hip as he'd slowly slipped down into the comfort of his chair.

He felt round behind him to his back pocket to discover what was digging into his buttock and giving him a pain like sciatica down the back of his right leg.

He grunted to himself to discover he still had the front door key in his pocket. He usually left it on the small shelf in the entrance hall. He ought to go and put it back there before he forgot and risked a scramble to find it, in the unlikely possibility of any unexpected callers. He always kept it double-locked from the inside whenever he was at home. Old habits.

Finally the lightbulb moment he'd been hoping for all day hit him in a flash. He sat staring at the key, now in the palm of his hand, his brain playing out images, like using fast forward on a DVD recorder to get to the scene he wanted.

A man. Coming out of a building. Pausing to rummage in his pockets, as if checking for keys.

Smith pressed pause on the replay in his head. Trying to capture a freeze frame of the moment. To see what features, if any, he could bring to mind.

Medium height, medium build. Dark hair. Glasses. Rimless. Features indistinct.

Because he turned his face away when he saw Smith coming.

Why?

Had he simply remembered something he'd left behind? Or had he recognised who was walking along the street towards him?

And what was the building? Not a pub, or a bar, or a shop of any kind, he was fairly certain.

An office, then? Or a block of offices? But where?

He needed to stop thinking about it. To concentrate on something else entirely, until the memory came back into clearer focus.

Because there was an outside chance that the man he had seen was their kidnapper, and that he had recognised Smith. And that might well mean that he'd seen Smith cruising the bars while he was looking for Lulu.

That in turn would suggest that if Smith used his powers of recall to the maximum, he might be able to pull up an image of where their paths could have crossed before that incident outside the building.

If their routes had crossed previously, in one of the pubs where he'd been asking about Lulu, there may be some sort of a game going on between the two of them. A game in which Smith was not yet aware of the rules.

Find the man and he might solve the mystery.

Get it wrong, and people might die.

33.

15:17 – THURSDAY AFTERNOON

Smith had again been up at the crack of dawn and donned his running gear. He was once more pacing himself at a slow and steady jog which once, when fit, he had been able to keep up for miles at a time. Those days were long behind him, but if he went steadily and took walking breaks whenever he needed to, he could still cover quite some distance.

What he needed to do was to find the building where he'd seen the man coming out, apparently looking for his keys. He'd so far not managed to pull up the right image to give him a location. He was out of practice. But he could remember every pub he'd been in, and where he'd parked the car each time, so he could simply retrace his steps from each visit and eventually, he'd find himself walking past the same building.

It might take him all day – maybe a few days - but he had nothing better to do with his time. At least it made him feel as if he was doing something.

It was mid-afternoon before he got lucky. He'd had some lunch at the coffee shop where both Gill Burrell and Kathy Morgan had been customers. He'd come across it on his way and decided mineral water would be better for him than an alcoholic drink so had gone in.

The optimistic part of his nature hoped he might get a

glimpse of the same man in there having a sandwich. The realistic side knew that such contrived coincidences only happened in crime fiction.

There was no sudden flash of inspiration. No anonymously bland features which rang a bell. The customers consisted in the main of older people making their drinks last, or younger women, sharing a hasty lunch before going back to work.

He hadn't jogged very far after his lunch break when he came across the building he recognised. An anonymous concrete slab, several storeys high. He stood across the street from it, pausing with a hand against his side, leaning slightly forward.

A runner with a stitch, getting his breath back mid training run. He didn't want to draw attention to himself, especially if the man he was still mentally calling Harold was in one of those upper-floor windows, looking out at him and recognising him as the copper he was trying to play mind games with.

He jogged on round the block, then crossed over so he was on the same side as the building, slowing to a walk to go past it.

There were blinds to all of the ground-floor windows so he couldn't see in, but by the same token, presumably, anyone working inside was unlikely to be able to see him.

Governmental, local authority and other similar offices, he saw from the brass plates on the wall in the porch. He didn't want to lurk about looking suspicious. There might be security on duty in such a building, for one thing, so he took a quick photo of the information on display, then carried on his way.

Now he'd found the building, he'd come back later, around the time he'd seen the man coming out. He might be someone completely innocent, nothing to do with the case at all. But the more Smith re-ran the scene in his head, the more he convinced himself there was something evasive about the way the man had turned away as he'd approached.

He still hadn't been able to call up any other scene in his head where the same man had appeared.

While he was killing time before coming back hoping to see him leaving, he'd cruise the pubs and bars around the area. If he went into some of them the familiarity might just kick-start a subliminal memory.

He stuck to drinking tonic water. He had a vague recollection that it was supposed to be effective against cramp, something he risked with all the unaccustomed exercise he was taking.

Not all of the pubs he'd visited previously were open at this time of day, but he sat in the bar of the ones that were, sipped his tonic and chatted sporadically to whoever was behind the counter.

He was in punter rather than policeman mode, so he was careful to keep it inconsequential. Football, the weather, the state of the economy.

He was in the third one when finally the lightning bolt hit him. He knew where he'd seen the man supposedly looking for his keys before. In this very bar. Sitting on a bar stool at the end of the counter whilst Smith himself was in the middle, talking to the man behind it about Lulu and giving him his card.

He'd only had him in his peripheral vision so his impression was fleeting. But the more he re-ran the memory, the more sure he became. Medium height, medium build, dark hair, rimless glasses. Nothing distinctive.

The invisible man.

Smith felt a sudden elation. He was getting close, he could feel it. He was now on his adversary's territory. He had the best lead so far.

He knew he should phone it in. But he was buggered if he was going to. Not yet, anyway.

What he was going to do was go back to that building he'd seen and lurk about until he saw the man again.

Always assuming that he actually worked there and hadn't just been visiting, perhaps to justify himself to a bureaucrat about claiming some benefit or another.

He had a quick look at the photo on his phone first, zooming in to study the listed closing times. Most of the offices seem to close fairly early. Around four-thirty was the latest he could see.

He knew it was later than that when he'd seen key-man coming out. That was hopeful. If he'd been leaving the building long after most of the offices had shut for the day, there was a strong chance that he worked there.

All Smith needed now was patience, which he had in abundance when he needed it most, and a little bit of luck on his side. Something which had been in short supply of late.

He finished his drink and retraced his steps to the building, looking for somewhere inconspicuous that he could plant himself and have the doorway in his vision. He just hoped there was no rear or side entrance he was unaware of.

His cover for lurking so long in one place was easy enough. He simply held his mobile phone to his ear and whenever anyone passed him, he made inconsequential small talk into it. It was such a common sight that no one would take any notice.

People were coming out of the building all the time. He'd discovered a convenient window opposite where he could turn his back on it so he wasn't quite so noticeable but still had something of a view of who was coming and going.

The whole time he stood there he kept his phone to his ear, talking into it occasionally.

It was just gone five when he saw the man he was waiting for walk out of the building. Smith kept his back turned, seemingly fascinated by the contents of the shop window. The man appeared not to notice him and turned left, walking briskly.

For a big man, Smith could do stealth. He'd had enough training in it. He moved from shop doorway to doorway, always ready to duck out of sight as the man he was hoping might be Harold walked on the opposite side of the road to him.

Whoever he was, he seemed unaware that he had a tail. He turned left at the next junction, walked another few yards to the entrance to a small private car park, then walked into that.

Smith knew he'd be too conspicuous following him into it, so he stayed where he was, phone ready, camera already zoomed in to the maximum, hoping he could at least get a couple of decent shots of the car as the man left. Preferably with a clear view of the registration number.

The man reappeared, driving out of the car park, and disappeared into the traffic. Smith checked his phone and found he had a good enough shot of the rear of the departing vehicle to read the full registration number. If he ran that through the system, he'd find out not only who the man was but also where he lived.

Then he realised. He couldn't run it through the system.

He dialled Tony's number. His call went to voicemail. He hadn't really hoped for an answer because his number would show up and he knew Tony wouldn't risk speaking to him if he was still in the nick.

'Tony, it's...' he hesitated, not sure what to call himself, as Tony was never on first-name terms with him. He tried an olive branch. 'It's Oscar, and I really need your help. It's urgent. I've spotted a potential suspect. By chance, one of those daft coincidences.'

He realised he was babbling, justifying himself. Something he never did. But he needed to say enough to make Tony take some action.

'I've got his car registration number and I need you to check it for me on the system and let me have an address. Please.'

That should let him know how desperate he was. He wouldn't be used to hearing a please or a thank you from the gaffer.

'Anyway, if you can help me out, I'd be grateful. This is the number.'

He rang off after he'd recited the registration number, before he reached the stage of grovelling.

Had the traffic been snarled up, he'd have a least had a try at following the car on foot for a bit. It might have given him an idea of where it was headed, if nothing else. But at the moment it was relatively light and free-flowing and the man, who may or may not have been Harold, was already out of sight.

All he could do now was wait and hope that Tony would come to the rescue. In the meantime he might as well head home for a shower and a change of clothes.

* * *

19:55 – THURSDAY EVENING

It was an unknown number calling him again. Smith was praying it was Tony Taylor, returning his call, with the information he'd asked him for. Just in case, he once again answered the call with nothing but a curt 'Schmidt'.

'Guv? It's Tony. Sorry it took me so long. Meetings and debriefs. You know what it's like. No leads yet, though. Now, about this info you wanted.'

'You got it for me, then? Thanks, Tony, I appreciate it. I owe you one. A big one. Fire away. What's the address?'

Taylor hesitated.

'Tell me first what you're planning to do with it.'

'I'm going to go round there, beat him to a pulp and drown his puppy, if he's got one,' Smith snapped before he could stop himself.

Then he paused to take a breath and get control of himself again.

'Sorry, Tony. Look, all I want to do is to go round there on a recce, to see what's what. It will save the team from wasting time if there's nothing to the man at all. He's just someone I saw in a pub where I was asking about Lulu and then I happened to pass him again in the street and he looked a bit shifty. As if he recognised me and was trying to avoid me.'

'The thing is, guv, I know what you're like. If you go round there, it will get messy. You're not supposed to be anywhere near this case, and if you get yourself arrested for assault, it will come out that it's me that's given you the info. And I don't feel inclined to chuck my career away for you. No offence, guv.'

Smith didn't blame him. He'd always treated him like shit and now it was coming back to bite him on the arse. The big problem was, without the information Tony could get, there was very little he could do.

Taylor was speaking again.

'I'll tell you what I will do for you, though, guv. I want a nice quiet evening in with the family. Nice meal, a bit of telly, feet up, a glass or two of wine. What I don't want is all hell breaking loose because you've gone round to some innocent bloke's house and started punching his lights out, in the mistaken belief he's our kidnapper.

'So what I'm going to do is, first thing in the morning, I'll text you the registered address for the owner of the car. On condition that you swear, on whatever you hold sacred, that you won't do anything - anything at all - without checking back with me first.

'Above all, that you won't make any attempt to enter the property without a warrant, nor to question a possible suspect in any way whilst you are officially off the case.

'Have we got a deal, guv?'

Taylor appeared to be loving this at least as much as Smith was hating it. Smith had never had him down for the vengeful type but was thinking that he needed to re-evaluate his opinion of the man who had been his DS for a number of years now.

'You know I have no choice but to agree,' Smith growled. 'Thanks, Tony. First thing tomorrow, though, eh?

34.

08:20 – FRIDAY MORNING

Smith was seething. Nearly half past bloody eight in the morning was not what he called fucking first thing. He knew Taylor would be in work by now so he couldn't understand what was holding him up and keeping him from sending the address like he promised.

Smith had been up for more than a couple of hours already, showered and dressed. This time, no running gear. On the off-chance someone saw him scouting around when he finally got the address, he had his warrant card and ID with him and, dressed in a suit which wouldn't stand out, he could simply use a cover story as close to the truth as possible, which was always best. A police officer, looking for somebody they needed to question.

He didn't need to mention the inconvenient fact that he was currently a police officer who wasn't supposed to be anywhere near this case or any other. Never mind sniffing round a house which might possibly be home to their serial kidnapper, or at least someone connected to them.

In desperation, Smith had tidied the house again, cleaned the kitchen, done the washing up and put a load of washing on while he waited for the message from Taylor.

Clive the cat was sitting on a chair, paws tucked

underneath him, watching his owner at work with a look of mild curiosity. Such domesticity was a rare sight.

The mobile phone was on the kitchen table. When its tone announced an incoming text message, Smith leapt across the small room with such haste that Clive jumped off his chair, spitting in fury, and rushed out through the cat flap.

The message was a short one. An address, then an order.

'If you spot anything, do NOT go in. Call me!!'

That was a first. His sergeant giving him orders smacked of a mouse ordering a predatory cat about and stood as much of a chance of success. But at least he now had an address to work from.

First he opened the back door and made a few 'chh-chh-chh' noises to try to appease Clive. He knew the little bugger could sulk for Britain and was likely to stay out all day and night just to make the point of how affronted he was.

'Suit yourself,' he said, in case the cat was still in earshot. 'I'm going out now. I'm sorry I scared you, all right?'

He wondered what the team would think if they could see their hard as nails gaffer apologising to a cat. But he had far more important things on his mind than an offended feline.

He jumped on a bus to save him some time and get him nearer to the address Taylor had sent him.

'*How are the mighty fallen,*' he thought to himself.

A couple of days ago he could have gone round there in a police car, with blue lights and sirens if he needed them. Now it was a bus ride and Shanks's pony to get where he needed to be.

The address he was looking for was in a quiet residential road, off the main drag. The properties were mostly respectable and semi-detached, probably worth a bob or two in the current market. He wondered what

'Harold's' job was which paid for a house like this.

Whatever he'd been expecting to find for a potential serial killer, this quietly refined taste of suburbia wasn't it. Although he knew from long experience that it was never wise to go in with preconceptions.

He walked the length of the road and back first of all, looking at each house in turn. Not too closely, but noting particularly details of the one he'd specifically come to see.

The first thing he spotted was that the upstairs front window had blinds on the inside and they were firmly closed.

There was no sign of a car on the driveway, but there was a garage, which was closed, and he had no way of seeing inside it without going up the drive.

He didn't feel constrained in any way by Taylor's message, but he was aware that if there were kidnap victims inside and if either 'Harold' or a possible accomplice was in there with them, his actions could potentially precipitate a bad outcome.

As he hesitated, the front door of the adjoining house opened and an older woman came trotting down the drive towards him. Late sixties, early seventies, he thought to himself. A sharp nose, twitching like a shrew.

A nosy neighbour was often a great way to get information. As long as she didn't call the police to report him as someone hanging around.

She was speaking to him as she approached. A slightly squeaky voice which went with the rodent image.

'Are you from the council? I didn't expect them to send anyone so soon.'

'That's right, madame,' he told her politely, giving her the briefest flash of his ID card, then pocketing it again before she had time to look too closely. 'We do always try to take calls like yours seriously and respond promptly. It's what you pay your rates for, after all.'

He was hoping she'd called to report drains smelling which would turn out to be evidence of the work of a serial killer, although realistically he knew that sort of thing tended only to happen in books.

'You'll need to go round through the side gate, and I'll have to go back inside to open it.'

For a moment, she looked suddenly suspicious as she asked, 'Where's your van, if you're from the council? You can't have walked here.'

He gave her his most disarming smile as he patted his midriff.

'I parked it a couple of streets away. The wife is always telling me I need to lose a few pounds, so I try to walk a bit whenever I can. Now then, do you want to go and let me in, please?'

She was chattering away as she hurried back towards the house.

'I thought it might be badgers, at first. But then I heard them barking at night. The foxes.'

Smith went to stand patiently by the gate while he waited for her to open it. Fascinating though anything to do with wildlife might be, it was not really what he'd been hoping for.

She resumed her monologue as if there had been no interruption as he heard her pull back a bolt and turn a key in the side gate.

'It's such a strange, eerie sound, isn't it? Foxes barking. And then they can do so much damage, digging like they do. My neighbour has some nice young trees at the bottom of his garden and I know they've been scratching all around there as well as in my garden.'

'What can you tell me about your neighbour, Mrs...?'

She turned towards him at that, looking suspicious again.

'Don't you know my name? Wasn't it on the form or whatever they gave you when they sent you out here?'

He laughed at that, trying his best to look unthreatening.

'You should see some of the handwriting and the

spelling I get on the forms. I've often no idea what someone's name is meant to be.'

'Oh, I see. Well, it's Harrison. Mrs Harrison.'

'I'd never have guessed that from the scribble. I thought it began with an M, for starters.'

'It's this way, right down at the bottom of the garden, where it's separated from the embankment. You can see where they've dug right underneath. And then they've dug through from here to my neighbour's side. I'm not sure if he's spotted it yet. I only saw it yesterday and I haven't seen him since to tell him. That's why I'm so surprised they sent someone so quickly.'

'Is he out at work at the moment, your neighbour? Only I noticed the upstairs front blinds are closed so I wondered if he perhaps works nights and is sleeping? He might not appreciate being woken up to be told about foxes in his garden, if so.'

'No, he's gone out to work. He comes home at lunchtime most days, though. And that blind has been closed for weeks now. Months, probably. I wondered if it had somehow got stuck like that. I don't know much about them.

'I think the neighbour sleeps in the back bedroom. I can see that well from the garden, and I often see him in that room.

'Look, you can see how much damage they've done, getting in. And they've been scratching all round my neighbour's lovely new trees. The last one he planted was a flowering cherry. He told me that's so I can look at the pretty blossom in the spring. He can be very thoughtful sometimes.'

Smith looked at the high wooden fence which separated the two gardens and wondered how she could know all of that. She saw his questioning look and said, 'I have a garden chair to stand on to look over the fence. The neighbour is kind to me and he's a very good cook. He often gives me the most wonderful stews and casseroles. I asked him where he gets his meat as it's the best I've ever tasted, but he said it was a long journey to his butcher so he doesn't go very often.'

'Would it be all right if I got the chair and stood on it? Just to see what the little devils have been up to on that side of the fence. Obviously I'm going to need to talk to your neighbour at some point.'

'There's the chair, look,' she pointed further up the garden. 'I keep it there so I can look over the fence and talk to the neighbour. He has one of those big barbecue things up that end of the garden and he's always cooking those spare ribs some people seem to like. I don't like the smell of those at all. He puts some sort of foreign sauce on them and they don't smell very nice. But the casseroles he makes are really delicious.'

Smith went to get the chair. First he stood on it at the top end of the garden and had a look over the fence. There was no sign of anyone. The big barrel-type barbecue was firmly closed up.

Next he carried it down to the bottom of the garden and put it close by where the foxes had dug a sizeable hole under the dividing fence.

When he climbed up on it, he could see the spinney of young trees Mrs Harrison had told him about much better, with clear evidence of where the animals had been scratching and digging around their bases. One in particular had quite a sizeable hole under it, causing it to lean slightly in a lop-sided fashion.

He got down from the chair, reaching in his pocket for the pair of latex gloves he had there. He never went anywhere without some, never knowing when next he might stumble upon a crime scene.

He crouched down to the hole under the dividing fence, stretched an arm into it and scrabbled round with his fingers.

He put four fingers and a thumb into the hole.

He withdrew five fingers.

What was lying in the palm of his hand was unmistakably a human index finger.

He closed his hand carefully around it to shield it from the inquisitive gaze of the woman as he stood up.

'Well, yes, Mrs Harrison, you clearly have quite a fox problem here, so I'm going to have to get on the phone to my office and summon up some reinforcements.'

Then he took out his phone, moving a few strides away from Mrs Harrison. He was hoping that, as Tony Taylor knew where he planned to be, he'd pick up as soon as he saw who was calling him.

He did, on the second ring.

Smith kept his voice low and his back turned to the neighbour, so she hopefully couldn't hear what he was saying.

'Tony? I'm at the house. Well, at the neighbour's, to be precise. There's been foxes digging about in the two gardens. I've found a human finger.

'Send in the cavalry. But the occupant, who's at work at the moment, is likely to come back home at lunchtime, so do it discreetly. No blues or twos. Park a bit up the road, preferably.

'Oh, and Tony, the blinds have been down in the front upstairs bedroom for weeks now. There's a chance there's someone in there. With any luck, they may be still alive.'

* * *

08:55 – FRIDAY MORNING

His call finished, Smith turned back to the woman and again took out his ID card. This time he held it out so she could have a proper look at it. He needed her on side and suspected a visit from the police might well be the most excitement she'd had in a long time.

'Mrs Harrison, I'm afraid I told you a small white lie in order to gain access to your property. You were right to be suspicious of me. I am actually a police officer, working undercover, and I need your help with our enquiries.'

The way her eyes widened as she looked from him to his card told him all he needed to know. She was going to be delighted to be caught up in all of this. Possibly less so as more grisly details began to emerge, as he was now sure they would.

But her expression told him that her first reaction was intrigue at what was going on.

'Oh, I see. Goodness me. So it's not about the foxes then?'

'I'm afraid I can't help you with those myself, but I will get one of my officers to chase it up with the council to see that someone comes and sorts it for you.

'We're actually making enquiries about your neighbour, Graham Johnson.'

He now knew the name of the person he'd been calling Harold. Tony Taylor had sent it to him together with the address and date of birth.

'Perhaps we could go inside and wait for my colleagues to arrive? And in the meantime, you could tell me everything you know about Mr Johnson. Would that be all right with you?'

'Oh, yes, of course. I expect you'd like a nice cup of tea while you're waiting. Come along.'

Smith made a face behind her retreating back. He suspected her idea of 'a nice cup of tea' might differ considerably from his. He could just about manage NATO standard tea, to be polite, but much preferred his paint-strippingly strong coffee.

He took a seat as indicated on one of the worryingly flimsy chairs around the kitchen table while she busied herself, fussing about finding a mug for him as she told him she expected he'd prefer that. When he saw the delicate bone china cup and saucer she put out for herself, he was grateful. He'd struggle holding the handle on one of those.

He took his mobile out of his pocket and asked her, 'Would you mind if I ask you a few questions about your neighbour and record the answers? That would be helpful.'

'Well, I don't know him at all well really, you must understand. Even though we've been neighbours for years. We don't exactly engage in social chit-chat. But he does kindly give me those wonderful meals he makes.

'I've lived here getting on for fifty years, so he must be well into his thirties now. He was born next door. His parents' house.

'The father was always feckless. I think he drank, you know. He just walked out one day and nobody ever saw him again.

'I used to chat to her. Graham's mother, you know. Timid mouse of a woman, but pleasant enough. Relieved to see the back of her husband, I suspect. It can't have been easy for her, living with a man like that. He was the reason we were never close. He didn't like her talking to anyone.'

'I think the mother went off to live with her sister or some other relative. A few years ago, now. I haven't seen or heard anything about her since, but as I said, we were only ever neighbours, never friends.'

'So does Graham live there alone now? No wife? Girlfriend? Boyfriend?'

She'd finished her fiddling now and put a mug in front of him, pushing the sugar bowl towards him. The contents looked like something Clive might produce but Smith tried to look grateful.

'No wife, that much I can tell you. I don't really know about his friends. I try not to be a nosy neighbour. Sometimes if I hear his car pull up in the drive in the evening, if I happen to be in the upstairs front bedroom, which is where I sleep, I might just glance out of the window.'

Smith interpreted that as meaning she spent a lot of lonely hours standing up there looking out at other people getting on with their lives.

'So did you happen to catch a glimpse of any visitors he may have brought back?'

She'd sat down opposite him now with her own cup of tea which was even paler than she'd made his. She took a dainty sip before replying.

'He did sometimes bring young women home with him. I didn't notice much about them, although I don't think I saw the same one more than once.

'About a week or two ago, though, I noticed he came back with a young man. They'd obviously been out drinking somewhere. Well, I don't expect Graham had had much to drink because he was driving, of course. But the young man was very unsteady on his feet and laughing a lot. As if he was rather tipsy. It was the noise which made me look out of the window. I haven't seen the young man since.'

They were interrupted by Smith's mobile phone ringing. Tony Taylor calling. He excused himself to Mrs Harrison, stood up and moved to the back door to answer. He knew she'd be hanging on to everything which was said.

'Tony,' he answered curtly.

'Guv, we're in the car at the top end of the road. Can you come and give us a sitrep?'

'On my way,' he told him, then, to the woman, 'Thank you for the tea, Mrs Harrison. My men are here, I have to go and brief them.

'Please stay in the house for now. Someone will come and tell you when it's all clear. And I'll get someone to get onto the council about your foxes, I promise.'

35.

09:15 – FRIDAY MORNING

Smith slid into the back seat of the black Ford parked at the end of the road. Sean Walsh was driving, Craig Stephens in the front passenger seat and Tony Taylor in the back, waiting to talk to the gaffer.

'I've got the Det. Sup. sorting out a warrant in case we need to gain entry,' Taylor told him. 'Tell me what grounds we have to do so.'

'Bugger waiting for a warrant, Tony. I found a fucking human finger in the back garden. That's grounds enough to enforce entry.

'Speaking of which, give me an evidence bag. I've got it in my pocket at the moment.'

He reached carefully into his jacket pocket. He'd removed his glove by turning it inside out from the wrist, so that the severed digit was preserved inside it, without risk of contamination.

It was reasonably fresh. It clearly hadn't been in the ground for all that long. Smith was nothing of a gardener but it seemed to him that the tree with the hole at its roots, which was starting to lean, looked like probably the most recent to have been planted in the small copse.

There were some bigger trees in front of the rear fence which looked as if they had been there for a long time. But in the little spinney in front of them, he had counted seven much younger saplings. Some people considered seven to be a lucky number. His policeman's intuition told him that it would not be so in this case. It also gave him a faint hope that Lulu might possibly be still alive somewhere in that house.

'I've been talking to the neighbour, who's helpfully nosy. Johnson lives alone, but she sometimes sees him bringing young women home. Nothing wrong with that. But she says he recently took a young man into the house and she hasn't seen him since.

'If that was Marcus, and Johnson now has Lulu as well, I think we could all make an educated guess as to why foxes are digging round the trees at the bottom of his garden and dropping body parts in the process.'

'Guv, if you're saying they're all dead, we effectively have even less reason to enforce entry. If it's bodies we're expecting to find inside, a short delay to get a warrant isn't going to make any difference,' Taylor told him, his tone reasonable.

'Tony, he doesn't come home until lunchtime. There's at least a possibility that Lulu is still alive in there. She's alone, afraid, probably tied up. She may even have been mutilated. And you're happy to leave her there another couple of hours or more?'

'We can't just break the door down on a hunch, though, guv. What if we're wrong?'

'Who said anything about breaking the door down? There's more than one way to enter a property. If you're windy about the prospect, Tony, leave it to me. I can get us in and out of there without anyone being any the wiser. Just give me some fresh gloves, and some shoe covers, so I don't cross-contaminate the scene with traces from the garden.

'But guv, you're...'

'Not supposed to be working,' Smith finished for him. 'I'm not working, I'm doing a spot of housebreaking while I'm off duty. So arrest me for it, if it makes you feel better.

But I'm going in. I need to know if there's anyone alive in there and if there is, I need to get them out before Johnson comes back.

'Oh, and if you're still unsure about going in without a bloody warrant, let me just tell you that the elderly woman next door was waxing lyrical about the wonderful stews her neighbour makes and shares with her. And how he loves to barbecue spare ribs in the garden all the time, although she doesn't like the smell of those because they smell sweet and sickly.'

Sean Walsh swivelled round in the driver's seat at that.

'Fuck, guv, are you saying he's a cannibal? He's killing his victims so he can eat them? And turning the old biddy next door into one as well, without her even knowing it?'

'I'm saying it's a distinct possibility, nothing more. Now, have any of you got the balls to come in with me – in and out clean, if necessary – or are you going to sit out here playing it safe and waiting on the paperwork?'

Whilst he was speaking he reached into the pocket of his jacket to pull out what looked like a standard jackknife. It was only when it was opened and fanned that the others could see it was an impressively professional-looking lock picking set.

Smith had learned all sorts of useful tricks in his past life, and had kept most of his skills up to date. Unless the front door had the security of Fort Knox, he should be able to have them inside in a couple of minutes, with no signs at all of entry.

Taylor hesitated for a moment before taking a decision. With Smith officially not allowed anywhere near the case, it was his own head on the block for anything and everything which went wrong or deviated in the slightest from the regulations, without a bloody good reason.

At least if he went in with him he stood an outside chance of keeping control of the system and stopping the gaffer from beating the crap out of any suspect they might find inside.

They were parked a short distance from the house, on the opposite side of the road, so he had clear line of sight to it. Particularly to that closed blind to the upstairs front window.

Taylor thought for a few short seconds about his own daughter being in that house. About what might have been happening to her inside it. He thought of all their Mispers, especially Lulu, the one with the best chance of being found alive.

It was all he needed.

'Sean, stay with the car and keep a close eye out for Johnson or anyone else approaching the house. Ring me to warn me if there's anything at all out of the way. Craig, you come with me.'

Then he was out of the car and following the gaffer's determined stride down the road towards the house and up the front drive.

Smith was already working on the lock. He was in luck. It was a basic one, nothing too sophisticated. It didn't take him long before it ceded and he was able to push the door cautiously wider, revealing a pleasantly light hallway in front of him.

There was not a sound from the interior. The three men stepped inside and Walsh carefully closed the door behind them. All three had donned gloves and shoe covers from the store in the car. If they found nothing at all in the house, they didn't want to leave anything to advertise their presence inside the property.

The stairs went up against the wall to the left and there were two doors which opened off the hallway on the right.

Smith silently signalled to Walsh to stay at the foot of the stairs and keep obo. He pointed to Taylor to check the first door on the right while he went down the hallway to the one in front of him at the end.

Nothing.

Nobody.

Quiet, tidy and orderly calm everywhere.

Again, without speaking, Smith motioned to Walsh to stay by the front door as he and Taylor moved soundlessly up the stairs.

A small, cramped landing, one door to the left, at the back of the house, one straight ahead, also towards the rear. The one on the right should logically be the front bedroom. The one where the blinds were drawn.

Smith and Taylor exchanged a look and a nod. No need for spoken communication. Start with the front bedroom and hope to heaven they might find someone still alive in there.

Smith went in first. Taylor was impressed by how silently the gaffer could move when he needed to, for such a big, heavy bloke.

At first Smith saw no one. Just a bed, a wardrobe and a chest of drawers. He noticed that the curtains were drawn on the inside, as well as the blinds being down. Someone was determined that no one would ever see into this room from outside the property.

Then he heard the quiet whimpers of fear.

He moved further into the room and there she was.

Lulu.

The girl he'd shagged and who had taken his wallet.

She was tied and gagged, trussed up to the radiator on the wall so she could barely move.

She was staring at him wide-eyed, as if confronting her worst nightmare which, considering what she must have been going through, could only be dire.

'Tony, get an ambulance first off. We need to get Lulu to hospital and get her checked out. Then we need CSI and the works. We need to start turning this place inside out and upside down.'

He was now crouching down in front of the young woman whose entire body was being shaken by tremors of fear, silent tears streaming down her face.

She cringed away as his big hands approached her head and face, then his fingers started to work on the fabric of the gag.

'Lulu, it's fine, don't be scared. I've come to rescue you, not to get my money back. Look, here's my police card. I think you already know I'm a copper. This is my sergeant, Tony. He's one of the good guys, but don't tell him I said that.

'I'm going to untie you and take your gag off so just stay calm and quiet, all right? I promise you we aren't going to hurt you. Tony's calling up an ambulance for you. Stay calm.'

She tried. She really did. But as soon as the gag was out of her mouth she started to scream until her throat hurt. There was a sudden warmth underneath her as she lost control of her bladder.

Smith ignored both. He simply wrapped strong arms round her and pulled her towards his chest, stroking her hair, talking soothing nonsense in her ear as she gradually calmed down and started to burrow against him, feeling the comfort and protection of being finally safe.

Smith threw a hard look at Taylor as he made the call for an ambulance and back-up. He needed no words. Taylor received and understood the clear message. Mention one word of seeing a soft side to the gaffer and he could live to regret it.

'Right, Lulu, listen to me. Everything's fine now. You're safe, I promise you, he can't hurt you ever again.

'Tony get Stephens to bring the car closer so Lulu can sit in there until the ambulance comes. The sooner she's out of this hellhole the better.

He called out for Walsh who sprinted up the stairs two at a time and came into the bedroom.

'This is Sean. He may look like a gorilla but he's harmless, I promise you. He's going to take you outside and put you in a car with Craig, who's also halfway civilised. You have my word. Craig will look after you until the medics come to take care of you.

'Trust me, Lulu, they both know what I'll do to them if

they don't look after you properly.'

He'd picked up a couple of covers from the bed and was helping her to drape them round herself so she was at least decent. She was still shaking from head to toe. It was likely to be a long time before she stopped, he knew.

Sean guided her towards the door, making no attempt to touch her nor to get too close into her personal space. He'd done the courses. He knew how to behave.

As Lulu reached the doorway, she turned and looked back at Smith.

'He raped me. Several times. With like a wooden pole. Both ways. You know. He called it something like Tinker. He spoke to it like it was a real pet or something, all the time he was doing it.'

She made to leave, then turned back and spoke again.

'Thank you. And I'm sorry I nicked your wallet.'

Smith smiled to himself and shook his head at her words. Then he was businesslike once more, addressing Tony.

'Right, next call, get someone round to the office where Johnson works and arrest him. Kidnap and false imprisonment charges for now, until we find out what else we can add to the mix.

'Meanwhile let's you and me have a quick shufti round the place and see what we can find for ourselves before CSI arrive and kick us out of our own crime scene.'

They found a door to the garage from the kitchen and decided to make a start in there.

It was obsessively tidy with, as Smith's grandmother was fond of saying, a place for everything and everything in its place.

Smith's eyes went straight to a wall where magnetic brackets held row upon row of well-maintained saws and assorted high quality chefs' knives.

Next he looked at the maximum size chest deep freeze against one wall.

'Tony,' he said quietly, 'you know when you get that

sort of a premonition where you're absolutely certain of something yet you're hoping to buggery that you're completely wrong?'

'Guv, I have exactly the same feeling. Shall I open it or will you? Or will we toss for it.'

36.

13:09 – FRIDAY AFTERNOON

There was nothing more Smith, Taylor or any of the team could do on site for the moment. Craig had gone with Lulu to hospital in the ambulance, where they'd be joined by DS Jody Mitchell. She had the specialist training to carry out at least an initial interview with her, once the medics gave the go-ahead for her to be questioned.

Crime investigators were swarming all over the house and garden now and tents had gone up outdoors to try to preserve as much evidence as possible.

Lifting the lid of the freezer had been as bad as either Smith or Taylor had anticipated. The number of body parts in there was going to be like the most complicated jigsaw puzzle imaginable for the pathology team, who were going to have to sort through them for identification purposes and to try to establish causes of death.

Tony Taylor was an experienced officer, not prone to losing control. The sight of the good-looking dark-haired severed head of Marcus Campbell staring sightlessly up at him from inside a frosty plastic bag nearly got the better of him. He had to rush out into the garden to take deep lungfuls of air in order to persuade his stomach contents, scant though they were, to stay put.

Smith was preoccupied with the thought that at some point someone was going to have to tell the next door neighbour, Mrs Harrison, what she'd been eating in the delicious stews and casseroles she'd waxed lyrical over, prepared for her by her seemingly bland and inoffensive next door neighbour.

He'd already been back round to see her and to reassure her as best he could without giving any details. He declined her offer of tea this time and also said no to coffee, fairly certain it would be far too weak to be of any interest or use to him.

He wanted to find out anything else she could tell him about Johnson's parents and exactly when she'd last seen them. He'd no way of knowing until DNA results could give some definite identification, but he had a strong intuition that one or both of them had been early victims of their son, the cannibal serial killer.

They'd reached the stage where there was really nothing more they could do at the scene. It was time to head back to the station to start writing up notes and plan the interview strategy with their prime suspect, most of which would be done, as usual, by DC Brian McMahon.

'D'you want a lift back to the nick with us, guv?' Taylor asked him. 'Or have you got your car somewhere nearby?'

'I'm not going back to the nick, Tony, I'm going back home,' Smith replied, deliberately ignoring the mention of a car. He wasn't going to admit that he didn't currently have one.

'You forget that the Det. Sup. gave me the whole "go and never darken these doors again until I give you permission" speech. Which he hasn't done so far.

'So I'm going home to shower and change, because that crime scene has left me feeling tainted. Then I'm going to book the first available flight to Germany to spend some time with my family. Which is what Aird told me to do in the first place. You can tell him from me when you see him that I'll be back sometime next week, but not to hold his breath.'

'But guv,' Tony looked worried now. 'You're a key witness in all of this. We need your statement, as soon as, so we can crack on. You're the one who found him, after all.'

'As I said, Tony, Aird's the one who told me to Foxtrot Oscar. This is me, Foxtrot Oscaring. And only he can issue an order to me to un-Foxtrot Oscar.

'You'll get my statement when I get back. And in the immortal words of Herr Schwarzenegger, I'll be back. Good luck with it all, Tony. You've got this.'

* * *

14:58 – FRIDAY AFTERNOON

Smith quite enjoyed the two short walks and even the bus ride in between to take him back to his flat. He felt surprisingly energized. It had been a bit of a petty victory, really, but for once it felt good to be putting work on the back burner and deciding to do something he wanted to do for a change.

Liberating. That's what it was.

Aird had tried several times to contact him but Smith was ignoring his calls. He knew he was behaving like a sulky adolescent but he couldn't help himself.

The Det. Sup. had been quick enough to put him on garden leave to protect the precious public image and it would be some time before Smith could forget, never mind forgive that.

So now that it was all over bar the shouting, he'd go and do what he'd been instructed to do in the first place. Spend some time with the person he cared most of all about. His Oma.

He stopped to buy himself a decent takeaway lunch from a Polish deli he'd not tried before. It looked good and made him realise how hungry he was.

When he let himself into his flat he found Clive curled up asleep on his recliner chair. The cat opened one eye, yawned and stretched, then went straight back to sleep.

At least he'd seen him before he went off and left him again for a couple of days.

He'd book his flight before he spoke to his Oma. No sense getting her hopes up if he found he couldn't get a seat at short notice.

It would be good to spend some time with her again. And with Anja. He had to admit to himself he was hoping that, even if she wasn't on the rota for the weekend, she could be persuaded to come and see him.

On a whim, he picked up his phone, found a saved number which had called him many times but which he had never called before.

'Don?' Smith said, when the journalist answered his call. 'Oscar Smith here.'

'Oscar. This is a rare and unexpected treat. To what do I owe the honour?'

'I have some information for you which you may not yet have. In return, I need a favour from you to call it quits.'

'I'm intrigued. Go on.'

'We found the missing woman, Lulu, this morning. Alive but very shaken. We've arrested a man on charges of kidnap and false imprisonment.'

'I know this, Oscar, a press release has already gone out. They weren't wasting any time to break a bit of good news, at least, on this case.

'If you want a favour, you'll have to do better.'

'What won't yet have been released is that we also found a freezer full of human body parts. I found a finger in the garden, dug up by foxes.

'What certainly won't go out into the public domain yet is that the presumed killer has been cooking and eating his victims, and feeding them to the elderly lady who lives next door.'

'Fuck, Oscar, this better not be some sort of a sick joke on your part because if it is, it's seriously unfunny.'

'Not a joke, Don, even I wouldn't come up with this for fun. You can check it out, of course, but you'll at least now be in a position to ask questions at the press conference that no other journalist to my knowledge has any clue about yet.'

'And the favour you want in return?'

'Lulu, the young woman. She's had a very bad time. Been to hell and back. The press pack are going to be baying for her exclusive story, naturally.

'I want you to take her under your wing and make sure she gets an exclusive deal from someone as reputable as any hack is, who will pay her a decent amount of money and keep the rest of the jackals away from her.

'Can you do that for me?'

'I can, of course. But I'm struggling to reconcile this request with the Oscar Smith I know and would struggle very hard to love. Bottom line – what's in it for you?'

'It's no secret that I had a one-night stand with Lulu and that the little bitch lifted my wallet. She owes me a hundred and fifty quid. I want to make sure she has the means to pay me back.'

Don Donovan chuckled down the phone.

'Now that is much more like the Oscar Smith I know.'

-o0o-

ABOUT THE AUTHOR

Carl Granger is an investigative journalist with a military background. When not working, he writes from his small, isolated cottage in the wilds of the East Midlands, where he lives alone with a one-eyed cat called Crippin.

Looking for Lulu is his first crime fiction novel.

Contact:

carlgranger@protonmail.com

www.carlgranger.uk

Milton Keynes UK
Ingram Content Group UK Ltd.
UKHW020129071124
2647UKWH00020B/374

9 782901 773511